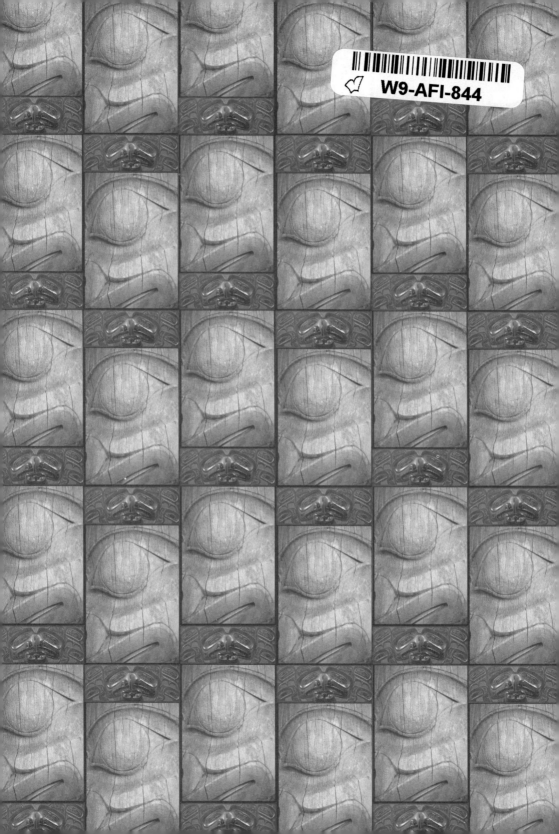

Skaay of the Qquuna Qiighawaay

The Collected Works

Edited & translated by Robert Bringhurst

The Collected Works

Being in Being

of Skaay of the Qquuna Qiighawaay

Edited & translated by Robert Bringhurst

DOUGLAS & MCINTYRE · Vancouver/Toronto

▸ DOUGLAS & MCINTYRE LTD.
Suite 201
2323 Quebec Street
Vancouver, BC V5T 4S7

Published simultaneously in the United States of America by the UNIVERSITY OF NEBRASKA PRESS, Lincoln, NE 68588-0484

We gratefully acknowledge the support of the Canada Council for the Arts and of the British Columbia Ministry of Tourism, Small Business and Culture. We also acknowledge the financial support of the Government of Canada through the Book Publishing Industry Development Program and of the Literary Translation Program of the Canada Council for the Arts.

Printed and bound in Canada by Friesens

01 02 03 04 05 · 5 4 3 2 1

Canadian Cataloguing in Publication Data:

Skaay, b. 1827?
  Being in being

(Masterworks of the classical Haida mythtellers)
Includes bibliographical references.
ISBN 1-55054-826-3

1. Haida Indians – Folklore.
2. Haida mythology.
3. Tales – British Columbia – Pacific Coast.
I. Bringhurst, Robert, 1946–
II. Title.
III. Series.
E99.H2S52 2001   C897'.2
  C00-911198-0

Frontispiece and cover:
Anonymous, *Rattle Fragment.*
Alder and paint, 16.5 cm high,
ca 1860? (American Museum of
Natural History, New York: E-1373)

Masterworks
of the Classical Haida Mythtellers

VOLUME 1
A Story as Sharp as a Knife:
The Classical Haida Mythtellers and Their World

VOLUME 2
Ghandl of the Qayahl Llaanas,
Nine Visits to the Mythworld

VOLUME 3
Skaay of the Qquuna Qiighawaay,
Being in Being

Haida *Skaay* is pronounced like English *sky* with the vowel prolonged. (The *y* in *sky* is actually a diphthong: one vowel blending into another. It is the first of the two that is lengthened: *skaaaaa-ee.*)

As a first approximation, *Qquuna* can be pronounced to begin like *cool* and end like *tuna.* To improve on this, pronounce the QQ like κ but deeper in the throat (down in the uvula, like the letters *qōph* in Hebrew and *qâf* in Arabic); then add to this sound a glottal catch or pop, like the unwritten catch in *uh oh!*). The first vowel, *uu,* is prolonged.

Qiighawaay, as a first approximation, can be pronounced *key-gaw-wye,* where *gaw* rhymes with *raw* and *wye* rhymes with *sky.* To improve on this, pronounce the Q like κ and the GH like G but move both deeper into the throat (into the uvula again, but without the glottal catch). The vowel *ii* (as in *key*) and the diphthong *aay* (as in *sky*) are both prolonged.

For more details of Haida pronunciation, see the appendix, page 359.

Preface

THIS IS THE THIRD OF THREE volumes under the general title *Masterworks of the Classical Haida Mythtellers*. The three books together provide a minimal introduction to one (one of the richest, to be sure, but only one) of the several hundred classical literatures that are native to North America.

Each volume is designed so that it can be read independently. This entails a degree of repetition, but the first work in the series – *A Story as Sharp as a Knife: The Classical Haida Mythtellers and Their World* – includes a large amount of cultural, historical and other information which is not repeated elsewhere and which readers of this volume may find useful.

In itself, volume three, like volume two, is designed for those prepared to read the texts pretty much on their own terms. Here the background information is confined to the endnotes, where readers can ignore or find it as they choose.

I have, of course, learned many things from Skaay and from his colleagues while making these translations and have therefore made revisions and corrections as I went. As a result, there are minor inconsistencies between translations in this volume and the excerpts published two years earlier in the first edition of *A Story as Sharp as a Knife*. The words sometimes differ slightly, and the line numbers do not always jibe. I hope these incidental variations will cause no inconvenience.

Illustrations

Anonymous   *Rattle fragment*   2
(Maynard)   Hlghagilda, 1884   12
(Dawson)   Qquuna, 1878   15–16
(Newcombe)   Qquuna, 1902   17
Anonymous   *Panel pipe*   26–27
Haida Gwaay and the adjacent coast   30–32

Anonymous   *Biform skyblanket: "The Swift Robe"*   36
Anonymous   *Oil dish in the form of a harbor-seal canoe*   38
Anonymous   *Naaxiin (figured blanket)*   102
Anonymous   *Bowl in the form of a redcedar dugout*   104
Anonymous   *Standing shaman*   150
Anonymous   *Raven amulet*   152
Ngiislaans   *Five-finned Killer Whale and Quartz Ribs*   174
Daxhiigang   *Waasghu (Seawolf)*   196
Daxhiigang   *Mask of the Lost Man (Gaagixiit Mask)*   198
Anonymous   *Tobacco mortar in the form of a frog*   246

Anonymous   *Raven rattle*   270
Anonymous   *Three black spoons*   272
Bill Reid   *Haida housepole (detail)*   282
Daxhiigang   *Model housepole (detail)*   296
Anonymous   *Pipe: The Raven in action*   308
Anonymous   *Xhyuu's housepole at Ttanuu*   328
Daxhiigang   *The Raven and His Bracket Fungus Steersman*   332
Anonymous   *The Raven as a ladle*   342

Anonymous   *Amulet: Killer whale and human*   346
Anonymous   *Mortar: Human in the mouth of the nonhuman*   350

Contents

Translator's Acknowledgements   *10*

Introduction: *The Hunter of Visions*   *13*

THE QQUUNA CYCLE

1   First Trilogy   *37*
2   Second Trilogy   *103*
3   Third Trilogy   *151*
4   Spirit Being Going Naked   *197*
5   Born through Her Wound   *245*

RAVEN TRAVELLING

1   Prologue: Skaay's Flyting with the Southeast Wind   *271*
2   Raven Travelling: The Old People's Poem   *281*
3   Epilogue: Ghandl's Conclusion   *341*

A FAMILY STORY

1   The Qquuna Qiighawaay   *345*

Appendix: *Haida Spelling and Pronunciation*   *359*
Notes to the Text   *361*
Notes to the Illustrations   *387*
Select Bibliography   *391*

Translator's Acknowledgements

SEVERAL PEOPLE have been kind enough to listen to or read early drafts of these translations and to talk with me at length about the form or substance of the text. I am particularly grateful to two Haida readers who, as a consequence of divisions within the community, after all their work, have asked to remain anonymous. I am permitted to thank by name Gudrun Dreher, Elizabeth McLean, Louise Mercer, and two of my colleagues at Trent University: Sarah Kinsley and Sean Kane.

I owe much to Trevor Goward – for the many fruitful and detailed conversations, and for providing the perfect workplace in the midst of the best society – of ravens, flickers, mallards, pied-bill grebes, frogs, sapsuckers, black bears, otters, mice and sandhill cranes. It was in their company that I completed these translations.

Some years ago, when I tried to unravel the mystery posed by the distorted bits of Nisgha (Nisga'a) and Tsimshian (Smalgyax) that occur in several classical Haida texts, Marie-Lucie Tarpent and Emmon Bach both listened to my questions and helped in finding answers. Nancy Turner, Randy Bouchard and Dick Dauenhauer helped me resolve other vital details.

Scott McIntyre has played a vital role in the incubation of this book and its two siblings. I take pleasure in the fact that in Canada the series is published with his imprint. It has also been a pleasure to work with Gary Dunham and Dan Ross at the University of Nebraska Press.

Mark Katzman, Kristen Mable and Laila Williamson at the American Museum of Natural History in New York went far out of their way on my behalf, arranging custom photographs of artefacts associated with Skaay and of drawings by Daxhiigang. For assistance in securing other photographs and some of the information in the captions, I am grateful to Steve Henrikson at the Alaska State Museum in Juneau;

Alison Deeprose and Phillip Taylor at the British Museum in London; Dan Savard at the Royal British Columbia Museum in Victoria; Rebecca Andrews and Lee Mueller at the Burke Museum in Seattle; Nadja Roby and Louis Campeau at the Canadian Museum of Civilization in Ottawa; Nina Cummings at the Field Museum in Chicago; Jacqueline Eliasson and Camille Owens at the Glenbow Museum in Calgary; Therese Babineau at the Phoebe Hearst Museum in Berkeley; Bill Holm in Seattle; Suzanne Morin and Stéphanie Poisson at the McCord Museum in Montréal; Francine Lahaie-Schreiner at the National Archives of Canada in Ottawa; Martha Labell at the Peabody Museum, Harvard University; and Bill McLennan at the University of British Columbia Museum of Anthropology, Vancouver.

These translations – and the larger project of which they are part – began for me in earnest in 1987, with a fellowship in poetry from the John Simon Guggenheim Memorial Foundation. Though I long ago exhausted the Foundation's monetary gift, I remain very thankful for the help and the momentum it allowed me to achieve. In recent years, my studies of Native American language and literature have been generously supported by the Symons Trust Fund for Canadian Studies, the American Philosophical Society Library, the Phillips Fund, and the Social Sciences and Humanities Research Council of Canada. To all of these agencies, I am grateful. And I am grateful to the Canada Council for the Arts, which has supported publication of this book through its program for literary translation.

Berkeley, California · 12 June 2001

Hlghagilda, 1884. Photograph by Richard Maynard.

Introduction:

The Hunter of Visions

SKAAY OF THE QQUUNA QIIGHAWAAY is one of the great poets, though his name has until recently been known to very few. It is easy to say that he would have been famous long ago if he had lived in a society where fame is something artists can expect. But poets of the kind Skaay was are only found in oral cultures. In oral cultures art is always local, and a poet's reputation is regional at most. Other poets as skilled and as brilliant as Skaay may well be living now in the ghettos of Los Angeles, the sidestreets of Bangkok or Lima, Yogjakarta or Dakar, or in United Nations tents, among the traumatized survivors of a dozen recent genocidal wars. The world in which fame is to be found cannot know that they are there – nor has it much to give them now, when fame has ceased to be a testament to value and come to mean a boldface listing in the catalogue of replicas for sale.

Skaay was born about 1827 in the Haida village of Qquuna, off the British Columbia coast. Until his early seventies, he lived in a world without writing. That is to say, a world in which voices were pure spirit, made of memory and breath, never captured by the hand nor by machines. It was a world in which stories far outnumbered human beings, and where the spirit beings of story were portrayed in innumerable carvings, paintings, masks. The mythtellers' visions and ideas were recalled in many forms, but words, like dancers' gestures, disappeared as they were formed.

Then on Monday, 8 October 1900, in the mission village of Skidegate, a little north of Qquuna, Skaay met a man some fifty years his junior who was trained as an ethnographer and linguist. The two men had, at first, no common language. A love of the mythteller's art was what they shared. And the linguist had the power to record, with his paper and his pencil, the sounds of human speech whether he understood them or not. Within a few weeks of that meeting, the poet had dictated to the linguist the contents of this book.

No one lives in Qquuna now, but in 1827 it was home to at least four hundred people. European ships began to call there late in the eighteenth century, chiefly to buy furs. British sailors came to know it as Skedans, from Gidansta, a name used by its headman. But in 1827 – even in 1860 – Europeans had not yet come to stay. No missionaries and no colonial agents were in residence, the Haida population was still high, and the people still controlled, as much as any people does, their land and fate. During Skaay's lifetime, the face of Haida Gwaay[1] – the Islands of the Haida – was transformed. He is, in that respect, a modern poet. But the traditions he was born to and grew up with were those of the precolonial, preindustrial, preliterate Haida world.

The endnotes begin on page 361.

Descent in that world was matrilineal. Skaay belonged, like his mother, to the Eagle side or moiety, and within that moiety to a lineage called the Qquuna Qiighawaay (the Progeny of Qquuna).

In the early or middle 1840s, Skaay moved from Qquuna to the nearby village of Ttanuu, where the headman of his lineage was "mother of the town" or headman of the village. Four decades later, in 1886, decimated by smallpox, measles and other imported diseases, those still living at Ttanuu gave up their village and built a new town on the old site of another, known as Qqaadasghu. Death pursued them there as well, and in 1897 the survivors moved to Skidegate Mission – a Christian settlement built where the big Haida village of Hlghagilda had stood.

Skaay himself was baptized on three occasions that we know of, but there is no sign whatsoever that he studied Christian doctrine or embraced the precepts of the church. In 1884, at Ttanuu, a visiting clergyman christened him Robert McKay. In 1889, at

Qquuna, 18 July 1878. The first photos ever taken of the village were taken on this date. Skaay was born here fifty years before. The population in the meantime had fallen by 60% or more. Photograph by George Dawson.

(National Archives of Canada: PA 44329)

Qqaadasghu, he was baptized again and entered in the register as Sky. On 31 January 1894, again at Qqaadasghu, he was baptized together with his wife, and their marriage was confirmed by yet another visiting Methodist. On this occasion, they were christened John and Esther Sky. This was wishful thinking on the missionary's part and constitutes a gross violation of older Haida protocol. Skaay and his wife necessarily belonged to opposite moieties – Eagle side and Raven side – and so could not, like English couples, share a name.

Skaay went on speaking Haida and using the Haida form of his name. As his poems attest, he also went on thinking in terms that the missionaries knew nothing whatever about. His experience of European contact had far more to do with destruction in

Qquuna, 18 July 1878. Skaay left the village thirty years before this photograph was taken, but these are some of the houses among which he was raised. Photograph by George Dawson.

(National Archives of Canada: PA 38148)

this world than with salvation in the next. When he was born, his group of Haida villages, including Qquuna, Ttanuu, Qqaadasghu and Hlkkyaa, had a combined population of close to a thousand. In 1897, when the last survivors of these villages gave in and moved to Skidegate, there were a total of 68. Skaay's work is a product not only of long tradition and personal genius. It is also a product of the Haida holocaust. Within his lifetime, the Haida population as a whole was reduced from something close to 12,000 to something closer to 800.[2]

John Reed Swanton, the linguist who transcribed these poems, was born on the coast of Maine and trained at Harvard and Columbia, where reading and writing were taken for granted and

Qquuna in September 1902. Though still used on occasion as a campsite, Skaay's birthplace had been empty of permanent residents for roughly twenty years. Photograph by C. F. Newcombe.

(Royal British Columbia Museum: PN 10)

the life of oral cultures was not well understood. When his work with Skaay began, Swanton had been in the Haida country for two weeks. He could write down almost anything Skaay said and work out later on, with help from other speakers, the grammar and vocabulary involved, but in taking down the poems, he was working, just as Skaay was, on pure faith.

Skaay had been forewarned that Swanton wanted to learn the Haida language by transcribing Haida stories. Swanton probably had not been fully warned that he would meet the greatest living Haida poet (and indeed the greatest poet, in any language, that he was ever going to meet). Yet even through the barrier of language, Skaay made an immediate and powerful impression on his visitor – one deepened and confirmed (as we know from Swanton's letters) over the weeks of their intense collaboration.

At their first meeting, speaking through an interpreter by the name of Henry Moody, Skaay explained to Swanton what he was going to do: tell a cycle of five stories connected with his birthplace, Qquuna, followed by a work called *Raven Travelling*, the story of the trickster, for which Swanton had particularly asked. Four weeks later, Swanton had in his notebooks precisely what Skaay told him he would have. He had the five-part Qquuna Cycle – a narrative poem of nearly 5500 lines – and *Raven Travelling*, in a version of some 1400 lines.

If the missionary records can be trusted, Skaay was 73 when he dictated these texts. As a young man he was strong enough to serve as steersman of his headman's war canoe during a raid on a mainland village,[3] but as an old man he was crippled, through some injury or deformity to his back. Despite the missionaries' grim determination to move everybody into European-style single-family dwellings and give everybody patrilineal names, Skaay remained, as he had for many years, in the household of the headman of his lineage. It was a household where the myths were still revered. The headman told them too, and with considerable skill. But immobility and age – together with his status as an honored commoner – had given Skaay the privilege of thinking at great length about the stories that still tied him to a disappearing world. While other men were occupied with hunting, fishing, carpentry or the cares of hereditary office in a time of devastating change, Skaay was thinking through the myths.

There is however always another side in the equation of oral literature. The listener's ability to listen, like the teller's ability to tell, governs the quality of the work. Swanton proved to have a gift for listening to stories and transcribing them that complemented Skaay's great gift for telling them. Henry Moody, the bilingual Haida colleague whom Swanton had hired on arrival, had a gift for listening too.

Moody's participation was vital. Skaay spoke sentence by sentence or stanza by stanza and listened while Moody repeated his words. This gave Swanton two chances to hear every word correctly and time enough to write the passage down. It gave Skaay a chance to check for errors. Into the bargain, it gave Moody a postgraduate course in his own culture.

In the fall of 1900, Moody was roughly thirty. He showed no unusual gifts as a poet himself, but he was admired for conscientiousness and intelligence, and he belonged to the aristocracy. In fact, he was the nephew and heir of Gidansta, the headman of Qquuna. Moody had never lived in Qquuna himself and could not have known it well. He was a child when it was abandoned. Yet it remained, like other village sites, a shrine.[4] His age, interests and family connections made Moody one of Skaay's ideal students, and the works Skaay chose to dictate were very likely chosen with Moody more than Swanton uppermost in mind.

All the better for us if this is so. Children learn far more from overhearing adults speak among themselves than from most things that adults say directly to their children. Outsiders likewise stand to learn far more from overhearing what insiders say to one another than from having things explained in terms outsiders are equipped to understand. This is why "children's literature" is so limiting a genre. It is also why stories told by Native Americans are so often misconceived by other people as stories just for children. Watered down to cross the membrane between cultures, stories lose their richness, their maturity. If Swanton had asked Skaay to tell the stories to *him,* he could well have remained merely a tourist in the realms of Haida literature – and if he had, so would we. By employing two insiders – one to speak and one to listen – Swanton eliminated the need for watering down. By sitting on the sidelines, he empowered himself to leap into the stream of Haida literature, where he was far over his head. We have to make the same leap. Only by going in over our heads can we allow Skaay's poetry to function.

By Saturday, 13 October, Skaay was well into the second trilogy of the Cycle. A week after that, he was somewhere in the midst of §4 of the same work, and the Cycle was finished before the end of the month.[5] When it was time for *Raven Travelling*, Skaay began in the spirit of the work, by playing a trick on Swanton and some others who had gathered there to listen. He began the poem at the end, with a light-hearted episode in which the Raven leads a flotilla of birds and fish against a character named Xhyuu, the Southeast Wind.

One of those present was Skaay's patron and protector, the headman of his lineage – whose name was Xhyuu, the Southeast Wind. After Skaay had been dictating for a while, Xhyuu himself took over, revelling in an episode in which the Raven is beaten to a pulp and then disguises himself as a Skaay-like little old man.

This jam session or flyting took a day of Swanton's time and left him thoroughly confused. Next morning, feigning perfect innocence, Skaay told the linguist he had started in the wrong place by mistake, an old woman had pointed out his error, and he was ready to try again. Then he unfolded his second masterpiece, *Raven Travelling*. By the beginning of November, Skaay had told Swanton very nearly all he chose to tell.

Many versions of the Raven story have been recorded on the Northwest Coast. Skaay's *Raven Travelling* is larger, richer, more complex, more self-aware than any of the others. It has been called the Haida version, the Skidegate version and the Skedans version of the Raven story. What it is in fact is Skaay's version: the work of a brilliant Native American artist. Not surprisingly, it is also the only version known in which the work itself pokes fun at its own literary nature.

While the Qquna Cycle and *Raven Travelling* are two of the longest works of Haida literature, they are also models of economy. Skaay could have made them both much longer. There is for example a nearly inexhaustible supply of mostly ribald trickster tales attaching to the Raven, Mink, Coyote, and other tricksters who inhabit North America. These tales can be woven into tapestries of any desired length. In Skidegate in 1900, such anthologies of trickster yarns were known as Youngsters' Tales. Skaay's flyting with Xhyuu is a taste of the genre – but when he started in for real on the following day, Skaay devoted himself instead to what he called *Nang qqayas qqaygaangghaay,* the Elders' Tale or the Old People's Poem. Though it includes an ample share of folk motifs, this is not a chain of yarns; it is a tightly organized account of how the world comes to have its present form and how the trickster comes of age.

At Swanton's invitation, Skaay's younger colleague Ghandl picked up where Skaay left off. In November, he dictated a Youngsters' Tale as a sequel to Skaay's masterpiece. Because the context – and the contrast – are informative, I have included the conclusion of Ghandl's tale as an epilogue to Skaay's.

The last and much the briefest work in the book is Skaay's account of his own lineage, the Qquuna Qiighawaay. Exactly when he dictated this poem I do not know, but it almost certainly came after the longer works, and at 200 lines, it would have needed only half a day to transcribe. Swanton had heard that every Haida lineage (or matrilineal clan) had a story of its own, and Skaay was one of many people from whom he sought examples.

Among some native nations on the Northwest Coast, especially in recent years, there is a tendency to consolidate the intellectual heritage into lineage tales, and in effect to treat the entire body of history and myth – including many stories shared by neighboring peoples – as if it were fenced and privately owned. This is a predictable response to threatening social conditions – but Swanton's Haida texts do not give any sign that such a process had begun in Haida Gwaay in 1900 or 1901. The lineage story was a recognized Haida literary genre at that time. It had its own name and its own conventional formulaic ending, but all the lineage stories Swanton heard from Haida elders were brief and episodic, while the myths and historical narratives sometimes went on for hours. Skaay's story of his lineage is episodic too, but it is the longest, and literarily much the richest, of all the Haida lineage stories Swanton heard.

Skaay's major work, the Qquuna Cycle, is the largest extant work of Haida literature, and one of the largest extant literary works in any native North American language. Mere size, however, is hardly the point. The Cycle is one of the great works of North American literature in any language, whether indigenous or colonial. It includes many themes addressed by other oral poets on the Northwest Coast, yet it is, like *Raven Travelling*, distinctively and singularly Skaay's. It constitutes some of the most potent mythic narrative I have met in any language from anywhere in the world.

In the notes, I have mentioned some of the related stories recorded in Haida and neighboring languages. Some readers may be interested in analogues as such, but I hope that others will seek them out in order to come to grips with the enormous differences in individual visions and performances of myths. In the study of European art and literature, it is generally taken for granted that two "versions" of one myth – two paintings of the Crucifixion, for example, or two plays or poems about Prometheus – can be profoundly different and acutely individual works of art. In the study of Native American art, this simple truth – a universal human truth – has been habitually forgotten or denied.

Many things distinguish Skaay from other mythtellers and poets, both within and beyond his immediate tradition. One of these is his intellectual reach. Though his only philosophical method is narrative, he is a skilled metaphysician. His psychological depth distinguishes him too. He is constantly probing his characters, examining what it means to be abandoned, what it means to be in love, what it means to be passed over. Then there is a third thing, practically forgotten in the literature of Europe; that is his hunterly manner. Hunterly in this sense means something similar to courtly. It suggests an extra ration of courtesy and care – directed not toward the non-*male*, as in the tradition of courtly love, but toward the nonhuman. The hunter, like the courtier, knows that he exists in a state of dependency from which there is no escape. Courtesy hedges this dependency and holds it up for inspection. Turn it over and you find its other side, which is predation. Finding that balance is one of Skaay's key themes.

This book includes Skaay's complete extant works, in the order in which their author chose to unfold them. This means the longest and most complex work comes first; the brief false start to *Raven Travelling* comes next, then *Raven Travelling* itself (*The Old People's Poem*), and then the short, poignant story of the Qquuna Qiighawaay. Readers encountering Haida literature here for the first time, or those overwhelmed by the mythological richness and density of the Cycle, may want to start at the back of the book and read forward. Better yet, readers daunted by the richness of Skaay's poems might begin with the first two volumes in this series. I hope, though, that readers more familiar with the Northwest Coast will appreciate a chance to encounter Skaay's work in something like the form and sequence that he chose.

His strengths are those that flourish in the long poem, which rarely gives immediate gratification. Poets of the kind Skaay was have an attention span measured in decades, not in minutes. After reading him for years, I know that while his poems can be spoken, heard or read in the space of a few hours, years are what it takes to perceive what they contain.

❧   ❧   ❧

Native American narrative poems are not prosodic machines, defined by repeating patterns of downbeats or syllables, nor are they little magnesium flares of emotion. Here the poem is a tree of meaning, flowering in the mouths and minds of human beings, yet rooted in a world in which we are only one of many species.

Like the best Haida spruce root baskets and cedarbark capes, Skaay's poems are densely woven fabrics. And like the best Haida sculpture and painting, they are spare, elegant, interlocking structures, at once strongly figured and powerfully abstract. The language is patterned, and the patterns can be found and verified by counting, in pretty much the same way students of English prosody count stressed and unstressed syllables. There are however two important differences. First, the patterns tend to repeat, like natural fractals, at varying scales. Second, the patterns are constructed out of images and ideas and events instead of metrical feet or syllables. They are noetic, not acoustic. The things you have to count are things perceptible directly by the mind, not necessarily detected by the ear.

In the translation, each English line corresponds, by and large, to a single Haida clause. The smaller clusters of clauses – the little narrative syllogisms through which the story is told – appear as individual stanzas. I have outlined what I take to be the overall structure of each work by giving numbers to the larger clusters of ideas and marking them with introductory capitals.[6]

In an oral performance, these patterns can't be seen and may not in fact be heard, because all they are made of is meaning. One can hear, even without knowing the language, certain aspects of the pattern, in the form of repetitive particles (*and then..., and then..., and then...*) and in the form of rhetorical pauses. But skilled performers do not always pause in the logically obvious places, just as skilled readers of verse do not always pause in the metrically obvious places. We have no acoustic recordings of Skaay and can therefore only guess at how he sounded, but we can follow the shapes of his thought from the transcripts alone.

I think most readers will come to sense these patterns soon enough, but in hopes of hastening the process, I have mapped the structure of one movement of the Cycle (§1.3) in considerable detail. Even here, however, the analysis does not exhaust the structure; the map could be made much finer yet.

Qquuna §1.3 is Skaay's Little Iliad: the story of a war between two towns, occasioned by the love of two too-well-connected men for the same woman. The theme was once a favorite on the Northwest Coast and well beyond, and many incarnations of this tale have been recorded. Like most coastal mythtellers, Skaay sets the scene in the Tsimshian country. Several of his characters have Tsimshian names, and one of them echoes a song that is either Tsimshian or Nishga in origin.

Skaay, in other words, did not invent the theme. He did not have to – just as Aeschylus did not have to invent the theme of Agamemnon's Return nor Botticelli the theme of the Annunciation. Like them, Skaay could begin with a well-known plot and end with a highly original work of art.

Because this poetry is oral, it is rich with repetition – something easy for modern readers to undervalue or misunderstand. Skaay's repetitions are not accidents or defects, any more than the repetitions in Mozart's string quartets or piano sonatas. The repetitions are never mechanical either. There are formulaic phrases that recur with some precision, but where larger motifs are repeated, Skaay always introduces variations. The key to understanding and enjoying repetitions of this kind lies, very simply, in learning to *hear* them. Faced with echoes and repetitions such as those which link §3.1 and §4.1 of the Cycle, a silent reader is apt to say with alarm, "There's some mistake. I've read this part already!" The *listener* – one who has learned to listen to literature in the way we listen to music – will say with delight, "Yes! I've heard this theme before – but never quite this way!"

Another kind of subtlety lies in Skaay's articulation of social and geographical space. He is concerned, first of all, with movement back and forth between the mainland and the Islands. As an islander, he speaks of the mainland towns as lying seaward, while the island towns (the villages of Haida Gwaay) are landward. The poems are set in a series of coastal villages, with frequent excursions into the forest behind, onto the sea in front, and down to the ocean floor. The village as Skaay conceives it is a line of big, square houses facing the beach, with the house of the village

headman or town mother at the center of the row. Within the headman's house, there is a three-part hierarchy of space, often mentioned in the poems. *Behind the fire* or *in the rear of the house* (Haida *tajxwaa*) is the area of greatest prestige, normally reserved for the headman and his wife (or the headwoman and her husband) and their children. The area *toward the door* (*hlkyaagwaa*) is for commoners and others of no account. Between these extremes is the area *midway along the side* or *midway along the wall* (*dangqayiitgha*). Unclassified or unclassifiable persons, such as shamans, are seated here. So are visitors whose importance is acknowledged but who are not, for some reason, admitted to the headman's or headwoman's private quarters.

If Swanton had come to the Haida country only twenty years earlier, he would have found such houses still in use, the villages still filled with massive housepoles and mortuary poles and still alive with drumming, dancing, face paint, masks. He would have found a people still quite sure that the holy land lay right there at their feet. By 1900, this had changed. In Swanton's words:

There is not an old house standing – all have modern frame structures with the regulation windows.... The missionary has suppressed all the dances and has been instrumental in having all the old houses destroyed – everything in short that makes life worth living....[7]

26

Anonymous Haida artist. *Panel pipe.*
Argillite, 46 cm long. ca 1850. (British Museum, London: De 5.)
The head of the leftmost figure – an eagle – is broken off, leaving only the lower
half of the beak. Altogether, there are fifteen interlocking figures.

That vanished world is the one that Skaay grew up in. It came
vividly to life the moment he began to tell a story – and the
stories that he told turned out to be as balanced, economical of
form and elaborately interwoven as the great works of sculpture
he had lived with until late middle age.[8]

Though Swanton's mentor, Franz Boas, took a lifelong interest in these texts, he never learned to read the Cycle as a whole.
Other students of Haida literature have suffered a similar blind-
ness. Yet the Cycle is on par with the masterworks of classical
Haida sculpture that Boas himself installed in the North Pacific
Hall at the American Museum of Natural History in New York.
It possesses much the same kind of energy – the animate and for-
mal interconnectedness, and the density of vision – that typifies
the greatest works of Haida visual art.

Nineteenth-century Haida carvers made such works not only
on commission from their headmen for installation at home but
for sale and trade to other native people up and down the coast,
and to visiting Europeans. Elaborate containers and utensils –
boxes and bowls, ladles and spoons – were favorite items for trade
within the region. For the European market, a new vehicle was

chosen: the tobacco pipe, sometimes made of wood but far more often of a soft black stone known as argillite. The more complex of these pipes form panels sometimes half a metre long. Most Haida pipes are constructed in such a way that they *can* be smoked, but few of them ever have been. Their makers and their purchasers alike routinely understood them as works of art, not as tools for the consumption of tobacco. They differ in this respect from the articles made for regional trade, which almost always functioned both as works of art *and* as very serviceable boxes, bowls or spoons.

There was no such market for literary goods. Europeans had been visiting the Islands for well over a century when Swanton came along, but he was the first outsider ever to ask for stories in Haida. No outsider asked again for seven decades after that – and by then there was no one alive who had actually known the pre-colonial Haida world.[9]

It is tempting to think of the Qquuna Cycle and *Raven Travelling*, with their interlocking sequences of characters and episodes, as panel pipes in words. And both these poems do in fact conclude with an abrupt and striking reference to tobacco. There is no reference, though, in any of Skaay's work, to the European custom of smoking. The tobacco he mentions is always native tobacco, which humans and spirit beings chew with calcined shell.

In his lineage history, using historical forms of the Haida verb, Skaay mentions things of European origin: a folding knife and smallpox. In the two larger poems – set in mythtime and told in timeless verbs – he mentions nothing whatsoever that the Haida took in trade from Europeans. There are no metal knives, no muskets, matches, kettles, cotton, tea or other trade goods. This lack of reference to contemporary life has been interpreted as escaping into mythtime. That is not what it is. The poems, it seems to me, are more like Haida spoons and boxes than like panel pipes: they are works of art that are truly meant to be used.

❧   ❧   ❧

Swanton first transcribed Skaay's words in pencil, double-spaced, in field notebooks, then went over the transcriptions with Henry Moody, correcting the Haida and adding an English gloss. From October 1901 through October 1903, in his office at the Bureau of American Ethnology, Washington, DC, he typed his Haida texts and made his prose translations, expecting to publish them all. As it happened, only the northern Haida texts were published in full. The Bureau published only a small sample of the southern texts, including Skaay's. The unpublished Haida manuscript went first to Boas, then to the American Philosophical Society Library, Philadelphia, where it remains.

Here, the entire Qquuna Cycle and all but the first 47 lines of *Raven Travelling* are translated from the Philadelphia manuscript. The opening of *Raven Travelling* is only to be found in Swanton's carbon copy (in fragile condition at the Smithsonian Institution in Washington, DC). "The Qquuna Qiighawaay" is translated from the Haida text that Swanton published in 1905.

Skaay's work, which fills this volume, is only about fifteen per cent of Swanton's Haida corpus. It is the cream of the collection, but there are five major classical Haida authors – Skaay, Ghandl, Kingagwaaw, Haayas and Kilxhawgins – each with a distinct voice, and each deserves a volume all his own.

Making these translations, together with the groundwork underlying them – studying the sources, building a working dictionary, and so on – has taken more than twelve years of my life. The results have been greeted with bafflement, joy, occasional rage, and sometimes with the blank stare of implacably racist disbelief. I am aware that the translations have their flaws, as all translations do. But in years of poring over the originals, I have never spent an hour without feeling deeply nourished, challenged and restored. That is why the translations exist.

1 Ghadaghaaxhiwaas
   (Ghaw, later *Masset*)
2 **Naay Kun**
   (*"House Point,"*
   later *Rose Spit*)
3 Ghahlins Kun
4 **Hlghaayxha**
5 **Hlghagilda**
   (*"Pool of Rocks,"*
   later *Skidegate*)

6 **Guuhlgha**
7 **Xayna** (*"Sunshine"*)
8 Qqaasta
9 **Kunji** (*"Facedown"*)
10 Ghaw Quns

11 Qqaadasghu
12 **Qquuna** (*"Edge,"*
   later *Skedans*)
13 Sghaana Kkyaalgha
   (*Shellheap of the Gods*)
14 Ttlxingas
15 **Ttanuu**

16 Hlkkyaa
   (later *Windy Bay*)
17 Xhuut Ttsiixwas
   (*"Seal Beach"*)
18 **Qinggi**
19 **Xhiina**
20 Ghangxhiit Kun

21 Sghan Gwaay
   (*"Red Rockfish Island,"*
   later *Anthony Island*)
22 **Qqaaghawaay**
23 **Hlghadan**
24 **Ttsiida Gwaay**
   (*"Skate Island"*)
25 **Qaysun**

26 Ttsaa'ahl
27 Kkyuusta
28 Yan

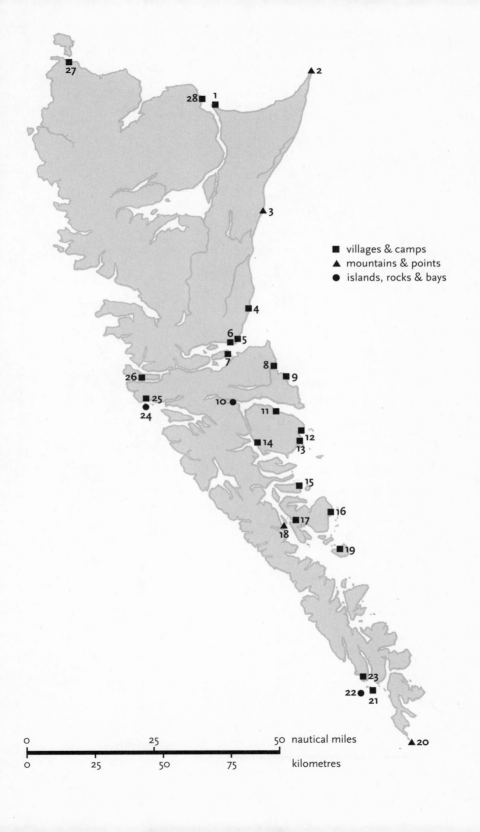

■ villages & camps
▲ mountains & points
● islands, rocks & bays

27

2

28 1

3

4

6
5
7

8
9

26

25
24

10

11

14

12
13

15

16
17
18

19

23
22 21

20

0   25   50 nautical miles
0   25   50   75   kilometres

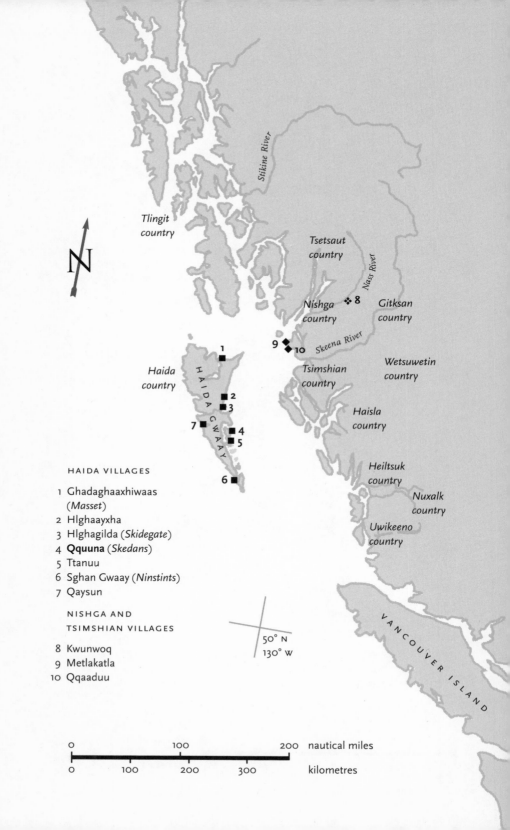

Tlingit
country

Tsetsaut
country

Nishga
country

Gitksan
country

❖ 8

9 ◆ ◆ 10   *Skeena River*

Haida
country

HAIDA GWAAY

1

2
3

7

4
5

6

Tsimshian
country

Wetsuwetin
country

Haisla
country

Heiltsuk
country

Nuxalk
country

Uwikeeno
country

Stikine River

Nass River

VANCOUVER ISLAND

HAIDA VILLAGES

1 Ghadaghaaxhiwaas
  (*Masset*)
2 Hlghaayxha
3 Hlghagilda (*Skidegate*)
4 **Qquuna** (*Skedans*)
5 Ttanuu
6 Sghan Gwaay (*Ninstints*)
7 Qaysun

NISHGA AND
TSIMSHIAN VILLAGES

8 Kwunwoq
9 Metlakatla
10 Qqaaduu

50° N
130° W

0   100   200   nautical miles
0   100   200   300   kilometres

BEING IN BEING

[▸]   square brackets mark editorial restorations
⟨▸⟩   angle brackets mark insertions
{▸}   curly braces mark deletions

The Qquuna Cycle

Anonymous Tlingit artist. *Biform skyblanket: "The Swift Robe."*
Mountain goat wool & yellowcedar bark, 146 × 100 cm + approx. 30 cm of fringe.
Late 18th century.
(Peabody Museum of Archaeology & Ethnology, Harvard University, Cambridge, Mass.:
N° 09-8-10/76401, neg. N-28168.) *See the note on page 387.*

The Qquuna Cycle §1

First Trilogy[1]

Anonymous Haida artist. *Oil dish in the form of a harbor-seal canoe.*
Alder, 30 × 16.5 × 12.5 cm. 19th century.
(Burke Museum, University of Washington, Seattle: N° 2211)

§1.1 The One They Hand Along

T HERE WAS ONE OF GOOD FAMILY, THEY SAY.   [1.1]
She was a woman, they say.
They wove the down of blue falcons[2]
    into her dancing blanket, they say.
Her father loved her, they say.

She had two brothers:
one who was grown
and one who was younger than she.

And then they came to dance at her father's town, they say,
in ten canoes,
and then they danced, they say,   10
and then they sat waiting, they tell me.

And someone – her father's head servant, they say –
went out and asked them,
«Why are these canoes here?»

«These canoes are here for the headman's daughter.»
The headman answered them, they tell me:
«Better look for other water.»
They left in tears, they say.

They came to dance again on the following day,
    in ten canoes, they say,

and again they were questioned, they say.   20
«Why are these canoes here?»

«These canoes are here for the headman's daughter.»
And then he refused them again,
and they went away weeping.

THEN, on the following day someone was there,   [1.2]
   in a harbor-seal canoe, in a broad hat,
      at early morning, they say.[3]
Surfbirds lived in his hat, they say.

After they had looked at him in his harbor-seal canoe,
they asked him, they say,
«Why is this canoe here?»   30

He said nothing, they say.
They refused him.
They said to him, they say,
«We cannot give you water.»

There was something white surrounding the crown
      of his hat, they tell me.
It moved like breaking surf, they say.
It was foaming and churning, they say.

And when they refused him,
the earth became different, they say.
Seawater started to boil out of the ground.   40

When they found themselves half underwater,
the villagers feared
that they might have to give him the woman.

There were ten more who attended her, they say.
And they dressed one to resemble her, they say.
They also painted her, they say.

They painted red cirrus clouds on her face, they say,
and gave her two skyblankets to wear[4]
and sent her to the headman on the water.
He turned her down, they say.   50
He wanted the headman's daughter, they say.

And yet again they painted one, they say.
They painted her with seaward dark clouds
and gave her two marten-skin capes to wear
and sent her out, they say.
He refused her too, they say.
He refused all ten the same way.

Then everyone in the village, including the children,
    hurried to her father's house, they say.
And they wept,
and they let her go down   60
without painting her, they say.
All ten of her companions went along, they say.

When she stood by the sea,
the canoe came ashore by itself, they say.
⟨And the visitor placed his hat on the shore
    as a gift for her father, they say.⟩[5]   64a

Now, when she had stepped aboard,   [1.3]
all ten of her companions crowded in with her, they say.

No one could see
what moved the canoe.

Once the women stepped aboard,
they saw him out there,   70
standing offshore in his boat
where they'd seen him before.

And then they yanked the stitches
    out of the boards in the housefront, they say.
They peered through the holes
to watch the canoe departing, they say.

After watching them go seaward for a time,
they could no longer see
what direction they'd taken, they say.

They did not see
that the canoe had gone back down.   80
And so they could not see
where the one of good family was taken.

D AY AFTER DAY, her father turned to the wall,   [1.4]
    and he cried and cried and cried.
And her mother turned to the wall
and cried and cried and cried.

Her father's head servant stood with them, day after day,
and after a time, when her father stopped weeping,
he said to him, «Search for the place
where my child was taken.»   90

«Wait. The signs will come together.
    I will find where your child was taken.»

ONE DAY later on, at first light,   [1.5]
  he stirred up the fire
and bathed, they say,
while the people in the house were still asleep.
He wanted none of them to see him,
since the shape of daybreak pleased him.

Now, when his skin was dry,
he turned to the wall   100
and spread out his fishing tackle, they say.

He opened a bundle,
took a stalk of skookum root[6]
and touched it to the fire.

It started to smolder,
and when he had watched it smoking awhile,
he quenched it,
smearing the ash on the stone floor,
and he marked himself with it.

Then he prepared for departure, they say.   110
He was going in search of the girl, they say –
and the girl's mother was with him, they say.

       ➤   ➤   ➤

FROM THEN ON, he moved like a hunter.   [2.1]
  He owned a sea-otter spear, they say.
He pushed off,
and he threw the sea-otter spear.

It wiggled its tail
and pulsed through the water
and towed him, they tell me.

After a time, the canoe ceased moving, they tell me.   120
So did the sea-otter spear, they say.
And then, they say, he pulled the canoe up on shore.

The lady stepped out of the boat
and he turned it keel-upward.
Sea-lettuce grew from the hull.
This is what slowed the canoe.
They had travelled for one year, they say.

And he took off his redcedar cape,
and he rubbed the canoe with it.
He rubbed the lady as well,   130
and he rubbed himself
until he was clean.

He launched the canoe again,
and he threw the sea-otter spear again,
and it started to wriggle again.

Again the sea otter towed them along.
They went on and on and on and on,
and then, once again, the canoe ceased moving, they say.

He pulled the canoe ashore once again,
and he turned it keel-upward.   140
Oarweed and wing kelp were growing all over it –
    and on the lady, and also on him.

He took off his cape once again,
and he rubbed the canoe and the lady.
He rubbed himself also.

When he was clean,
he launched the canoe.
And again he threw the sea-otter spear,
and it towed them along.

When it had pulled him along for a time,
he came to where charcoal was floating, they say.   150
There was no passage through it, they say.
He brought out his tackle box
and looked in.

He had old scraps
from repairing his halibut hooks.
When he scattered spruceroot lashings on the water,
the channel was opened,
and then he passed through it, they say.

Not far away, he came to a place
where the channel closed in again.   160
When he scattered more lashings,
the passage was opened, they say.
Then he went through it, they say.

And he came to the rim of the sky.
Now, when it had opened and shut four times,
he thrust in his spear, propping it open.

He got under it that way, they tell me.
Then he pulled out the spear
and put it inside the canoe.
Then he took out his paddle   170
and started to use it, they say.

SOON, they say, he saw smoke from a large town.   [2.2]
He beached the canoe to one side of the village, they say.
He turned it keel-upward
and seated the lady beneath it, they say.
After that, he walked to the village, they say.

The tide was out
when he came to the edge of the village.
A woman with a child on her back had come down
    on the foreshore.

She was clutching a basket   180
and using a digging stick,
probing here and there for something.

As she put something into her basket,
she looked at him
sitting there.
After looking him over,
she went back to what she was doing.

She was prying up the beach rocks,
putting sea-pickles into her basket.[7]
It was Wealth Woman.   190

When she looked up again
to where he was sitting,
she spoke to him, they say.
She said, «I know who you are.»

Then he stood up, they say,
and went down on the beach
and stood near her.

Then, they say, she asked him,
«Have you come here in search of the one of good family?»
«Yes,» he said.   200

«You see this town.
  The one who took the girl for his wife
  gave away his father's hat.
  Because of that, his father poured grease
      into his son's wife's mind.[8]
  She lies in that cave.

«After you enter the headman's house,
  go around to the right
  and walk behind the screen.
  What you hear there may please you.»

Then he set out,   210
  leaving Wealth Woman there,
  and he entered the cave where the girl was lying.
  She lay still,
  but her eyelids were fluttering.

He took off his redcedar cape
  and massaged her with that,
  and tried to pull her to her feet.

Nothing happened.
  Second time round, he got angry
  and failed again.   220
  Then, having failed,
  he went on his way.

He put a pair of figured blankets on his back
  and wandered among them.

None of them saw him.
Then he went into the headman's house, they say,
going round to the right.

They say that the floor descended in ten tiers to the fire.
Midway along the side, on the rim of the housepit,
    someone was weaving a figured blanket,
and from the blanket she was weaving,   230
something whispered to him this:
«Tomorrow again, part of my face will still be
    unfinished, unfinished.»

THEN, they say, he went back of the screen.   [2.3]
    What he found there surprised him, they say:
a large bay ringed with sandy beaches,
cranberries ripening on the outcrops,
women's songs and songs of joy rolling up from it in waves.

Close to the stream flowing into the bay,
a fire was built for heating salt water, they say.[9]

Then some people came along with baskets of berries.   240
Walking past him, they say,
the last of them wrinkled her nose.
«I smell a human being ...»

«Excuse me,» he said. «Are you speaking of me?»

« ... but I'm wearing a dancing blanket that came
        from one of the young woman's ten companions –
the ones who were eaten.
It must be myself that I smell.»
It was Mink Woman speaking.

48

And now he went up to the fire
built for heating salt water.   250
When he came near,
one of those who were sitting there said,
«What will he do
when they come here to look for the girl?»

«What are you saying?
If the ones who come seeking the girl
bring back the hat
that his son left among them,
he'll bring her back out near the sea and the fire.»

Pleased with what he heard,   260
he hurried off.

H E RAN BACK to the canoe   [2.4]
where he had left the girl's mother,
and lifted up the hull.
Nothing was there but the headwoman's bones.

When he took off his redcedar cape
and rubbed it across her,
she woke
just as though she'd been sleeping.
She was sweating.   270

He put his arm in the canoe
and pulled it to the water.
When the lady came aboard,
he approached the town by sea.

He tied the lady down, they say.
He tied himself down too.

Wealth Woman told him to tie himself down –
    and the lady as well.

They were tied in their seats, directly offshore
    from the headman's house.
As they floated there,
someone came out   280
and said to them, «Wait!
They ask that the headwoman's boat hold its position.
They will bring you in from there.»

When they had floated there awhile,
thunder sounded from the house, they say.
Right after that, feathers came up from the smokehole,
    forming a point.

As they rose,
they broke free of the house.
When the feathers veered toward them
and settled around them,   290
both he and the lady lost track of themselves.

Now, when he came to himself,   [2.5]
his boat was at rest on the rim of the housepit.
There, they say, he untied himself, and the lady besides.
When he could walk,
he came and untied her.

Her son-in-law sat there in back of the fire,
and they spread out a mat for her close to the fire, they say.
Then she went down there and sat,
midway along one side.   300

And she carried a small basket, they say,

It held one pair of horseclam shells, butterclam shells
    and mussel shells also, they say.
And they came to serve the lady.
They offered her food.

After food had been served
and consumed,
they brought a water basket out
and filled it with water,
and then they put stones in the fire.

When the stones were glowing hot,   310
they lifted them into the basket,
using their tongs.

Now it was boiling.
The headman gave orders
to one of the youngsters who stood near the basket.

The boy went into a storage pit
that was there in one corner.
He returned with humpback whale on the end of a stick.
This he put into the basket.

Now after testing it with the stick   320
and finding it soft,
he lifted the whaleflesh onto a dish
    shaped like a giant red chiton
and set it in front of the lady.

Now, when the headman spoke to him again,
the boy brought the lady the rotten shell of a horseclam
for sipping the broth.
She refused to use that as a spoon.

Now when she reached into her own basket
and brought out a fresh pair of clam shells and mussel shells,
silence fell in the house.   330

The headman himself was looking at nothing except the shells.
When she noticed his eyes fastened upon them,
she paused.

Then she handed the shells to her husband's head servant,
who passed them in turn to her son-in-law.
He cradled them in his cape.

Now, when he had admired them for a while,
he gave another order.
The boy came to take them
and put them in back of the screen.   340

Then evening fell,
and the house went to sleep,
and this one went to sleep as well, they say.

         ➤   ➤   ➤

W HEN day was just breaking,   [3.1]
   a seal pup cried in the corner, they say.
As daylight arrived,
he began to prepare for departure, they say.

Now the canoe sat on the rim of the housepit.
There he tied the lady into her seat,
and he tied himself into the stern.   350

Behind the screens set end to end,
  a clap of thunder boomed, they say,
and feathers came out in a point

52

and settled around them,
and then they lost track of themselves, they say.

They were floating on the open sea, they say,
when they came to their senses.

Now he untied himself,
and he went to the headwoman, too,
and untied her.

They had left in midsummer, they say,   360
when the seal pups cry.

Now he took up his paddle   [3.2]
and started to use it, they say.
After taking two strokes,
he had come up offshore of his master's town, they say.

The lady went into the house and sat down.
She explained to her husband
what this one had seen
in the place where her daughter was lying, they say.

Then the head servant went to his master.   370
He explained to him then
the predictions they'd made
by the fire they built for heating salt water.
He told him precisely the words they had spoken.

He spoke to the firekeepers at once, they say.
Two of them went through the village
inviting the people, they say.
They rushed right in.
They filled the house, they say.

Then he served them food, they say.   380
He fed them and fed them.
When the food had been consumed,
he told the people of the town
what he was thinking, they say.

He told the people of the town
that he was going in search of his daughter.
All of them approved, they say.
He proposed that the headmen travel in ten canoes.
They agreed to do it, they say.

ON the following day, his elder son vanished, they say.   390
The day after that, as they started   [3.3]
        to load up the boats,
the younger boy had vanished too, they say.

For the father and mother, cumulus clouds
    were painted on ten sets of clamshells, they say,
with ten sets of mussel shells nested inside them.
They painted ten for the elder son
and ten for the younger as well.

Every man in the village preparing to go
gathered ten sets of shells, and every woman five.
After they gathered them,
they sat waiting for both of the boys,   400
who had gone to get married, they say.

They were waiting to go bring their sister back up
    to the surface,
and now they were tired of waiting, they say.
The people had everything ready,
and there they sat waiting.

54

Her elder brother returned at midday
with redcedar twigs tied in his hair.
«Mother, I bring you my wife.
  She is standing outside.
  Please bring her in.»   410
That's what he said to his mother, they say.

«Well now! My son has come home!»
  When she went out to look,
a woman with her hair well done
    and big round eyes was standing there.
It was Mouse Woman, they say.

Though the younger was gone somewhat longer,
he also, they say, came back at midday.
He entered with fern fronds tied in his hair.
Hai hai hai hai haiiiii!

«Mother, I bring you my wife.   420
  She is standing outside.
  Please bring her in.»

Something astonishing stood there, they say.
No one could look at her.
A creature with short hair, wearing armor.[10]

«Lady, come in.»
  She wouldn't come in.

«She won't come in.
  She refused!
  My child, your wife just refused!»   430

«She's a contrary woman.»

Then he went out to his wife
and brought her inside
and sat down beside her.

              ➤   ➤   ➤

NEXT DAY at first light, they set off in search of the girl. [4.1]
The people of the village launched their boats
and went to sea.

The elder son's wife sat on a thwart toward the bow.
The wife of the younger concealed herself in the crowd.
The first sat up high   440
to see how they were headed, they say.
She kept a close hand on her purse
wherever she was.

As they headed to sea,
she reached into the purse
and brought out a needle, they say.
She tossed it into the water, they say,
It threw up a wake of its own, they say.

They lined up behind it, they say,
and the needle towed them, they say.   450

After it towed them and towed them and towed them along,
they saw smoke from a town
drifting seaward, they say

Some distance away, the elder son's wife told them to land.
She gave them directions.
They say she had married the elder son
in order to do so.
Mouse Woman had.

They paddled ashore,
and she told them, they say, to cut pairs of long poles.   460
It was there that they got them.
The younger son's wife stayed in hiding
while the wife of the elder was guiding them with her words.

While the ten canoes stood offshore,
they linked them with poles at the bow and amidships.
They lashed the poles to the thwarts.
It worked.
Then they brought them about all together, they say,
   just offshore of the town.

There they were riding, they say,
offshore from the headman's house,   470
and someone, they say, came out and stood there.
«Wait. They ask that the boats hold their position.
They will bring you in from there.»

AFTER floating in place for a time,   [4.2]
they lost track of themselves, they say.

They came to themselves on the rim of the housepit
as if they'd been resting, they say.
They untied themselves from their places.
They unfastened the lashings tying the poles across the canoes.

They spread mats on the rim of the housepit.   480
There were crowds on the ten tiers
   on both sides of the housepit.

The headman's daughter was not to be seen –
the one they had come to reclaim.
Only her husband was seated there.

Then they spread out two mats right in front
of where he was sitting, they say.
In front of him, people from all ten canoes
    piled their clamshells, they say.

They piled them up as high as the house.
Hu hu hu hu hu! To the roof!
Next, they intended to top off the stack   490
with the hat they'd brought back to him.

«Call in my father,
    and ask him to come right away.»
One of his brothers set off on the run, they say.

«Isn't he coming?»
«He's just about here.»

Hwuuuuuuuuuu!
The house quivered, they say,
and the earth shook.
Among all who had come there in search of the woman,   500
not one raised his eyes.

Then the youngest son's wife raised her head
while the rest of them cowered, they say.
She looked behind the fire and then toward the door.

«Raise yourselves up!
Have you no power?»
Those were her words.

In a moment, the house shook again,
and the earth along with it.

Hwuuuuuuuu!   510
Those in the house put their heads down again.

  Now, they say, she told them once more,
«Raise yourselves up!
Have you no powers?
Have you no powers?»

  At that moment he came in and stood there, they say.
Something amazing came in and stood there, they say.
His eyeballs stuck out
so that no one could look at him.
When he planted his foot,   520
it stayed where he put it, they say.

  As he took one more step,
the earth and the house shuddered, they say.

  As he took yet one more,
the house and the earth quivered,
and all together they cowered.
She said once again,
«Raise yourselves up!»

  As she lifted her chin,
the spirit being entering the house   530
reached up and clutched his head.
«A powerful woman you are.»

  As he came further in,
nothing more happened.
He sat near his son.
But he snatched up his hat
just before he sat down.

With his father's staff, the son divided the shells.
He took less for himself.
He gave more to his father.   540

«Haven't you sent for your wife, my young headman?»
«No. I have waited for you.»
«Send someone now for your wife, my young headman.»
  One of his brothers went to call her then, they say.

«Isn't she coming?»
«Yes. She's nearly here.»

Soon she came in, they say,   [4.3]
  the one they had come to reclaim,
who had been in the cave.
And she went to her mother directly, they say.   550
She didn't go down to sit next to her husband.

Then his father started to call on his powers, they say.
After a time he fell over, they say,
breaking in two.

Feathers came swirling out of his body and out of his neck.
One of the woman's companions came out of his body
and one from his neck.
One out of his body, one out of his neck,
and another one out of his body, and one from his neck.

He restored all ten that he had eaten.   560
He called on his powers to do that, they say.

Because of the hat, he had eaten her women, they say,
and put grease, they say, in the mind of the one of good family.
Because of the hat, they say, he had put her away in the cave.

After a time, he knit back together, they say.
His powers withdrew.
He sat up.

Next, they built up the fire
and called them to come
and started to feed them, they say.   570
They were still busy eating when midnight arrived.
Then it ended, it ended.
They went to bed, they say.

    ➤   ➤   ➤

W^HEN day was just breaking,   [5.1]
  a seal pup cried
in the place where it had cried before, they say.
Then they prepared for departure, they say,
with their boats on the rim of the housepit.

Her husband's father called her then, they say.
«Lady, come here. I have something to tell you.»   580

Then she went to him, they say.
She sat beside him,
and he gave her directions, they say.
«Lady, you will give birth to me.
Don't be afraid of me.»

He gave her a nugget of copper, they say,
with spines sticking out of the side.
Its name, they say, is Down the Throat.

«Have Master Carver make my cradle, lady.[11]
Put scattered cumulus clouds on the top of it, lady,   590
and across the bottom too.

Let the clouds be flat on the bottom.
When the sky is like this,
even good-for-nothing humans may come out to me to feed.
Whenever they see me like this,
the common surface birds will come to me to feed.»

Her parents were there on the rim of the housepit, they say,
    ready to take her.
But down where they were looking,
she was listening to her father-in-law, they say.

After he had finished his instructions,   600
she stepped aboard the same boat as her father.
They had already lashed the canoes together
and roped themselves into their seats.

When the headman's daughter stepped aboard, they say,
they forgot where they were.
When they came to themselves,
they were out on the open water, they say.

THEY set off at once, they say,   [5.2]
and they came to the village directly, they say.

When they had been there for a time,   610
the one of good family was pregnant, they say.

When she started her labor,
they built her a shelter apart from the houses, they say.
They drove in a birthing stake,[12]
told her to hold it,
and left her, they say.

Now he emerged,
and she caught her first glimpse of him.
Yes. Oh yes. It stopped her heart, they say.

Something stuck out from under his eyelids.   620
She raised herself up
and scrambled for safety, they say.

«Awaaayaaaaa!» she cried.
and the village flipped over, they say.

Then she went toward him again, they say,
and reached out to him.
«Aiii! Grandfather, it's me,»
she said as she lifted him into her arms, they say,
and the town was as quiet
    as something that someone has dropped.

She brought him into the house, they say.   630
Her father put cooking stones
into a urinal that he owned,
and they bathed him in it, they say.[13]

⟨ Then, they say, she asked for Master Carver. ⟩   633a
As soon as they called him,
he came to them, they say.
He had already started his work in the forest
and brought it half-finished, they say.

As soon as he entered,
he made the design, they say,
as the one of good family described it.   640

He drew cumulus clouds together in pairs.
He drilled holes for the laces
to straighten the baby's legs.

And they fastened him in it, they say.
They brought a pair of skyblankets out,
and they wrapped them around him, there in his cradle.

T HEN, without waiting, they launched the canoe.   [5.3]
A crew of five, the woman and her child went aboard.
And they started seaward, they say.
They went farther and farther and farther to seaward.   650

To the landward towns and the seaward towns[14]
    it was equally far,
they could see that it was,
when they put him over the side, they say.

When they put him over the side,
he turned round and around and around and around
    to the right four times
and lay quiet, they say,
like something that someone has dropped.

And then they made for shore
and settled this place here, they say.   659

§1.2 One Who Acquired a Wolverine for a Mother[15]

THERE LAY THE VILLAGE OF KWUNWOQ, THEY SAY,   [1.1]
   on the Nass.
Four servants of the one who owned the town
   came out of the house.
Downstream from Kwunwoq, on a sandbar, where they went
   to cut some firewood,
they saw a stand of young redcedars too, they say.
They noticed it because of the headman's wife.
It surprised them, they say.

They finished their cutting
and loaded the boat
and caught the rising tide, they say.

At sunset, they came home again.   10
The people of the town came out and carried up the wood,
and the head of the village invited them in, they say.

When food had been served,
he mentioned the news,
that they had seen a stand of young redcedars.
Then and there the headman's wife proposed
that they should go for cedarbark, they say.

T HEY headed for bed,   [1.2]
     and they launched her husband's canoe
          in the morning, they say.
The villagers, the rich men's daughters, and the young men
     went along.   20

They caught the falling tide at once, they say.
Hu hu hu hu hu!
Plenty of food with them too: cranberries, salmon.
They went downriver right away, they say.

They landed at the cedar stand,
and the women went inland to strip it.
They stripped it for her.
When they had taken what was nearest,
they went further inland, they say.

And she sat with her back to the sunshine,   30
splitting the cedarbark.
She was a sniffer instead of an eater, they say.
Her fingers were slender.
She turned away food.

W HEN the voices of the other men and women   [1.3]
      were dwindling away,
someone wrapped in the skin of a black bear, fur side out,
     came up and stood there next to her, they say.
He carried something long.
The tip of it was sharp.
Half its length was reddish brown, the other half bluegreen.[16]

He was staring at the lady.   40
She did not so much as glance at him in return.
And he asked the lady a question, they say.

«When your husband is hosting the people,
  what do you do?»

«When my husband is hosting the people,
  I stuff my face
  with everything placed in front
  of whoever sits next to me.»

  She had children: two boys.
  One of these was a toddler.   50

«What did you say you do
  when your husband is hosting the people?»

«When my husband is hosting the people,
  I dish up the food
  and stick my face right into it and gobble.»

«What do you do
  when your husband arrives with his catch?»

«I run right down,
  pull up my dress,
  wade out to the boat,   60
  take two spring salmon off the top
  and swallow them whole.»

  He pressed his pole against her brow,
  and when it came out through the back of her head,
  he lifted his arm.
  All the flesh and bones and innards fell out of her skin.

  He sat right down
  and put it on, they say.

And he picked up her innards
and buried them in the sand
    at the base of the trees, they say.   70

W<small>HEN</small> he was sitting   [1.4]
    where the headman's wife just sat,
they came back out and gathered round, they say.
All of them were busy splitting cedarbark.
There in the crowd – hu hu huuu –
the one of high rank was doing it with them.

«My dear, I'm starting to feel a little bit peckish.»
«Well, I have something fresh here.»
«Me too!»
«Me too!»
They wanted her to eat, they say.   80

The one who was quickest broke food into pieces
and set it there in front of her, they say.
And now she ate all that they gave her.

They couldn't get going
while she was still hungry, they say.
They got home after bedtime, they say.

The headman's wife was finally eating, they say.
That's why it was getting toward dark when they started –
and so they explained it, they say.

T<small>HE HEADMAN</small> gave orders to build up the fire, they say, 90
    and invited them in.   [1.5]
Her youngest had cried himself nearly to death
in her absence, they say.

They handed him over,
and when she uncovered her breast
and offered it to the child,
he jerked away and bawled, they say.
The breast he was offered belonged to a man.
That's why he jerked his head away and bawled.

The townspeople gathered in the house.   100
They roasted the salmon
and broke it in pieces.

They set down a dish
in front of a person who sat just beside her.
She grabbed it and – huuu! –
she upended it.
She didn't bother to chew.

When she scooped up the dish,
those serving food to the people froze in their places.
The way she had started to eat   110
left them speechless.
That is the wife of the headman?

Very next day, his wife was hungry again,
and again he invited the people.
The elder boy surprised them too,
as he carried his younger brother up on his shoulders
    back and forth in front of the town.
Both of them were bawling.

The headman invited them all.
They asked her to dish up the berries, they say,
and, yes, she bent over and ate them.   120
The servers came back in a bunch with the empty trays.

They gaped in amazement, they say.
It wasn't the headman's wife they were seeing.

E ARLY NEXT DAY, this one launched a canoe   [2]
    that belonged to his father
and set his little brother in the bow, they say.
He headed for anywhere out of the Nass –
    away from the village of Kwunwoq, that is.

He'd been riding the falling tide for a time
when a woman, who leaned halfway out
    of a house up ahead,
said, «Come in!»
The front of her house was painted and sewn.[17]   130

And then he steered toward it, they say.
When he landed, she said,
«Stick around.
    You'll go on with your journey tomorrow.»
She spread out mats with colored borders in their honor.

The headwoman sat on one side.
The elder brother took the seat beside her,
    while the younger one sprawled directly across.
    And then, they say, she said to him,
«Let the younger one sit next to me.»   140
    He picked him up
and set him beside her, they say.

He'd gone hungry some while, they say –
since the moment their mother began to surprise them.
Now, for the first time since then, the woman beside them
    was going to feed them.

She turned toward the back,
poked through her purse
and brought out a dish in the form of a mouse.
Into the dish she put one bite of salmon.
She set it before him, they say.   150

He looked downward, they say, and thought,
«After going without for this long,
 is this what I'm eating?
 How much of that do I leave for my brother?»

When she noticed his face,
 she said to him, they say,
«Small as it is,
 even those who are spirit beings from birth
     cannot finish it off.»

He picked it up.
His little brother picked it up too.   160
Still, it remained there.

After they had eaten it awhile
and had their fill,
she took away as much as she had served.

When they'd eaten their fish,
she served them a cranberry.
Then the same thought crossed his mind.

She looked at his face again
and said, «Eat it.
Those who are spirit beings from birth
     cannot finish it off.»   170

Then they began to spoon it up.
They ate and went on eating.
When they were filled,
she returned it to its place.

Evening fell,
and she brought out the mats.
Then the headwoman lay down.

The older boy came up to lie beside her,
and she said to him,
«Lay your little brother down beside me.»   180
He picked him up
and set him next to her, they say.

As soon as he had set him there,
his baby brother slept
just as if someone had clubbed him, they say.
He slept for the first time
since he'd started to cry.

Now, as this one was sleeping,
he heard a woman laughing.
He was wakened by the voice, they say.   190
His little brother – yes! – was playing with the woman.

When his brother made a certain move,
«Yuuuwiiiii!
There's the One Who Acquired a Wolverine for a Mother
but here next to me is the One Who Is Coming up Strong.»

When the elder brother heard that,
he started shedding tears,
and at that moment, daylight came.

Daylight came,
and then he prepared to go somewhere, they say,   200
wherever that somewhere might be.
She told him to sit down again, they say.
«Before you go, I have something to tell you.»

She brought her purse up by the fire,
took out something bluegreen
and bit off part of it, they say.

«Grandson, if they ever overpower you,
chew on this
and lather it over your body.»

Then, they say, she told him,   210
«Farther down the inlet lives the one whose daughter
 you are bound for.
Your brother can stay here.
I'll marry him later.»

T HEN he rode the falling tide alone, they say.   [3.1]
     He was destined, they say, for Sqaaghahl's Daughter.[18]

And here lay that one's town –
the town of the one whose daughter he'd come there
to marry, they say.

Darkness was falling, they say,   220
as he walked into town.
He walked into Sqaaghahl's house then, they say.

He sat down just inside the door.
The one of good family was sitting
farther back, between the screens
     that formed a point behind the fire.

There were women with their hair done up in dreadlocks
moving here and there around her.
They were watching her, they say, on her father's behalf,
to keep her from doing anything wild.

W HEN day began to break,   230
he had not got in to see her.   [3.2]
Instead, he went outside.

He went around the corner of the house
and walked along a narrow trail.
In the meadow he came to, bones
    were heaped beside a waterhole.
Behind them stood a pine.
He perched in one of the upper branches, they say.

When he'd been sitting there awhile,
sunshine fell in patches in the meadow.
Then the one of good family arrived.   240

The one who came first wore a bone in her nose.
She carried a bludgeon.
The one in the rear was equipped the same way.
A scalp, they say, hung from the club of the one in the lead.
She was Tlingit.
The one behind was one from far away.

The one of good family knelt
and slipped out of her clothes
and was nude.

Then she entered the water,   250
went round in a circle four times
and came out.

74

The Tlingit woman dried her back,
the foreign woman dried her breasts,
and after they had rubbed her up and down,
she went back in the water.

After going around to the right in a circle four times,
she sat down in the meadow,
letting the sunshine fall on her back.

As her skin was just starting to dry,   260
he seized her, they say,
and the moment he seized her,
he kissed her, they say.

The first of her women lunged for her club –
    the one with the scalp on it –
and was ready to clonk him.
The other one was set to club him too,
but the lady called them off, they say.

«Don't kill him.
I'm going to marry him.»

All the others who had seen her,   270
and afterwards had seized her,
had been murdered by her women.
Those heaps of bones were theirs, they say.

They lay together then and there, beside the pine, they say.
The Tlingit woman sat at their feet,
the one from far away sat at their head,
and they watched her, amazed.

The sunlight left the meadow,
and the four of them went back to town, they say.

T HEN she went into her father's house.   280
    As she came in,   [3.3]
she hid her husband in her clothes.
Her father was watching.

«My dear, why are you limping?»
«Daddy, a shell went into my foot and hurt me.»
    They went together behind the screens, they say.

Then evening fell,
and the one of good family went to bed
        behind the screens, they say.
And then they kept on making love.
In the night, the headman heard   290
someone speaking very sweetly to his daughter.

Morning came,
and the headman gave orders to build up the fire.
Two servants piled on the wood.

When it was burning well, he said,
«Now let me see
who talks so sweetly to my child.»

Right away, another of the headman's children
        went behind the screen, they say,
and said, «There's someone in her bed.»

Then her father said,   300
«Aiiiii! Where did this spirit being come from?
The one I sired my child for
is the One Who Acquired a Wolverine for a Mother.»

«Wait. It could be him.»

76

«Daddy, he says that's who he is.»

He spread out a mat next to his own and said,
«My dear, you and your husband come and sit down.»
Soon she came out with her husband.

They put four quartz pebbles into the fire, they say.
When they were glowing,   310
he pulled them out with fire tongs
    and set them in a dish, they say.
Then he placed them in front of his son-in-law.
A white stone spoon was in the dish.

She sobbed, they say.
«Aaa, aaa, aaa.»
She was speaking through her tears, they say.
«Every time I find a man who pleases me,
    he murders him.»

«Say no more,»
    he told his wife, they say.   320

Then he took the spoon
and scooped up one of the hot stones
and swallowed it.

His stomach was unharmed.
He did it with all four.
He polished them right off.

His spirit powers were that strong.
If his powers had been weak,
he would have died right there, they say.

Since his spirit powers were strong,   330
that one allowed him to marry his daughter, they say.

Then for a time, while he lived there with his wife,
Mouse Woman's plan to take his brother for her husband
and his mother's strange behavior
all vanished from his mind.

O NE DAY later on, he stayed in bed, they say.   [4]
  He was still there at evening.
He was there when the others went to bed.

The next day again, he stayed in bed –
right up until the others came to bed again.   340
He lay in bed for two whole nights and days.

«My dear, why is your husband so unhappy?»
«Mmmmmmmmmmm,» is all she said.
  Then she went to her husband
  and, sitting by his side,
  she chatted with him sweetly for a while.

  Then she told her father,
«He can't stop thinking of his brother,
  whom he left a ways upriver.»

«My lady, take your husband   350
  to that useless old canoe of mine, up beside the trees.»

They went out together then, they say,
but that canoe – you know, they couldn't find it.
The only thing that lay there was a humpback whale's skeleton,
     in among the salmonberry vines.
Even its tailbones were there.[19]

Then they both came back.
«Daddy,» she said,
«we couldn't find it.
    There's nothing there except a humpback whale's skull.»

And then he said to her,   360
«My dear young lady, that's her.
    You must say to her nicely, *Seaward, father's canoe!*»

When she went back to it with her husband,
    she kicked it.
«Seaward, father's canoe!» she said.

Now it rode there on the water: a whale canoe.
Along the gunwales were carvings of migrating geese
who knew how to paddle by beating their wings.

And now they loaded her, they say.
Nothing but the best food!   370
    Cranberries, sweet berries, soapberries,
the marbled meat of mammals of the land –
    grizzly, mountain goat and deer, marmot, beaver –
prime cuts of all the mainland mammals.[20]

When the canoe was piled high,
this one went aboard
and put his foot against the cargo and shoved it toward the bow.

When the canoe was getting genuinely full,
the servants went up to the house
and filled a basket with the meat of humpback whale.

After it was heaped beyond the brim,

they took it down.   380
Then they set it on the top, they say.

When they were set,
her father came out of the house, they say.
«My darling, when the creatures on the port and starboard sides
    start to call across the beam,
toss cranberries into their mouths.
When they get hungry,
they keep talking.»

As soon as their wings started beating,
the boat started moving, they say.
As long as their wings kept on beating,   390
the boat kept on going.

A FTER A TIME, they came up abreast   [5.1]
    of the house of their sister-in-law.
There too, they were preparing to launch a canoe –
one that Mouse Woman owned.

They were loading that one up with food as well.
When it got full,
that one also used his feet to shove the cargo toward the bow.
Once it was loaded,
they set off in tandem, they say.

The very instant that the geese along the gunwales
    of the elder brother's boat began to call,   400
he brought cranberries out
and ladled them into their mouths.

All along the gunwales of his younger brother's boat
    were tiny human beings,
clutching little painted paddles in their hands.

They were paddling with those.
The moment they began to smack their lips,
that one fed them the same way.

As they came near the stand of young cedars,   [5.2]
the wives of both brothers sat upright, they say,
and then they gave the order, «Head for shore.»   410

Here, they say, the women got off.
They had poles in their hands,
and they probed from the water's edge inland.

After a time, up by the grass, just in front of the trees,
    they dug up human bones.
The canoes rode at anchor offshore.
Their husbands were watching from there.

Mouse Woman brought out her purse,
and Sqaaghahl's Daughter brought out her purse.
Sqaaghahl's Daughter took out of her purse
    a mat with a fringe of cumulus cloud,
and Mouse Woman took something out of her purse   420
and bit off a part of it.

Next, they spread the mat across the top,
and beneath it, they say, they started to jostle her bones.
Mouse Woman spat underneath it repeatedly.

Then she told Sqaaghahl's Daughter to hurry.
«Quick! Get a move on, my lady.»

She answered, «How about you, my lady?
You get a move on.»
They were sisters-in-law.

Then she pulled off the mat.   430
Hey! Their husbands' mother sat there wide awake.
This one sat there on the water, staring at his mother.
The pair of them did.

They put her aboard the younger brother's canoe
and rode the rising tide to the village of Kwunwoq –
the two brothers' father's town.

The younger brother's wife arranged
    for her husband's mother to hide, they say.
They were concerned about their other mother now.
They wondered how their other mother would react
when they arrived.   440

As soon as they came near the town,   [5.3]
    the younger brother's wife gave the order
        to bring the canoes alongside one another, they say.

There was commotion in the town.
«The favored child and his younger brother too,
    who ran away together down the river,
are coming back with wives!»
they said to one another.

They descended upon them
as though they expected a hostile canoe.
In front came their mother, donning her belt
to help them carry up the load.   450
She didn't mingle with the crowd.

The elder brother brought his boat to shore,
and Sqaaghahl's Daughter stood next to the basket.

«Come this way, my lady.
 This basket goes up to the house.»

She went to her as she asked
and began to settle the tumpline over her forehead.
Sqaaghahl's Daughter insisted that this wouldn't do.
Better, she said, with the straps crossed over the shoulders.

She did as she asked, put her arms through the straps,   460
and staggered uphill with the load.
It was all she could do to get up to the house with it.
It was huge.
After that, they carried up everything else in one load.

After they pulled the empty canoe high up the beach,
the younger brother brought his boat to shore.

The biggest basket, sitting on the top of the load,
had carrying straps made of thorns.
She was standing right next to it,
Mouse Woman was.   470

Then she called to her mother-in-law, they say,
who was still up the hill.
«Come this way, my lady.
 This basket goes up to the house.»

And her mother-in-law came down to her
and started to fix the basket straps over her forehead.
Mouse Woman said that this was improper, they say,
and then she put the straps across her shoulders.

When she started uphill with the basket,

the straps went round her throat and cut her head off.   480
It rolled a ways away.

Mouse Woman pulled a whetstone out of her purse
and raced up the beach
and dropped it there between the trunk and the head,
which were drawing together already, they say.

When head and trunk had ground themselves away,
there was foam, just foam, heaped up on either side.

She brought her husband's mother
    out of hiding then, they say.
They swarmed around her
to show they were happy to see her.   490

Killing her mother-in-law
was her reason for marriage, they say –
Mouse Woman's reason, that is.

A crowd of people lugged her giant basket to the house.
    Then, they say, she said to her husband,
«Forget me.
    The only reason I married you
was to restore your mother to life.»

She pushed her boat off just like that,
and it went waaaaay downstream.   500
Not a trace of her remained.
The elder brother's wife, however, lived there
    as a headman's wife –
the other one's successor.   503

84

§1.3 Ghaawaxh

THEN SHE CONCEIVED A CHILD,   [1.1.1]
Sqaaghahl's Daughter, that is.
She gave birth to a boy.
She conceived again.   [1.1.2]
She gave birth to a boy.

She conceived again.   [1.1.3]
She gave birth to a boy.
She conceived again.   [1.1.4]
She gave birth to a boy.

She conceived again.   [1.1.5] 10
She gave birth to a boy.
She conceived again.   [1.1.6]
She gave birth to a boy.

She conceived again.   [1.1.7]
She gave birth to a boy.
She conceived again.   [1.1.8]
She gave birth to a boy.

In addition to these, she gave birth to a daughter.   [1.1.9]

At Qqaaduu, just across from Metlakatla,[21]   [1.1.10]
   they built their house, they say,

the sons of Sqaaghahl's Daughter.   20
Their mother and their sister joined them there.

⟨T HEN they decided to go for beaver, they say.⟩[22]   21a
I The eight of them went together to get them, they say. [1.2.1]

When they came to the pond
and broke open one end of the dam,
a pole impaled the oldest one's shoulder, they say.
And he died on the spot.

They hurried back, they say.   [1.2.2]
And they arrived behind the house
    in the middle of the night, they say.
They sent the youngest brother in
to see what he could see.   30

«Speak to our mother.
    And keep a close eye on our elder brother's wife.
    She must be unfaithful.
    She must have made him weak.
    That has to be what happened to our brother.»

He came out of the trees   [1.2.3]
    and went in to see his mother,
    and he touched his mother's head
    and said to his mother,
«The beaver dam broke right on top of my oldest brother. 40
    A piece of it went through his neck.
    He was gone in an instant.»

And she cried out, «Aiiiiiiiiii! My son...»

«Hush! We will keep it a secret.
  Say nothing.»

Her cry woke the rest of the house
  and they asked her,
«Why did you scream?»

She answered them,
«My dreams came up too close.   50
  I dreamed that a beaver dam broke right on top
      of my oldest son
  and he died on the spot.
  That's why I screamed.»

Now, when he'd been lying there in silence   [1.3.1]
          near his mother,
he began to hear a person
speaking sweetly to his eldest brother's wife.

When dawn was close to breaking,   [1.3.2]
the talking had stopped.
Then he crept up close,
and without ever waking the man,   60
he sliced off his head.

When they had waited all together for a while,   [1.3.3]
daylight came,
and then, they say, they all came in together.

They were carrying a human head.
The youngest brother stuck the head up near the door.
Blood continued dribbling out of it.

Tʜᴇʀᴇ across the water lay the town of Metlakatla.   [2.1.1] 73
    Because the headman's son had disappeared,   68
they were searching all around, they say.

They asked about him everywhere.   [2.1.2] 70
They asked for him in vain.
And then, they say, they gave up asking.   72

Later on, the north wind started blowing.   [2.1.3] 74
The sea was frozen all the way to Qqaaduu.
They started walking back and forth across the ice, they say.

Tʜᴇɴ early one morning a slave   [2.2.1]
        crossed over to Qqaaduu for fire, they say.
«Go into the middle house,»
    they said to him, they say.
And when he went into the middle house   80
a drop of blood landed on his foot, they say.

Nudging the stump of his firebrand into the fire,
he glanced away from the rear of the house,
    back in the direction of the door.
Hanging just above the doorway – yes! – it was the head
    of the missing headman's son.
He knew it was him, they say,
by the abalone earrings that he wore.

He gathered up the glowing coals
and carried them outside.
When he reached the ice,
he threw the coals away.   90

Then he went back in again, they say.   [2.2.2]
Though he had looked right at it,

he didn't trust his eyes.
And he went inside again
and nudged the stump of his firebrand into the fire.

When he had gazed around the house a little while,
he ran his eyes across it once again.
It was the headman's son.
He saw it plainly once again.
Then he went out with the coals, they say.   100

When he was halfway back across,
he threw the coals away again.
He thought, «I must be wrong.»

Then he went back there again.   [2.2.3]
He went inside
and went up to the fire.

Without waiting, he looked.
That was truly who it was.
He saw it with his own eyes.
Then he went off with the coals.   110

Right outside the door, he threw them away.
And right away he ran off yelling,
«The headman's son who disappeared,
his severed head is right up therrrrre!»
He kept on yelling as he ran.

THERE in the town, as soon as they heard what he said,   [2.3.1]
they leapt to their feet.
They got ready for battle.
They dressed in their helmets and shields.
They started to gather their spears and bows and arrows.   120

They went after Sqaaghahl's Children.
None survived except the daughter and her mother.
They took the lives of all the brothers.

The two who lived, lived farther inland then, they say,   [2.3.2]
    at the foot of a hill in back the village.
They lived in a hut made of brushwood.

She lived there with her daughter quite some time,   [2.3.3]
and every day at sunset she was weeping.
The daughter lay in bed beside her mother,
and they stayed in bed a long, long time.

O NE DAY, as morning came,   130
she called for suitors for her daughter.   [3.1.1]
«Sisssterrrrs! *Who will marry Ghaawaxh's child?*»[23]
    A large creature ran in from out front.
«I'll marry your daughter.»

«Supposing you marry my daughter,
    what will you do?»

«When I've married your daughter,
    I'll head for the beach at one end of town
    and eat them up from one end to the other.
    I'll chew them limb from limb.»   140
    That was the Grizzly, they say.

Again at once she called in all directions,   [3.1.2]
«Sisssterrrrs! *Who will marry Ghaawaxh's child?*»
    Something bandylegged arrived.
«I'll marry your daughter.»

«Supposing you marry my daughter,
  what will you do?»

«I'll tip the village over.
  I'll chew right through the base.»
That was the Beaver, they say.   150

«Sisssterrrrrs! *Who will marry Ghaawaxh's child?*» ...   [3.1.3]
«Supposing you marry my daughter,
  what will you do?»

«I'll swim out from one end of town,
  and when they all come out to take me,
  they'll fight about who gets me.
  Those in the town will destroy one another.»
That was Deer, they say.

Again at once,   [3.1.4]
«Sisssterrrrrs! *Who will marry Ghaawaxh's child?*»   160

A creature came in and stood.
He carried a bow.
There were circlets of birds' down around it.

He held the arrows with it in his hand.
He wore a quiver on his back,
dancing leggings on his legs,
a dancing frontlet on his head.
He didn't say a word.

«Supposing you marry my daughter,
  what will you do?»   170
He moved his right foot forward.
The earth broke into pieces.

«Yes, your lordship, you're the one.»
Then the earth came back together.
«You conceived and bore your daughter just for me, I think.»

He took his frontlet off.   [3.1.5]
He laid his arrowcase aside.
He went off with only his bow and two arrows.
He brought in a grizzly,
a mountain goat too.   180

He went out again.
Then he hauled in a deer,
a beaver as well.

H E WENT out again.   [3.2.1]
He carried a corner post back on his shoulder.
He set it in place
and instantly lifted another one out of it.

He took it across to the opposite side
and did the same thing there.
and again toward the front, and again at the opposite side,   190
where he left it.

He went out again.   [3.2.2]
He brought back an interior pillar.
He planted it once toward the rear of the house
and again on the opposite side,
again toward the front, and again on the opposite side.

He went out.   [3.2.3]
He brought back a beam.
He set it in place on one side.

After nudging and pulling it this way and that,   200
he placed it on the other side as well:
first on the pillars on one side
and then on the other.

He went out again.   [3.2.4]
He brought back a roofplank.
He set it in place at the back on one side.

Then he rolled it right over
and fixed it in place, again and again and again.
In that way he finished off half of the roof.
He did the same thing, front to back, on the other side.   210
That part was done.

He went out again.   [3.2.5]
He brought back a plank for the housefront.
He set it in place.

Then he rolled it and rolled it again
and finished one side.
The other side too.

He built the back wall the same way.
Then he did the same with both the side walls,
and the house was done.   220

H E WENT out again.   [3.3.1]
He came back with two pieces of quartz in his hands.
He rubbed them together
and set them just under the smokehole.

The flame was steady and even.
It never went out.

His mother-in-law was occupied from then on   [3.3.2]
    quartering grizzly and mountain goat.
She got them cooking them right away.

He took up his quiver and also his bow.   [3.3.3]
He put on his frontlet.   230
Next he put his wife beneath his arm
and went away with her, they say.
He was the son, they say,
    of One Who Cuts Across the Stars.[24]

WHEN he'd lived with his wife   [4.1.1]
    in his father's house for a time,
Ghaawaxh's Daughter bore him a child.

She gave birth to a boy.
And then she gave birth to another.
And then to another.
And then to another.

And then she gave birth to another.   240
Then to another.
Then to another.
Then to another.

And then she gave birth again.
She gave birth to a girl.
Again she gave birth.
She gave birth to a girl.

He named the eldest boy Tornado.   [4.1.2]
He named the younger girl Cleaning the Wounds.
He named the other Healing the Injured.   250

Their grandfather summoned the eldest   [4.1.3]
and pulled out his bones
and put stones in their places.
He filled his whole body with stones.

O NE DAY he gave ten servants to the eldest   [4.2.1]
      of his grandsons.
Then he gave ten servants to the next.
He gave ten to all eight.
And then he made houses for each, arranged in a row.
All the housefronts were sewn.

On the eldest one's housefront he painted a thunderbird.   260
On the next, he painted the sealion.
On the next, he painted a rainbow.
On the next, he painted a killer whale.

On the next, he painted a human.
On the next, he painted stars.
On the next, he painted a cormorant.
On the next, he painted a gull.

He presented a chest full of spears to the eldest.   [4.2.2]
He gave him a box full of arrows as well.
He gave the same things to all eight.   270
And as for their sisters,
he dressed each of the two
      in two marten-skin blankets, they say.

Then he sat down in front of his grandchildren's town,   [4.2.3]
and he called them to come.
They picked up their weapons
and went at each other.

A little later, one of them was hit.
The elder girl went to him
and drew the arrow out.

The younger went to him next   280
and spat on her palms
and rubbed his wounds.
At once, there were ten of them back in the fray.

The two were moving freely among them.
Then they all tried shooting at the girls.
The arrows just bounced off the marten skins.
That's why their grandfather gave them
    the marten-skin blankets.

They stayed on their feet,
and he called off the fighting.

ONE DAY he got ready to lower   290
       his grandchildren's town.   [4.3.1]
He pulled apart the floor planks
and looked down.
He could see people close to the houses
    of Metlakatla and Qqaaduu.

When midnight came   [4.3.2]
he lowered the house of the eldest.
When it had almost reached the ground,
a voice from Metlakatla said,
«Huuuwaaaaa! Ghosts are pitching camp!»
He heard someone say that, they say.

He lowered a second.   300
He lowered a third.

Then he gave the youngest some instructions.   [4.3.3]
«If they're proving too much for you,
  and you ever have to fall back,
  make a sketch for me on a wedge,
  and when you feed it to the fire,
  you say, *Let my grandfather know*,»
his grandfather said.[25]

A LL THIS WHILE, those at Metlakatla were saying,   [5.1.1]
      «Huuuwaaaaa! Ghosts are pitching camp!»   310

All eight came down.
Next morning – yes! – the smoke rose over top of them.
They strolled back and forth in front of the town
wearing feathers in their hair.
The others wondered who they were.

They sent a servant over by canoe to ask for fire.   [5.1.2]
«Go to the one in the middle,
      the one with the thunderbird on it,»
they said to him, they say.

He landed in front of it
⟨and went in⟩   319a
and put his cold coals in the fire.   320

Toward the door, he saw – yes!
it was Ghaawaxh doing the cooking.
The same one whose sons they killed.

A line of gamblers stretched from the rear of the house
      all the way to the door.
Other people clustered near the players.
He stared at them.

One of them threw him a good piece of meat.
«Here, try the food of the ghosts.»

He left.
And then he threw away the coals, they say,   330
and paddled off.
He went straight back.
He kept the meat, however.

He went into his master's house,   [5.1.3]
and he said, «Did you really kill Ghaawaxh?»

Right away, they called in everyone in town, they say,
and asked, «Did you kill Ghaawaxh?»
Yes, said some, and others, no.
Some said she might have escaped.

When it was time to go to bed,   340
a brainless one bit off a piece of the mountain goat meat.   [5.1.4]
They expected to see him
drop dead where he stood.

A bit later, he said,
«It went down very well.
Taste it. Chew it. This is human food.»

One of the bunch started talking, they say.
«Well, go there and gamble.
Then you'll be able to see for yourselves
whether Ghaawaxh escaped.»   350

They went to bed,   [5.1.5]
and early next day the town mother's boat
    rode on the water.

The leaders of the town and all the young men went along.
They followed that canoe across.

A s soon as they beached the canoes,   [5.2.1]
they went into the middle house,
and those who were playing each other
ended their games.
They started right away to play
    against their guests instead.[26]

The mother of the town played against the eldest brother.   360
Ghaawaxh spread grizzly skins all throughout the house,
    which they didn't do at their place.
She and the rest of the women began to serve food.

Being left-handed,
the elder brother handled the sticks on that side.
His war club lay on that side too.

When they had been working the sticks for a while,   [5.2.2]
he stopped the mother of the town,
    who was just, they say, in the midst of his turn.
«You're cheating me.»

«No,» the one who was facing him said,   370
«I am not cheating you.»
    This one persisted, ignoring his answer.

After they had argued for a while,
the mother of the town threw cedarbark dust
    in this one's face, they say.
Then this one clonked him on the head.
He killed him.

There was commotion in the house.   [5.2.3]
The ones on that side grabbed their weapons,
those from Metlakatla too.
They started at it right away.   380

As the battle continued,
the sisters were moving among them.
Whenever any of the others hit them with a spear,
the spearhead simply bounced away.

After the battle had raged for a while,
one got an arrowhead lodged in his body.
The wound was bad.

As he was starting to keel over,
the younger sister sucked his wound
and sucked the arrowhead right out.   390

The other also sucked his wound,
and she spat on her palm
and rubbed.
Then he got up,
and the ten went on fighting.

They were still going at it the next day at dawn,
and the day after that,
and they began to push the Qqaaduu people back.

I T WAS THEN that the youngest brother   [5.3.1]
        went back in the house
and sketched a figure on the butt end of a wedge.   400
He said, «Let my grandfather know,»
and then he fed it to the fire.

In an instant, it was standing in his doorway, [5.3.2]
and this is what it said:
«Your grandsons are losing.»

Then he looked down through the floor planks.
It was true: they were starting to drive his grandchildren back
when they'd only begun to even the score.

The elder brother was naked,
taking swings at them with his fists. 410
When he landed a blow,
there was one who didn't get up again.

His grandfather kept looking down. [5.3.3]
He reached around behind him
and took down his bentwood box.

After pulling four more boxes from inside it,
he lifted something out of it
that bristled with tufts of thunderhead
    and wads of matted goat hair.

After gazing down a little while longer,
he dropped it on the ones from Metlakatla. 420
Nothing was visible then except their legs.

The others struck at them
and killed them.
That was the Avenger's Cloud, they say. 424

Anonymous Tlingit artist. *Naaxiin (figured blanket or Chilkat blanket).*
Mountain goat wool & yellowcedar bark, 167 × 91 cm + approx. 45 cm of fringe. ca 1875.
(American Museum of Natural History, New York: 16.1/869)

The Qquuna Cycle §2

Second Trilogy[1]

Anonymous Tlingit artist. *Bowl in the form of a redcedar dugout.*
Alder, 32 cm long. 19th century.
(Phoebe Apperson Hearst Museum, University of California, Berkeley: N° 2-4634)

§2.1 The One They Abandoned
for Eating a Seal Flipper

THERE WAS ONE OF GOOD FAMILY, THEY SAY. [1.1]
He was forever making arrows, way up high behind the fire
    in his father's house.
He was a sniffer instead of an eater, they say.
He lived in Metlakatla, where his father
    owned the town, they say.
His father was the mother of the town.

Then someone in the village shot some seals, they say.
He boiled the meat
and invited the people, they say.

The high-class arrowmaker's father came.
The whole town flowed into the house. 10
They had a feast there.

As the guests were heading home,
they sent some seal meat over to his lady,
who had stayed back in the headman's house, they say.
When they carried it in,
one of the flippers lay on the top.

Now he looked down from up above
where he was always making arrows.
Then he came down

and called to his mother,   20
«Give me a fingerbowl.
I want to wash my hands.»

Then he said,
«Pass me that.»
He ate it.
He polished it right off
and passed the empty platter back.

Now the headman came back in
and said to his wife,
«Mother of my child, let me have a little taste
        of that harbor seal flipper   30
that I had left over from the feast.»

«My son just ate it,»
she said to her husband, they say.

From up where he was always making arrows,
he could hear his mother's words.
When she had spoken to her husband,
he didn't make a sound.

Later, he said, «The town is moving tomorrow.
Pass the word.»
Instantly, a slave went out   40
and cried, «His father says we leeeeeeeeeave
        the favored child behind tomorrow.»

D ARKNESS fell,   [1.2]
    and he went out to see the wife
        of one of the ten brothers of his mother –
the one that he was sleeping with, they say.

When he had been in bed with her awhile,
she told him what to do, they say.

«When they're just about to leave,
I'll get off to go outside.²
Dig around with your toe
in the place where I squat.   50
I will hide something there on your behalf.»   51

Around his ankles, he wore amulets, they say,
     made out of copper.   733
He had a younger brother who could just sit up, they say.   52
He also had a dog.

W HEN dawn began to spread its wings,   [1.3]
     the noise they made preparing for departure
          echoed up the beach.

Then, when they were just about to leave,
he took over the care of his baby brother, they say.
He also kept the dog
which he had raised since it was born.

They were just setting off   60
when his uncle's wife climbed out of the canoe
     and walked away, they say.
She squatted down just behind the driftwood.
The moment she was back on board,
they started on their way.

When they had gone around the point,
he walked to where she'd gone.
Nothing but a rotted stick was lying there.

Then he started poking with his toe.
He found a small box
laced around with cord. 70

He set the box beside his baby brother,
and he gathered up some planks.
Next he built a hut,
just big enough to sleep in.

After it was made,
he sat beside his baby brother
and opened up the box.

There was a square-cornered oil dish inside it,
and both halves of a mussel shell
    wrapped and tied with twine.
He untied them. 80
Yes! They held live coals.

He looked inside the oil dish.
Only half the space was taken up with oil.
There were cranberries too,
and in the bottom of the dish, ten salmon.

He didn't eat a bite of that food.
He kept it all to last his little brother through the winter.
Meantime, he continued making arrows.

⸼   ⸼   ⸼

SOME TIME LATER, there was one salmon left, [2.1]
and a little bit of oil, 90
and only a few berries.

Then he started fretting.

There was going to be nothing
to feed his little brother.
He was also sharing with the dog.
That's the reason it was almost gone.

There was just one salmon fillet left,
a very little bit of oil left,
the cranberries very nearly gone.

Then nothing but the scraps were left.   100
He gave them to his brother,
together with the last bit of oil.

Darkness fell,
and he lay down,
and then he wept and wept and wept.
He cried into the night
that he had nothing left to feed his little brother.

LATER ON, his dog went out.   [2.2]
It started barking just behind the hut.

He sat up quickly   110
where he lay, beside his little brother.
Then he grabbed his bow,
which rested right close by.

There in the hut he moistened an arrowshaft with his lips.
Right outside the hut he set it to his bow.
Then he crept forward steadily.

The dog was barking into the hole
below the base of a redcedar blown over by the wind.
When he crept up close,

there was not a sign of anything.   120
The dog was barking at the ground.

When he was right there beside it,
it was barking at the rainwater standing in the hole.
A salmon – yes! – was floating there.
He speared it with his arrow.
He also broke its neck.

He brought it back
and laid it on a plank beside the hut
and split it.
Then he boiled the head, the body, the liver, the heart.   130

He fed the body and head to his little brother.
He fed the liver and heart to the dog.
He himself ate nothing.

He went back to bed,
but when the dawn came, the dog
was barking there again.

He went back there with his bow,
and looked in the pool of water.
Two salmon floated there.
He speared them with an arrow.   140
Then he brought them to the hut.

After he had split them,
he boiled the fillets, heads and livers,
and he fed his brother and his dog.
He himself again ate nothing.

Next day it was barking there again.
He grabbed his bow.
Just outside the hut, he nocked his arrow.

He went there,
and three salmon lay in the same place.   150
Each morning there was one more.

There were eventually ten there,
and he speared them with his arrow.
He hauled them all back
and split them.
He threw the guts and gills away.[3]   156

When the dawn came again,   160
and the dog was barking there again,
he left his bow behind.
He only took the arrows.

There was one more salmon than before.
Next day, one more still.
It continued like that until there were twenty.
Those he had split on the previous day,
he cut into strips on the next.

He split some planks up into poles
and hung the fish.   170
He dried it.

Food entered his belly then, they say,
for the first time since the others had abandoned him.
There was now enough to feed his younger brother.

Next day again, the dog was barking there.
He went there again.
There was one more salmon than before.
The next day, there was one more yet.
It continued until there were thirty.

Next day again, the dog was barking there.   180
He went there again,
and there was one more yet,
and another again the following day,
and there came to be forty.

A GAIN, as he was lying in the bed beside his brother,   [2.3]
  and the day was just about to break,
he heard the dog go out.

He listened to the sound a little while.
This was different from the bark
that he had heard before.   190

After yapping for a time,
it started growling.
Then he grabbed a pair of arrows and his bow.

Right outside the hut, he rubbed an arrowshaft with spit.
Then, bow and arrow at the ready,
he crept steadily along.

It was barking at the water, in the same place as before,
and he peered there in the water.
There was not a sign of anything.

At the edge of the water it started digging for something.   200
After it had dug there for a time,

the roots snagged in its teeth,
and after it had tugged a little while,
it pulled loose.

Then he joined in, digging right behind the dog.
The dog was digging in the lead.
As soon as they dug their way down to the tideline,
a salmon creek formed.
And as soon as it did so, it started to seethe.
He was standing there amazed.   210

Then he went to work.   [2.4.1]
He gathered the planks left behind by the villagers
and split them and split them and split them.
He made them into poles.
Then he trimmed the poles and notched them.

All this while, the salmon were running, they say.
That's what he was up to.

He measured the poles with his arms.
He made them two spans long.
Others he made one span.   220
There were twenty of each,
with notches along them at intervals.

He painted the longer ones at the top,
where they tapered and flattened.
The image he made was that of a salmon.
These, they say, were the seaward teeth of the trap.[4]

All the while he was making these,
he kept on caring for his brother and the dog, they say.
He did the cooking all this while.

When he finished the poles,   230
he went out and dug spruce roots.
Then he came back
and built a big fire out of dry branches
for scorching the roots.

At once, he split them with his teeth.
As soon as that was done,
he cut some hemlock saplings into half-rounds.
As soon as those were made,
he lashed them crosswise to the poles.

He put four crossties in the back walls of the trap   240
and made the baffles of the entranceway with three.
He put three across the seaward teeth as well,
     to make the downstream walls.

Next he cut stakes for both wings of the fish fence.[5]
Then he lashed them together
and was finished that far.

H E WENT inland,   [2.4.2]
     cut trees for his pilings,
and sharpened them at one end,
wrapping the other with bark-fiber braid.

Next he waded in and drove the pilings,   250
laying the tapered shape of the trap.
Next he put the upstream walls in place.
He tied them onto the pilings with cedarlimb line.

Next he put the baffles in the entranceway.
And then he put the downstream walls in place.
From that moment on it worked like a funnel.

WHEN he was happy with the salmon trap,   [2.4.3]
       he went to get more planks.
He pulled them from their places.
He cut some of them down into poles.   260

Then he built a larger house, they say.
And then he set up drying racks, one above another.
He made the rack supports.
He notched them.

The drying racks filled up the front and the rear of the house,
reaching up to the ridgepole.
Below the beams, they went from wall to wall.

Though he had now begun to eat,
he had no time to do so.
Still, all the while he was working,   270
he did not forget his brother and the dog.
He kept on feeding them.

As soon as the drying racks were finished   [2.4.4]
        and everything else was just as he wished,
he went to the salmon trap, they say.

He hauled and hauled and hauled them out.
He strung them right away.
He strung them on ten strings.

When evening came,
he roasted salmon for his brother,   280
and that night he didn't sleep, they say.

He hauled and hauled and hauled them out again

when the next day came,
and strung them too.

And still they kept on running.
Hu hu hu hu hu!
When had they ever been hungry?, they say.

WHEN the house was full again   [2.5]
    and he had everything he needed,
and had stayed up more than ten nights splitting fish,   290

once again, before he went to work another night,
he roasted salmon to feed his little brother
while he stayed out and worked.
He hauled out more and more and more.

Then he came back in,
and both rows of the fish that he had roasted
had disappeared, they say.

He went up near his little brother.
After shedding several tears right close beside him,
he went back out to split some fish, they say.   300

Evening fell,
and he roasted some more fish.
There was still more in the trap,
and so he worked through yet another night.
He was going and going and going.

Then he came back in,
and once again, the food he'd cooked
had simply vanished.

He shed another tear up close beside his little brother,
and then he went back out to split some fish.   310

He split them,
working through the night,
and also set three rows of fish to roast.

On and on and on he went, hauling in the fish.
Then he came inside,
and – yes! – the roasted salmon had just vanished.
Half of what was hanging in the racks
was also gone.

Then he called his younger brother,
and he said, «Brother dear, have you been eating   320
all the things that I've been roasting for you?»

«No. Just after you go out,
  some creature, big like you, comes in
  and scoops it up
  and grabs some from the racks
  and wolfs it down.»

«And I've been thinking it was you!»

He gave up trying to keep up with all the salmon.
He gave up splitting salmon too.
He was glum.   330

He sat there waiting,
watching,
wanting to see what would take his fish.

Then evening fell,

and he took out his bow
and strung it.

He brought two chests of arrows out
and set one on the left side of the door,
and he sat with his bow on the other one, to the right.

When he'd been sitting for a while,   340
and it was pitch dark,
a pair of flaming torches came up close beside the house.

After coming round the front –
yes! – they stood there in the doorway.
A face was in the doorway, fires blazing in its eyes.

It stood there and it stood there.
Then it scooped up every scrap of roasted fish
and wolfed it down.

Then it stood there looking up,
and then it reached for what was there   350
and wolfed it down.
And as it did so, this one shot it
underneath first one arm, then the other.

This was Gawgiila, they say.

And as Gawgiila kept on reaching up and turning,
this one kept on shooting.
He shot him many times.

Just as he was emptying the first chest of arrows,
that one moved to get the salmon on the other side,
and this one shifted over to the second chest.   360

When he had emptied that one too,
it was the middle of the night,
and that one went away.

This one went out after him at once.
He took more arrows with him,
and after he had shot him many times both back and front,
the other stood up straight
and – yes! – stepped right across a mountain.

Then this one came back home.
He came inside   370
and bounced his little brother on his knee.
He scratched the dog behind the ears,
and the dog ran his tongue around his jowls.

Then he held his father's drum above his brother and the dog
and laid it down on top of them.

And then he left again.

       ➤   ➤   ➤

H E FOLLOWED the trail of headless arrowshafts.[6]   [3.1]
After he had loped along a ways,
he heard a rapid noise.

He stood stock-still,   380
and after he had listened for a while,
what he heard turned into something
like the sound of someone working with an adze.
Then he went in that direction.

Someone – yes! – was roughing out the hull of a canoe.

The crown of his head was the only part of him showing.
This one stared at it intently.

Then he crept up toward him.
Then the head went down inside the hull,
and then it staaaaayed inside awhile,   390
and the adze lay out there in plain view.

Then this one nicked it
and ran with it and hid
beneath some ferns that stood nearby.

When he had kept on watching for a time,
the other one stood up
right in the midst of what he was doing
and looked around for something.
He swept the chips aside,
and this one kept on staring at him hard.   400

That one closed his eyes
and sucked his fingernails.
After that, he spoke.

«Grandson, come and see me.
News of you has come here by canoe.
News has come that they abandoned you
because you ate a harbor seal flipper
    that your father had left over.
Come see me, grandson,
if it's you.»

He came out then, they say, and stood there   410
and handed him his adze.
That one took it right away.

It was Master Carver making that canoe, they say.

« You know, you could get four crooked wedges
   and rig a pair of loops both fore and aft
   and split one hull out from the inside of the other. »

   That one hadn't ever managed
   to split them out from inside one another, so they say,
   because his wedges were too straight.

   So that one went to get the wedges   420
   while this one rigged the loops.
   When that one brought the wedges back,
   this one told him how to place them fore and aft.
   Then he began to drive them in.

   When he had worked his way around,
        pounding them in sequence for a time,
   the hulls began to – yes! – come loose from one another.
   And after he continued this awhile,
   they sprang apart from one another.

« I'm not surprised they want my salmon! »
   He was odd, you know, from being all alone
        with no one but his brother.   430

   Then the other said,
« Now, grandson, come with me.
   You're going to marry my daughter. »

THEN he went with him.   [3.2]
   Oooooh yes! There was smoke going up in a row,
        like the teeth of a comb.
   This was that one's town, they say,

and that one took him to his house,
at the center of the row.

Seated – yes indeed – behind the fire, between the screens
was someone lovely as a spirit-being's daughter.   440
And her father said to her,
«Princess, my dear, come and sit next to your husband.»

She rose at once
and came and sat beside him.

After his father-in-law had fed him and fed him and fed him,
it was starting to get dark,
and then she said to him,
«Let's go outside.»

«I don't know where they go when they go out.»

«If only there were not so many going there,» she said,   450
«where they go out.»

He said to her, «I'll go with you.»

It was dark then,
and he went with her.
He stayed out with her quite a while.
Then they came back in and sat back down.

A drum kept sounding all the while
from the town straight across on the opposite shore.

His wife's father fed him very well.
He went outside each evening with his wife,   460
and the drum was always beating in the same place.

One day, he had heard the sound enough.
When he was outside, squatting with his wife,
he asked her, «Why is that drum
    forever beating in the same place?»

«They're working on the one who owns the town, they say.»
  Then, they say, he said to his wife,
«Let's go over there and see.»

W HEN they came back in,   [3.3.1]
    she asked her father,
«Daddy, don't you own a small canoe?»   470

«Yes, my princess, one is sitting on the beach.»
  Then a pair of servants launched the boat
while his wife and he walked down.

They climbed aboard
and let the servants do the paddling.
He rode amidships with his wife.

They came ashore
and brought up the canoe.
His wife and he went up the beach together.

The moment they saw him,   480
the crowd that was standing in front of the house,
peering by turns through the door,
opened suddenly before him.
Then he peered inside, together with his wife.

The one he had riddled with arrows – yes! –
    hung slumped and swollen in a sling
made out of kelp stipes looped from poles

lashed together into a frame
that was hanging on ropes from one of the beams.

His toes were in the lower loops,
his fingers twined around the loops above.   490
There were arrows sticking out of him all over.
He was in enormous pain.

A FTER watching for a time,   [3.3.2]
   this one thought,
«Why can't the shaman see
what's sticking out of him, I wonder?»

When he thought this,
someone else who stood nearby
turned and looked him in the face,
and said aloud, they say,   500

«You ought to hear
what someone standing here is saying:
*Why can't the shaman who is working on him see
what's sticking out of him, I wonder?*»

The one who spoke his thought aloud
was one of the Land Otter people who read minds, they say.
The shaman doing the doctoring
was a Land Otter person too, they say –
and yet they couldn't see what he saw
sticking out of him, they say.   510

After a bit, someone stood up
and proposed that he should take a turn, they say.
Then he got ready to leave, along with his wife.

They came back over,
and he asked her to ask her mother for something, they say.

«Mother, don't you have some cedarbark?»
«Yes, my princess.»

Then she gave him some.
They dried it by the fire,
and they pounded it   520
and plaited it into fine cedarbark bands.
It was finished.

THEN they were ready to come for him, they say.   [3.3.3]
  There in the house he wrapped the bands
     of cedarbark around himself.
He wrapped his arms and chest and legs.

When they offered him ten moose skins,
he agreed to go.

Then they took him over there, they say.
When he came in,
the other was still slumped there in his sling.   530

After dancing around him awhile,
he pulled all the arrowheads from his back,
slipping them quickly into the bands around his arms.

That one had been hanging there in never-ending pain.

Then he pulled them out on either side from head to toe.
He tucked them in the wrappings on his body and his back.

Then he took him down
and set him on the floorplanks.
The creature who could not sit down was sitting.

He asked them for some cushions then,   540
and laid him down.
He rested there in comfort.

It was then – yes! – that he saw the other's daughter,
and he stared.
He looked straight at her.

Then he picked the other up
and hooked his toes back on the lower rungs,
the fingers of both hands on those above.

He stuck the arrowheads back
where they had come from, in his buttocks and his sides,   550
and he was in great pain again.

Then this one turned away.
He wouldn't look at him again.
They brought him back across in their canoe.

As soon as he returned,   [3.3.4]
two of them were standing in the doorway.
They made it twice ten moosehides
and a pair of copper shields.
He turned them down.

Then they came again   560
to ask if he would do it in exchange
    for all the property in town.
He turned them down each time.

Then that one saw what this one had in mind.
The one whose daughter was about to be his wife
 thought very highly of his daughter,
since his own wealth was so great.
But after this one turned down all his property,
he said that he could marry his daughter, they say.

H E GOT READY to go there again.   [3.3.5]
 He wrapped himself in cedarbark again,
and then they ferried him across, they say.   570

He went inside
and started dancing round and round
the one who hung there in a sling.

As he continued going round,
he pulled them out from all across his back,
and then he pulled them from the left side of his body.
Then he took him down
and let him sit.

While that one sat there,
he continued to remove them from his right side
 and his shoulders and his chest   580
until none of them remained.

There he sat.
Then he said to his daughter,
«My princess, come out and sit next to your husband.»

She married the one of good family,
and Master Carver's Daughter crossed the channel right away.
That quick, he had two wives.

    ➤   ➤   ➤

AFTER he'd been living with his wives a little while,   [4.1]
a day came when he lingered in his bed.
He was still there when they came to bed again.   590

He was the same on the following day.
Both his wives pretended not to notice.
There in the bed, he was constantly weeping.

Then, they say, the old one asked his daughter,
«Why is your husband behaving this way?»

Then she went to her husband gently
and used her gracious voice on him awhile.
Then she came back and answered her father,
«He acts this way because he's homesick
for the place where he left his little brother.»   600

«My princess, you should go there with your husband –
both of you, I mean.
Take your husband out to look
for the canoe I own
that sits out at the edge of town.»

Then they went there with their husband.
They reached the place together.
Nothing lay there but a humpback whale skull.

Then they all came back.
She said to her father,   610
«Daddy, nothing's there except a humpback whale skull.»

«That's it.
A person has to say to it, *Seaward, father's canoe!*»

Yes! It lay there waiting, just offshore.
Hu hu hu hu hu!
A big canoe, broad in the beam, a sockeye on the prow.

They loaded it with fine food,
and another one was launched across the channel
    for Master Carver's Daughter.
They loaded it and loaded it and loaded it with fine food too.
It was piled high with cranberries, sweet berries,
    prime cuts of mountain goat,
        berrycakes of all the different kinds.   620

They brought the boats alongside one another
and set off on their way.
Both wives went along with him, they say.

WHEN they were coming near the townsite,   [4.2]
    this one strung his bow.
He held two arrows in his hand.

He leaped ashore, they say,
at a rocky point not far from town.
Then he ran up to his house.

When he went in,   630
he lifted up the drum
that he had placed there to protect his little brother.
His little brother and his dog lay underneath it,
with nothing but the ligaments still linking up their bones.

When the canoes came up to shore,
he went back down to meet them.
He drew his bow to shoot Gawgiila's Daughter.

Then she said to him, «Don't kill us.
We are going up to wake your younger brother.»
Then he acted otherwise.   640

They all went up together then
and sat above his brother.

Gawgiila's Daughter took something out of her purse
and bit off the tip of it.
It was blue.

Then Master Carver's Daughter brought out a mat
        with a border of cumulus clouds
and laid it over his younger brother.
The one kept spraying something through her teeth
        at what was underneath it.

This one told Gawgiila's Daughter to hurry.
That one answered, «You might wish to do so, lady.   650
Get a move on.»

Then she lifted up the mat.
His brother got up from where he had lain.
The dog was glad to see him too.

Then they unloaded both canoes.
The crew had made no move to do so until then,
        they always say.
And there were scads of them
that his fathers-in-law had given him.

The next day, they rebuilt the house.
They made a bigger place for him.   660
It was sewn.

In the house that stood there now
they ate nothing but the best food,
day after day after day.

When juicy venison was served,
prime cuts of mountain goat were waiting to be served.
They sliced it up and handed it around.
They barbecued it right there on the fire.
He was eating.

O NE DAY they said to their husband,   670
   «Let us have some digging sticks.»   [4.3]

What they said to him excited him.
He climbed a spruce.
He cut some gummy limbs.

He worked them,
and he finished them.
Fresh from the woods, the sticks were leaking sap.

When he brought them to the house,
they simply laughed at him and said,
«Give us real digging sticks – our fathers' kind.»   680

He went out once again
and used redcedar limbs.
The women turned them down again.
He tried all kinds of wood.
He had no luck.

Then he tried some spurs of yellowcedar.
He roughed them out right there,
and then he brought them back

and finished them.
The women said, «Make the lower part red
    and the upper part blue.»   690

They were hung behind the fire.
They had egg-shaped grips on top.

They ate their breakfast early the next morning.
The crowd was like a mass of hatching eggs.
The young men flirted with his wives.
He just pretended not to see.

Then both women left the house
    with digging sticks laid across their shoulders.
They took no baskets, though.
And he went with them.

The butter clams were spitting,   700
and he said, «Hey! Over here!»

When he called out to them,
the women both came over.
Then he heard them snicker there together.
They embarrassed him.

They had walked along together for a while
and then went separate ways,
and then they headed inland, toward the trees.
They both came suddenly to a standstill,
facing one another from the two ends of the town.   710

They pushed down on their digging sticks.
By prying up the ground,
they pried another town up,

even bigger than the village that they had.
They restored their husband's father's town.

>   ❯   ❯   ❯

SUDDENLY NOW, there were crowds   [5.1]
    strolling along in front of the town.
He became town mother of his father's town.
Both women were still his.

They walked the beach again next day,
and when he spoke to them of clams   720
the way he spoke the day before,
they laughed at him out loud.
They embarrassed him still more.

When they had gone along together for a while,
they drove their digging sticks into the ground again.
They turned up two humpback whales,
and the people of the town came down to flense them.

They went down again the next day
and dug up another two.
They went down every day for five days,   730
and they dug up ten in all.
They dug up five on either side.[7]   732

The one of good family
    distributed five whales to the people,   734
and they flensed and flensed and flensed, day after day.
He left the other five alone,
and kept them tethered to his house.

The gulls that came to feed there

hovered thick as smoke
above the whale flesh that lay there.   740

Then he got his bow and arrows.
After watching them awhile,
he picked a little gull.
He shot it in the head
and brought it in.

He slit it open from the tail
and took the skin.
He pegged it out to dry.
When it was starting to get dry,
he put it on.   750

Wearing it, he hopped across the floorplanks.
Then he tried his wings.
He flew right out.
He left the town behind.
Neither of his wives had any notion where he was.

N ASS INLET is the place he flew, they say.   [5.2]
       He wanted to see
how his father's people were faring.

They were doing very poorly with their fish rakes.
His father's men had only one fish in their boat.   760
He snatched it up
as one of them was watching.
«Aiiiii! He's going to eat the eulachon!»[8]

They all looked up at him.
They saw around his legs
the very things the favored child –

the one they had abandoned –
used to wear around his ankles.

They paddled off
and hit the beach bow-first.[9]   770

They told the headman that his child –
the one they had abandoned –
had been changed into a gull
and that he'd flown just above them.
That's precisely what they said, they say.

Then his father and his mother turned away,
and after they had wept,
the headman said to his head servant,
«Tomorrow, go and find my child's bones.»

T HE SERVANTS headed off,   780
and after they had ridden down the inlet on the tide,   [5.3]
they found a rotting chunk of whale blubber floating.
When they had paddled farther on,
they found two more.

After scouting for a hiding place,
they cached it there, they say.
They were hungry in Nass Inlet,
in the days before the heavy runs of eulachon.
They cached it to come back to it, they say.

They continued on from there   790
and then their headman's town came into view.
The town was larger than before.
There were crowds along the beachfront.

The servants' bones, as they came closer, turned to water.
The stern man was the only one whose paddle
    kept moving in his hands.

Then this one came outside.
His father's servants – yes! a crew of four –
    were just about to land.
He went back in
and strung his bow
and got four arrows too.   800

He ran out, shoving everyone aside.
He drew his bow.
Then Gawgiila's Daughter and Master Carver's Daughter
    held tight to both his shoulders.

«Wait! Let them land.
 Then bring them to the house.
 It would be best for you to send them back in style.»
Then the women took his weapons.
He went on standing where he was.

As they were coming up on shore,
he went to them and said,   810
«Come ashore, all four of you.
 Strip naked,
 and then come with me.»

They stripped,
and then they went with him.
He gave them seats midway along the wall,
and then he fed them.

When they had eaten nearly everything he gave them,
he offered them some humpback whale too.
They ate it up as if the heaps were scraps.   820

He made them strip
in order to be sure
they took no leftovers home with them, they say.

When they began to take their leave,
one of them was doubled over almost to the ground.
He went up to him and asked,
«Why do you look like someone punched you in the belly?»

That one spoke when he was spoken to.
«My lord, the reason is, I'm stuffed.»

When they were ready to set off,   830
he spoke to them again.
«Don't touch those rotting chunks of whale
        you saw drifting on the water.
I'll be watching the whole way.»

Then he told them something more:
«Say you could not find my bones.»

THEY headed off,   [5.4]
    and it was nighttime when they got there.
They said, «We found no bones.»

Then his parents wept,
and after they had wept,   840
they went to sleep.

Then the head servant's child – yes! – began to cry.
It cried the way a child does
when something catches in its throat.

The headman's wife said, «Bring the child here!»
and she bounced it on her knee.
Then she put her finger in its mouth,
and she discovered something there.

And then they stared at it.
They didn't understand   850
how it could be.
Then the baby's father said, «You ought to see
how much there is!

«The town that was your own
has grown larger.
His two wives dug the whole thing up again.

«They go to get some water
and they get ten whales too.
There are five of them there now, floating on a tether.»

Then, though it was midnight,   860
the headman ordered wood put on the fire, they say,
and they went out to call the people.

Right away, they came and came and came.
When they had polished off the one remaining salmon
and the last handful of cranberries, he said,

«You ought to hear what I am thinking.
I think you should prepare yourselves to go
to a kinsman of yours whom I abandoned.

I should give the town to him.»[10]
The village headmen all approved.   870

Then another plan was made.
His mother's ten brothers planned to offer him
    their daughters as his brides.
Each father had his daughter fitted out.

Next day, the town was taken down.
Hu hu hu hu hu!
They launched their big canoes.
They painted up his uncles' daughters' faces.

They rafted up the boats.
They laid redcedar planks across the gunwales.
Then they perched their daughters up on those.   880

T HEY rode the falling tide a ways,   [5.5]
  and came across those rotting chunks of whale.

They went ashore
and boiled some right there
and ate it,
and they took some to their daughters
who remained in the canoes.

But the youngest uncle's daughter was unpainted.
Her father left her plain,
the way she was.   890

He handed her a little piece of bark cake,[11]
and told her she should bite off half of that.
She did as she was told.

Then they paddled on in the canoes,
and then the town came into view, they say.
It lay there – yes! –
and there the whales floated too.

The moment that he saw them,
the headman got his bow,
but when his two wives talked to him awhile,   900
he started to calm down.

They landed,
and a good-looking woman was the first to come up toward him.
He told her to open her mouth.

The smell was strong,
and he turned her away.
He turned all nine of them away.

Then the daughter of the youngest came ashore.
She opened her mouth.
It was sweet,   910
and then he smiled
and led her inside.

Then the others came ashore.
His father gave him all the people of his town,
and they settled alongside those who were there.

This one gave five whales
to the people who had come.
Day after day they were flensing them.
Day after day after day, they were flensing and flensing.
As though the heaps of food were scraps, they ate them.   920

§2.2 The Man Who Married a Bear[12]

Then, out behind of the town,   [1]
    a man began to hunt with dogs, they say.
When he'd been hunting there awhile,
his dog caught a scent.
He got up close.
The dog – yes! – was barking at a grizzly.

This one went right up to him,
and that one threw him down inside the den.
His mate was sitting in the house.
This one tumbled in and sprawled against her breast.

Then she dug a hole for him   10
and put him there.
She kept his cedarbark cape between her teeth,
    and nothing more.

The other came inside,
and then he asked her,
«Where's the human I threw in to you?»

«This is what you threw me,
and I've ripped it all to shreds.»

He went out after him again
and couldn't find him.

Then he asked her once again,   20
and she gave him the same answer.

Before daybreak, that one went to hunt, they say.
He slung a big basket on his back,
and she was handling his thread.[13]
It started to uncoil.

Then she let the hunter out
and gave him food,
and then they lay with one another in the house.

When it started coiling in again,
she lifted up a floorplank   30
and put him underneath
and sat on top.

The other one came in.
There were a few small crabs in the bottom of the basket.
His luck had changed.

He sat there in the house,
and he did not know why
he captured nothing.

Again the following day, she was paying out his thread
while he went out to hunt some more.   40
While it was still unrolling from the skein,
she cut it.

Then she brought the human out
and married him, they say.
She showed him where and how

her former husband hunted,
and she told him what to use.

Next day, he took the basket
and headed through the woods.

When he had gone along a ways,   50
he came upon a bay.
In the midst of it, a shoal was just awash.
He swam there
and loaded up with crab.

With the basket filled, he left.
His wife's eyes opened wide,
his basket was so full.

He went on living with the grizzly as his wife.
That was the only life he lived in all that while.

AFTER A TIME, she conceived a child, they say.   60
She bore a boy.   [2]
She conceived again
and bore another boy.
She had the two.

Now he had to work to get enough.
Pretty soon, he gave up catching crabs
and started hunting harbor seal.

He stayed out hunting once for four nights
laying in a store,
and then he took his leave.   70

She told him what he was to do.

«When you go out to hunt,
 get enough for my children.
 We'll be at the head of the inlet, waiting.»

Then she said to him,
«Don't speak sweetly to another woman.»
 She handed him a basket made of spruce root,
 brimming with fresh water.
 A blue falcon's feather floated there.

She said to him,   80
«Don't mess with other women.
 I will see it by this means.
 Drink from it after you've eaten.»
 This is what she told him.

He left her then
 and walked back to his father's town.

W HEN he had sat beside a waterhole   [3]
      behind the town awhile,
 his mother came.
 He told her who he was.

His mother came out of the timber in tears.   90
 Then his father got a silver otter skin he owned
      and sent it out to him.
 With that, he came inside.

They made a place for him to sleep,
 and he lay down.
 They were continuously offering him food.
 He wouldn't eat a thing.

Sometime later, he went out at night with two men
to go hunting.
He was spearing harbor seal.

When the canoe was full –   100
that is, when it was truly full –
he headed up the inlet.
The others who were with him wondered what was going on.

When they reached the head of the inlet,
a grizzly was sitting there.
Those who paddled with him
spun and faced the other way.
He held his course
and came to shore.

He went to where the grizzly was   110
and sat beside her there.
Both cubs were with her, frolicking.
They licked him up and down.

He went to the boat
and unloaded the seals
and paddled away.

After many nights passed,
he went hunting again,
and those who had gone with him before
went out with him again.   120
He speared more seals.

The canoe was brim full,
and they kindled a fire
and pit-cooked the seals right there.

Then they loaded the boat
and went up the inlet again.

When they came near the shore,
those who were with him backpaddled again.

He went ashore again
and sat beside the grizzly.   130
The youngsters licked him up and down,
but their mother wouldn't look in his direction.

When he had sat with her awhile,
he stood up and unloaded the seals
and paddled away.

THEN came the time he went for water by himself   [4]
and slept with one he was in love with.[14]
Then he went back to the house.

After going there again,
he went out hunting.   140
Then he cooked the harbor seal
and went to the inlet again.

The grizzly was different this time.
Her hackles went up as soon as she saw him.
«Turn back!» his stern man said.
«She's not the same! Her back is up.»

But this one paddled toward the beach.
He went ashore,
and once again he sat beside her.
She wouldn't look in his direction,   150
though the cubs were just as happy as before.

He sat beside her for a time,
and then she went for him,
whacking him back and forth with her paws
until she'd ripped him limb from limb.

Then the cubs started in on their mother,
one on each side,
and tore her to pieces.

Then they wanted her back.
They were acting like dogs   160
that have medicine smeared on their noses.
Then they went away together.

LATER, they tackled some people and killed them   [5]
just as the people were starting a fire.
Then they went away again together.
After that, they killed some others.

Then once, when they'd been doing this awhile –
going here and there together for a while –
they came along behind some people
who were kindling a fire,   170
and the child who was with the people cried.

One of the people said to the child,
«Hold your tongue!
Your uncle's children might come by and kill us.»
When they heard those words,
they went away, they say.   176

§2.3 The Sapsucker[15]

WHAT'S ENCIRCLED BY THE TIDE
was grassy all around, they say.
He was always going back and forth along it –
the Sapsucker was.
He had no feathers whatsoever.

Then, up above, there was a big spruce sloughing off its skin.
He whacked it with his beak.
And as he drummed his beak against it,
something said,
«Your father's father asks you in.»   10

Then he looked for what had spoken.
No one was there.
Then, after something said the same thing again,
when he peeked inside the hollow of the tree,
someone shrunken and sunken, white as a gull, sat at the back.

Then he stepped inside.
The elder lifted the lid from a little round basket.
When he had opened up the five nested one inside another,
he presented him with feathers for his wings.
Ooooooooooh my!   20

Then he gave him tailfeathers too.
Then he shaped him with his hands.
He colored the upper part of him red.

Then he said to him,
«Now, my little grandson, you should go.
This is why you have been with me.»

Then he went back out,
and then he flew,
and then he did the same thing as before.
He clutched the tree,   30
and then he struck it with his beak.

And so it ends.

Anonymous Haida or Tlingit artist. *Standing shaman.*

Alder, 48 cm tall. Late 19th century.

(Museum of Anthropology, University of British Columbia, Vancouver: A 2615.

Photograph by Bill McLennan.)

The Qquuna Cycle §3

Third Trilogy[1]

Anonymous Tlingit artist. *Raven amulet.*

Killer whale tooth, 15.5 cm long. ca 1890.

(American Museum of Natural History, New York: E 2715, neg. 291556)

§3.1 Standing Traveller

Aᴛ sᴇᴀʟɪᴏɴ ᴛᴏᴡɴ, sᴏᴍᴇᴏɴᴇ ᴡᴀs ᴛʜɪɴᴋɪɴɢ   [1.1]
        of ritual bathing, they say.[2]
Things, they say, were going on within him.

He lived in a house with his eight younger brothers.
So did his mother.
After a time, his younger brothers disappeared.

Nobody knew where they'd gone.
When daylight came, their mother wept.
When daylight came again, she wept again.

Later, when her crying stopped, she said,
«If the eldest of my sons were also gone,   10
    my heart would ache a little less
    when day is breaking.»

After she'd been saying this in front of him awhile,
he couldn't bear to hear it anymore.

Then he said to his sister,
«Sister, get out one of the stone boxes
    that my mother owns
    and fill it with water so I can get in.»

So she tied on her belt.
She set her mother's stone chest beside the door   20
and filled it up with water.

Her brother crawled to where it was.
He was just barely able to climb in.

When he'd been floating there awhile,
his butt was sticking up
like something someone tosses in the air.
His sister pushed it down
with a poker that was lying near the fire.

When she had held it down awhile,
she took the stick away.   30
His butt stayed just beneath the water.

She took the stick and pushed it down again,
and when she took the stick away,
it stayed way down beneath the water.
Then he broke the box wide open with his knees.

Then he called his sister again.
«Sister, get another one from mother
and fill it up with water.»

She filled another one with water.
He got in that one too   40
and pressed his knees against it.
He shattered that one also with his knees.

Then he called his sister again.
«Sister, fill another one with water.»
Then he broke that also with his knees.

He did the same thing again.
He broke four boxes with his knees.

T HEN he went into the sea.   [1.2]
  When he had floated there and floated there awhile,
something brushed against him.   50
He grabbed it with his hand.
He had the backfin of a flounder.

Then he called out to his sister,
«Sister, cook this
and then eat it.»

When he had gone on floating there awhile,
something nudged him.
He grabbed it.

He had one side of a halibut.
He tossed it to his sister,   60
and he said to her,
«Roast that.
Don't cook it in water.»

He got a harbor porpoise tail and a Dall's porpoise tail.
After he had taken one of every other mammal of the sea,
he tossed ashore a humpback whale's tail.
And then he said to his sister,
«This one now, you ought to cook in water.»

After he had gone on floating there awhile,
something stroked itself against him.   70
He reached for it.
Nothing was there.

After the same thing had happened yet again,
he grabbed ahead of it.
He felt it slipping through his fingers.
Then he clenched it with both hands.

After it had towed him right out of Xhaana Inlet,
he lay back and braced himself at Hlghaayxha.[3]
Then something cracked at the base of the Islands.

In his hands there was a strand of something sweet
    that he could see through.   80
He tied it in his hair.
It was one of the plumes of Hlghutghu, they say.

When he had tied it in his hair,
he swam back into the inlet, they say.
He swam along in front of Guuhlgha.[4]

Then he came to Xhaana.
The creek was backed up in a lake then.
He opened up the channel with a single motion of his hand
and hung around the creek mouth.

WHEN he had floated there awhile,   90
  he heard heavy footsteps coming toward him.   [1.3]
Someone faced him from the shore.

In his right hand, that one had a spruce knot
    and a maplewood bludgeon.
In the other, soggy seaweed and a rose-thorn club.[5]
«So, grandson, come and see me.»

He went to him at once.
«Grandson, face this way.»
He faced that way at once.

That one hit him with the spruce knot.
It was just the way it is   100
when you squeeze and crumble something in your fist.
Then he hit him with the maplewood.
That was just the same.

Then he said to him,
«Now, grandson, turn your back this way.»[6]
He did as he was told.

That one whipped him with the rose thorns.
He didn't feel a thing.
Then he hit him with the seaweed.
That nearly knocked him off his feet.   110
He straightened up some ways away.

«Wait there a moment, grandson.
We will wrestle with each other.»
That was what he said to him.

«Now let's wrestle, grandson.»
Then they laid their hands on one another.

After he tried for a while to throw him,
this one finally pinned the other to the ground.
That one smiled at him.
«What you've got is stronger, grandson.   120
Swim back down the inlet.»

After he had swum   [2.1]
and gone on swimming for a while,
he came ashore at Sealion Town.
When he had warmed himself awhile,
he lay down.

After lying there awhile,
when the day began to break,
he went outside.

He took an overgrown trail.   130
After walking for a time,
he saw a shrew
stopped in her tracks by a fallen tree.

He lifted her across,
and then he watched her.
She went beneath a clump of fern some distance off.[7]

He went there.
He spread the fronds aside.
There was – yes! – the sewn and painted front of a house.

Then that one said to him,   140
«Come in and see me, grandson.
The birds have been singing
that you would be borrowing something from me.»

She hunted through her storage box.
and bit off part of something for him.
«Yes, grandson, here it is.»

And then she told him this:
«After you have left here,
go to Guuhlgha Lake,
and take your bow along.   150

«You'll shoot a mallard there.
Blow the stomach up,
and fill it with the oil.

«I know the place well
  where something killed your younger brothers.
  After you revive your younger brothers,
  you may eat, but not before.»

H E WENT on his way   [2.2]
  and went back to his house.
After sitting there awhile,   160
he lay down.
Early the next morning, he went up to Guuhlgha Lake.

A mallard drake was there beside his mate.
Oooooooooooh yes.
He drew the bow,
  aiming just above its head,
  and there it lay like something tossed aside.

Then he brought it ashore
  and kindled a fire
  and plucked it   170
  and cooked it in water.
He saved the entrails.

Just like that, he went to the beach
  and came back with the shell of a horseclam.
Just like that, it boiled.
He skimmed the mallard grease with the shell.

He dished up the meat of the mallard,
  and just like that, he put one of the cooking rocks
      into the mallard grease.
Just like that, it splattered and seethed.

The creatures who live in the forest spoke.   180

«Oh-oh! Oh-oh! The mallard oil might spill!»[8]
Just like that, they cut him down to size.

He didn't eat the mallard meat.
As soon as the oil started to cool,
he put it in the mallard paunch.[9]   185

Then he headed off.   190
He took the oil and the mallard feathers too.
He went back home,
and then he went to bed.

W HEN daylight spread its wings,   [2.3]
    he went to Guuhlgha.
From there he took two children.
Then he went inland from one end of Sealion Town.

When he came to the lake,
he scouted around.
Then he pulled a two-headed redcedar out of the ground,
    roots and all,   200
and wrapped the base of the tree with cedarlimb line.

He tied the heads of the tree together too.
Then he spread the trunks apart and braced them.
Then he set it in the lake
and tied both children by the feet
and hung them there, dangling over the opening.[10]

It quivered and jerked
when the creature – a seawolf it was – came up in the middle.
This one kicked the brace out,
and the trap snapped tight around its throat.   210

Then it pulled everything under.
As if someone were scattering something in handfuls,
up came the splinters and shreds of redcedar.

He went away.
He leaned his tackle – two dead children and a pole –
    against the housefront.
He was thinking about using them tomorrow.

And so he went again.
He took the pair of children once again.
Again he looked around awhile,
and again he uprooted a big two-headed redcedar.   220

He spread the trunks apart,
and then a wren sang steadily, a little ways away from him,
«*Ttsii! ttsii!* my sinews! my sinews!»

Then he caught it
and pulled out its sinews
and spliced them together
and wrapped them round the base and head of the cedar.
Then he put it in the water.

When he dangled the children over the mouth of the trap
    on the end of the pole,
the seawolf came to take them.   230
He yanked out the brace.

Then it pulled everything under.
After everything went down a second time,
it came up dead.

He went out after it

and brought it in.
He pulled it up on shore.

When he started to cut from the muzzle,
thunder crashed,
and lightning bolts exploded too.   240
When he started on its back,
it was the same.

When he turned to the base of its tail,
there wasn't a sound.
Then he slit its belly open.
Out spewed his younger brothers' bones.

He assembled all his younger brothers' bones,
and chewed the leaves that Mouse Woman had given him[11]
and lathered the juices over the bones.
His brothers sat right up.   250

Then he said to them,
«Go back and take the same names and places that you had.»
They were glad to see each other.

THINGS went on and on and on and on and on –   [3.1]
   and one of them, after a while, was missing, they say.
Next morning another was missing.
This went on until all eight of them were gone again,
and this one's mind was sick.

Then he went to Guuhlgha.
He went out on a point toward the head of the inlet.   260
Across the water – yes! – he heard them
   chattering and laughing as the birds do in the morning.[12]
He pulled the ribbon out of his hair
and tossed it across.

He walked all the way over on that,
and there outside the middle house,
where their voices poured out through the door,
a crowd was milling.

He moved through the people
and looked through the door.

Behind the fire: someone lying on his back,   270
and something hanging down from up above him.
Flames were licking out of it.
It sizzled and it hissed.

After he'd been watching for a while,
the one who lay under it ran from the heat.
Behind the fire were those who are spirit beings from birth.

H E CONTINUED to sit there,   [3.2]
and then someone stood up and said,
«He should be here – Quartz Ribs should –
so he could try to lie there underneath it.»   280
He was listening to everything they said.

A little later, someone left the house.
He kept on sitting there.
The other one returned,
and they said, «Isn't anyone coming?»

«He's on his way,» the other said.
After that, he entered.

Like a favored child of the gods,
dressed in a medicine coat, he entered.
He was dressed in a garment of marten skins besides.   290

He lay down underneath it
the moment he entered the house.
His ribcage was glowing.
Sparks were exploding out of his skin.

Someone stood on one side toward the door,
and someone on the other side too.
Behind the fire, Jilaquns, the mother of the one
    who'd just come in, was sitting.
The one who was closest to the door said,
«How the tongues are wagging! How
    the tongues are wagging!»

The one on the other side said,   300
«It isssssn't over yet!
  The talk is going round,
  even while those who are spirit beings from birth
  are busy debating their future locations.»

Jilaquns called an attendant – one of the several
who were sitting there among them.
«You Who Make Waves in the Daylight by Walking,
    bring the Swimming Hermit Thrush here.
Exactly *where* I slept with him
is what I want to ask him.»

He'd been saying he'd slept with the lady, they say.   310
She told the other to go get him
so that she herself could ask him to explain himself, they say.

There was no one living underneath
    What's Encircled by the Tide.

Now Quartz Ribs had lasted one day.   [3.3]
Because they could see he was going to last another,
those who are spirit beings from birth
    were shaking as though they were out in the cold.

They were worried.
They were worried that he would take the supporting position,
    right underneath them,
although he belonged to the other side.[13]

The ones near the door were talking again,   320
saying the same things.
Then She Who Makes Waves in the Daylight by Walking
    went to get the Swimming Hermit Thrush.

Later, she returned.
Jilaquns asked if he were coming.
«He's coming,» said the other.

«Maybe I made love to him at Goose Cove
    when I went to eat some orchid bulbs.
Or did I make love to him at The Yews?»

At that moment he entered, they say.
He was a pretty one.   330
He'd been gambling.
He kept patting his face with cedarbark powder
and wiping it off.

He went straight to the lady.
He wormed his way instantly into her clothes.
He kept looking straight at her.
She glanced at him once,
and it lasted forever.

Quartz Ribs was ready to do one more day.
Those who are spirit beings from birth
    were shaking as though they were cold,   340
thinking Quartz Ribs would last one more day
and live right underneath them.
When dawn was just breaking, the heat drove him out.

Now, when they had considered it for a while,   [3.4]
    someone stood up and said,
«Go after Honored Standing Traveller.
They say he was bathing for strength
in order to live underneath here.»

Then he got ready to leave.
He threw his headband back across   350
and started running.

He said to his mother,
«They're ready to come get me.
You should come with me.
My sister, Riches Tinkle Round Her Ankles,
    should come with me too.»

As soon as he said this,
they came there to get him.
He said he would go in his own canoe.

Then he went to get the seawolf skin
which he had stored in a two-headed cedar.   360
He dressed himself up in it there in the house.
A being that no one could look at was strutting around.

Then they started paddling across.
His mother took the stern,

his sister the bow.
He stood there amidships.

Then his sister stepped ashore, along with his mother.
He was the last to disembark.

They went up to the house.
His sister led the way.   370
She held the mallard paunch.
His mother had the feathers folded in her robe.

They entered.
Those who are spirit beings from birth
    bowed their heads to him.
He was stunning.
He entered dressed in the skin of the seawolf.

He lay down underneath it right away.
He sizzled and hissed.
Flames spurted up.
Every time the flames went down again,   380
his sister came and smeared him with the mallard grease.
His mother also dusted him with the feathers.

Later on, when he'd lasted one night.
Those who are spirit beings from birth
    started watching him closely.
Hu hu hu hu hu! He was just about to last another night.

The ones who are spirit beings from birth
    were debating their future locations.
They discussed among themselves
where they would go to make their homes.

Just then, one of them stood up.
He asked, «Where is that sister of the spirit beings,
    Woman Lips are Licked For,   390
going to make her home?»[14]

«Somewhere, your eminence, somewhere
    just along the shore among the windfalls
along with my attendants, I am going to make my home.»

A while later, when day was close to breaking,
they were watching him intently.
A while after that, the Raven called.
The dawn became the day.

All the while he lay underneath it,
they watched him.
So he made his home below.   400

THEN they sent the news to Outruns Trout   [3.5]
    and Ordinary Marten.
They tied a line to one and sent him up.
It wasn't long enough.
He lengthened it with hemlock root.
Plain Old Marten took the other end below.[15]

Then those who are spirit beings from birth,
    after debating where they would live,
went off in different directions
leaving the town of Xayna behind.   408

§3.2 Quartz Ribs

T HEN QUARTZ RIBS STARTED TRAVELLING AROUND   [1]
    What's Encircled by the Tide, they say.
After he'd been walking quite a while,
he came inside and told his mother,
«Mother, down at Ghangxhiit Point
    someone keeps on wailing and calling my name.»[16]

The following day he went out to shoot birds
    on What's Encircled by the Tide.
He walked around it all
as people walk around a small space.

Then he said to his mother again,
«Mother, she's constantly wailing and calling my name
as though she couldn't stop.»   10
Then he said to her,
«I'm going there to help her.»

«Don't do it, prince, my son, don't do it.
They will call you Little Fat Boy.»[17]

«That's fine, mother.
I'm going there to help her.»

Early the following morning he left again.
He walked past Qqaadasghu,

and then he walked along by Qquuna Point
and came to Shellheap of the Gods.[18]   20

He picked up the pace then.
He jogged as far as Stretchout Town
and went right by.
Then he reached the edge of Whiteshell Beach.
Out to sea an eagle – yes! – was tugging
    unsuccessfully at something with its talons.

He watched it.
Then it grabbed again at something with its talons.
He wondered what it was and went to see.

There was a creature swimming in the cove.
Its fins were sheathed in copper.   30
An ermine dangled from its nose.
He caught it with his hands.
He was thrilled with it.

As he was just about to slit it down the edges with his nails,
a clap of thunder boomed.
When he was just about to slit it on the lower side,
it thundered once again.
When he was just about to do it on the upper side,
it thundered yet again,
and lightning flashed.   40

Then he skinned it from the tail,
and when he had the skin,
he put it on.

Dressed in the skin, he went into the cove.
The sculpins darted away from him.

When he opened his mouth,
he sucked the sculpins in.

Then he opened it
and spewed the sculpins out again.
Belly up, they floated there.   50
He stepped out of the skin
and folded it under his arm.

He had two other coats, they say.
There was the medicine coat.
There was also the marten-skin coat.
Before he left the house,
when he displayed them for his mother,
he almost burst her house apart,
and she has asked him to put them away.

H E TRAVELLED on,   60
and he came to Hlghadan.[19]   [2.1]
There a woman had just given birth.

He took the infant's skin,
and he became the newborn child.
He grew the way a puppy does.
He started walking right away.

One day, after he had been outside,
he came in bawling.
She tried to stop him.
He refused to be consoled.   70

After bawling for a while
he started snivelling over and over,
    «Waaaaa b-b-b-b-b! Waaaaa b-b-b-b-b!»

Then she tried to stop him all the harder.
After trying hard to speak,
he started miming with his hands.

A while after that, his mother hammered a bow
    from a copper bracelet.
She made the arrows for him too.
Then he was always hunting birds.
He didn't take time out to sleep.

THEN one day the weather was calm,   80
    and they went out to gather shellfish.   [2.2]
They didn't take his mother.
Then the storms blew in again,
and then again the weather was calm,
and they went out again for shellfish.

Then he asked his mother if she had her own canoe,
and she told him that she had one.
Then he and his mother went along
    with the rest of them for shellfish.

The lead canoes had already arrived,
and they were tagging along after.   90
He put his mother ashore
near where the other canoes were riding at anchor,
and he anchored his behind them.

Now when the baskets of the lead canoes were full,
he sat there on the water,
took his hunting bow, and drummed on the canoe.

From shore they waved at him to stop.
They spoke in whispers.

Then they loaded their canoes
and raced away.   100

Before he even reached the shore,
he told his mother to hurry.
He loaded the mussels into the bow.
Then he put his mother in the stern,
and they paddled fast away from Qqaaghawaay.[20]

When they had raced away some distance,
that one came up after them.
As he started closing in on them,
he opened up his jaws.

When they had almost floated down his throat,   110
this one grabbed his hunting bow
and poked the other in the lip.
He pushed him back,
and that one dived.
They came to shore,

The people started down to meet them,
and his mother told them she'd escaped
by blowing through her labret hole[21]
and swishing her toes in the water.
This one was listening closely.   120

WHEN they had gone on living there awhile,   [2.3]
stormy weather came again.
It was foul. It was foul. It was foul.

When the uneaten mussels had spoiled,
the weather turned fair,

Ngiislaans (John Cross). *Qqaaghawaay at Ghuudang Xhiiwaat*
  (*Five-finned Killer Whale and Quartz Ribs*).

Argillite plate inlaid with whalebone & abalone shell, 24 × 36 cm. ca 1890.

(Alaska State Museum, Juneau: 11-B-824.)

See the note on page 387.

and they went again for shellfish.
He and his mother paddled behind them.

When the baskets of the lead canoes were full,
he drummed on the gunwales of his boat again.
They waved at him to stop.   130

He just stared back at them,
and then they raced away.
Once again he paddled after them.

When he had paddled some distance toward the shore,
that one came up after him again.
He had five dorsal fins.

Again the current hurtled down his gullet,
carrying them in.
This one grabbed his jaws and squeezed them shut,
pushing him away.   140

When they landed on the beach,
the others came again to meet them.
They asked if he had surfaced.
His mother said she'd whistled through her labret hole
and dabbled her toes in the water.
That's how they escaped, she said.

T HEN it was foul weather again.   [3.1]
    After the foul weather went on for days and days,
this one went out on a point at the edge of town
and dressed in his halibut skin.   150
Dressed like that, he dived.

A little after that, he came to a broad trail,

and after he had followed it awhile
he came upon the town – the town of Qqaaghawaay.

After snooping here and there,
he peered into that one's place.
Between the screens forming a point behind the fire
sat his daughter.
When he saw her, this one quivered with desire.

When he had paced around the town a while longer,   160
evening came,
and he went into that one's house.

She was there, sitting down, behind the fire.
Her skin had five dorsal fins as well.[22]
He stared at her.
Then they went to bed.
The moment he approached her,
they went to bed together.

THEN came the dawn,   [3.2]
and the people of the town went out to fish.   170
When the talking had gone on for quite a while,
he got out of bed.
Yes! They were catching their fish
   right in front of the town!

He got into the halibut skin.
After swimming there beside them for a while,
he swallowed a few of them.
They tumbled into his gullet.
After chewing them awhile,
he opened up his mouth.

Then he went ashore   180
and walked back toward the house.
He went inside.

When he had sat there for a while,
evening fell,
and they went back to making love.

He was fascinated by her.
He went to her over and over again.
And there in bed again with that one's daughter,
he listened to them talking on and on – of nothing but himself.

WHEN they went out to fish again,   190
he dressed himself again.   [3.3]
He swallowed two canoes
and spat them up on shore.

Then he went back in,
and after he had sat there for a while,
evening fell,
and then he went to her again.
He slept with that one's daughter.

Then that one gathered up his gear
to go fishing with the others.   200
They brought his skin to him
and handed him his spears and box of arrows.

They smeared pine sap on the bindings
to increase that one's power over this one.
And this one heard the other say
that he would crunch this one's head between his teeth.

SOMETIME LATER, day was breaking,   [3.4]
    and he heard the talk of people going fishing.
When the talk stopped,
he got up   210
and went into the water again.
He surfaced close to two canoes
who were out at the edge of the group.

One waved a paddle back and forth.
They were signalling to Qqaaghawaay, they say.
That one wasn't doing any fishing,
only cruising back and forth among them.

He paddled straight to where they were,
and they pointed at the water with their paddles.
«It's on the surface over there,» they said.   220

He picked up a fishing spear.
He looked the quarry over.
It wasn't very big.
So then he took an arrow in his hand.

He speared it on the surface.
He stuck it in the side
and hauled it out of the water.

Then he said,
«Is this the creature that's been killing you?»
They said to him,   230
«Don't talk that way! That's him!»

THAT ONE told them to keep fishing,   [3.5]
    and they hauled in halibut and clubbed them.
This one lay in the canoe.

The skin of Qqaaghawaay was lying there as well.
They saw him creeping toward it.
Then that one grabbed his spear and speared him.

Spearing him just made him swell up huge,
and the canoe capsized.
The open sea was boiling,   240
but this one kept the skin.

And then he swallowed them.
The many that were fishing there
tumbled down his throat,
and only two canoes escaped.

He headed off with all those he had swallowed.
He spat them up on shore in a narrow cove
    at the edge of town.
They tumbled backward toward the water from the trees.
From the tideline up, the corpses had no skins,
but dorsal fins were on them.   250

Then he went back to his mother's house.

O N THE FOLLOWING DAY, he said to his mother,   [4.1]
    «Mother, I'm going to leave you now.
It wasn't you who bore me.
I came to give you help
because you were wailing and crying my name.
My other mother's home is in the middle of these islands.»

His mother started singing lamentations right away.
He liked her voice so much
he stayed the night beside her,   260
and he left her the next day.

Right away, as he was leaving,
he dressed in his medicine coat,
with the marten-skin coat over that.

On top of those he wore the skin of Qqaaghawaay,
and dressed like that, he started up the West Coast.
The spirit beings living there opened up their doors.

After travelling awhile,
he came to one who lived midway along the coast
and had his door shut tight.   270

Going by,
he reached out sideways with his hand,
and the house tumbled toward him in a heap.

A FTER travelling some more,   [4.2]
he came upon a person
who was fishing for black cod.[23]

As this one passed him on the seaward side,
the other said, «Your lordship,
inasmuch as you are Quartz Ribs,
passing on parade,   280
cut me off a head.
That's what I need here, sitting on the water.»[24]

Then this one turned to face him.
He thrust his arm straight into the cliff face
and twisted it, drilling a hole.

Next, he started scooping up black cod.
When he had gathered a huge armload,

he heaved it into the cave.
Then he stuffed the one who spoke to him in with them.

That one strung some on a line   290
and put some more in the canoe
and paddled off.
He towed the string of cod behind him.

F ROM THERE he travelled on.   [4.3]
     From there he travelled on awhile,
and he reached the bay at Ttsaa'ahl.

At the narrows of the bay – yes! – it lay there face up, waiting.
One branch of each of its pincers was copper.
It lay there waiting for him.

Halting there in front of it,   300
he looked at it.
It had five dorsal fins.²⁵

He steered across its body even so,
and then it grabbed him.
It squeezed right through to his insides.
Even the medicine coat was punctured by its claws.

He tried growing into something huge.
Nothing happened.
Then he shrank back into the halibut skin
and slithered out between the claws.   310

That one took away the other skin, they say,
since he belonged to the same side as Qqaaghawaay.

THEN he passed through the Narrows.   [5]
    As he was coming up to Kkil Point,
the sandspit dried on his account.
He halted there in front of it.

After he had floated there awhile,
he started slashing at its waist
and cutting it across.

When he had done this for a time,   320
he reached the water on the other side.
That's how there came to be a passage there, they say.[26]

After he had travelled on a ways,
he came to Rock Point's house.
A swimaway was sticking out the doorway.[27]
His spines looked fierce.

This one looked at him a long, long time,
and then he said,
«Swim away, big man, or I'll kill you.»
Because of what he said,   330
that one swam away along the far side, near the other island.

When he had travelled farther on,
there were two men fishing out of one boat
in the Bright Earth fishing ground, off Taawghahl.[28]

The bow man began to think aloud:
«I wonder if the one they say was travelling the West Coast
is coming over this way.»

The stern man yelled at him,
«Aiiiii! Why do you have to talk that way?

We're going home!»   340
He cut the lines himself,
and then they raced away.

This one bit off half of their canoe
and let the stern man escape on what remained of it.
That one made it to the shore at one end of Taawghahl.
He's the boulder sitting there, they say.

Then he went away from there.
At Qquuna Bay he stood up straight.
Going ashore, up near the trees,
    he turned to catch the sunshine on his back.

Then he started – yes! – dozing off   350
and losing track of where he was.
While he was feeling that way,
he started hearing something – yes! – going *xuuuuu*.
He looked up.

Yes! It had the halibut skin in its claws.
Dressed in his medicine coat,
he chased it.[29]

The eagle led him inland,
and someone stood there, waiting for him.
That one had a spear.   360
He wore the helmet of a warrior.

This one ran right past him,
and after he had passed him,
that one grabbed him.
Then this one's head dropped into that one's hand,
and that one tossed it up the river.   366

§3.3 Floating Overhead

T HERE LAY THE VILLAGE OF QQUUNA, THEY SAY. [1.1]
And the one who was the mother of the town
   held title to Sand Reef.
Early one day, he went there hunting harbor seal.
Then he issued invitations to a feast.

They came in droves.
He kept dispatching invitations.
The one who was the mother of the town
   was known as Floating Overhead, they say.

One day, he was heading over there,
and where the overfalls form, on the landward side
   of Gwaay Jats, just offshore from Qinggi Hluu,
there were people on the water singing something.   10
They were drumming on their gunwales.

He headed over there,
and they were singing – yes! – of him!
«Floating Overhead can taste his o-o-own
   reflection in the o-o-o-o-ocean,»[30]
they were singing as they paddled.

He arrested them.

He asked them why it was
they'd taken seals from his reef.

The seals they had were their canoes.
He tied them underneath his thwarts,   20
and then he headed back to shore with them.

Then, when the canoe came just abreast of Mallard Grease,
    north of Turn-of-the-Tide,
One of them said to the other,
«Get ready, little brother.»
«You get ready,» he replied.

Then they jumped him, both together.
They tied him down to the canoe,
and then they took their seals
and turned back the way they'd come.

A ND THEN they took him to their father's house.   30
    He had arrested Way Out Seaward's sons, they say.[31] [1.2]
They set him down inside their father's house,
    midway along the wall,
and gave their father all the news.

«Father,» they said, «he spoke to us
of something that you gave to us.
He hauled us in.
He tried to tie us up.»

Their father said,
«My dear young gentlemen,
    your feebleminded father holds his tongue   40
    if ordinary surface birds are speaking.»
Just like that, he put an end to the discussion.

Then they brought him forward.
Then they brought a giant cooking basket out
and heated stones.
When they were hot,
they put them into the fresh water in the basket using tongs.

When it had reached a rolling boil,
they dropped him in, canoe and all.
They shook the basket to and fro with him inside,   50
and when the waves rose up
he hunkered down in his canoe.

Then they came and got him.
They laughed at him
because he was afraid.

W HEN they had had their laugh,   [1.3]
        his wife arrived, landing with a thump
            on the roof of the house.
She was shrieking.
Besides that, she was shaking up the roof,
which was exposed by the low tide.   60

She asked what they were doing to her husband.
Just as she was asking,
he brought to mind the copper drum he owned.

As he was just about to strike it with his hand,
the headman said,
«Gentlemen, my children, go and get him,
and pitch him out the door.»

Then they went and got him
and threw him out along with his canoe.

That's how she got her husband back,   70
and then they both went off together.

W HEN he had lived there with his wife a certain time,   [2]
he brought to mind the song
that Way Out Seaward's children had composed.
Then he began to sleep alone.

When he had kept this up awhile,
he woke once in the darkness.
He could hear someone – yes! – talking nicely to his wife.
He didn't move.

Then morning came,   80
and he put a keener edge
on a clamshell knife he owned.

Then they went to bed,
and then he lay awake.
Wide awake he lay.

The moon came up.
As it got lighter,
one end of a rainbow pierced the smokehole.

He watched it.
It reached down and touched his wife,   90
and then the rainbow drew itself back out.

Once again, a while after this had happened,
he heard someone speaking very nicely to his wife.
When the sweettalking stopped,
he slithered over.

He took hold of the man's hair
and sliced his head off.
Then he walked outside
and tied the head above the door.

A FTER many nights went by,   100
there was someone on the water, just offshore.   [3]
It was a woman.

She waited there offshore a little while.
«Sir,» she said, «throw down your sister's child's head.»
He paid her no attention.

It was Jilaquns's son who had slept with his wife
and whose head he had taken, they say.

She called ashore again,
«Sir,» she said, «put your sister's child's head aboard my boat.»
He utterly ignored her.   110

She was angry after that.
Swinging something long and thin,
    bluegreen for half its length,
she gave the town a whack.

The town of Qquuna lurched and tilted partway over.
Then he walked outside
and stomped it back in place.

The woman said the same thing again,
and then she struck the town again,
and once again it tilted partway over.

Then he tromped it down again   120

and went and got the head
and tossed it toward the sea.

The harbor-seal canoe that she was in
moved across the water of its own accord,
and he remained there watching.

Then he headed up the Step Aside Trail.[32]
Out at Xhaaghusgha, he dived.
He stretched his arms up to the surface.

Her companions were paddling slowly by then.
As they were passing over top of him,   130
he grabbed them.

Then, turning in their seats,
they paddled her astern.
They didn't budge.

Then the lady said to him,
«Sir, if that is you, come aboard.
Something other than you think will happen.»

Then Floating Overhead – yes! – vaulted
    through the bailing hole.
He didn't wait; he went amidships,
and the lady made a place for him.   140
The moment he reached over with his arm,
the two of them were lying side by side.

They went to where she lived.
And when she set her child's head back into place,
he came back to the surface.

AFTER Floating Overhead had lived there   [4]
        with her for a time,
when it was autumn,
she and her companions started digging orchid bulbs.

One day, coming home at evening,
they were happy.   150
He heard the noise they made.
He didn't understand
what would make them act that way.

While they were out digging orchid bulbs,
he was busy getting firewood.
They trooped back in
and kept on being happy.

After that, when they headed off again,
he trailed them.

They went along slowly, single-file,   160
beating time with digging sticks, and singing.
They were swaying like the treetops in the breeze.
The lady walked slowly in the lead.
He was spying on them, creeping up behind.

They came out on a point and faced to seaward,
and they sang together there.
The lady sat beside the water.
He was watching.

Someone glided from the sky
and perched beside her: 170
someone who had bushy eyebrows,

someone who was handsome.
The two of them lay down together there.

This one turned and went back up the trail.

Soon they all came back,
and he spoke to the woman he was living with.
«Don't you go tomorrow.
I will go.
I'll get a bigger load of bulbs.»

On the following day, he borrowed her dress and her sash,   180
and he fixed up his hair, there in the house.

They walked along together, singing.
He went slowly in the lead.
He sauntered to the tideline
and pried up a rock
and picked a sea-pickle up from where it lay.[33]

Then he sat down, facing the sea,
just where the lady was sitting before.
Farther up the shore, her companions were singing.

A moment later, that one glided down   190
and sat there close beside him,
and the two lay down together.

Then he snipped the other's penis off,
shoving the sea-pickle into its place.
That one bolted away from him making a noise.

Then he was murderously happy.

He went back to the house,
returning the dress and the sash to the lady.[34]

Her companions were up early the next morning,
and when the primping had continued for a while,   200
they went outside together.

Just outside the door, they were composing a new song.
Again, they started singing as they walked.
Then he walked behind them, as before.

The lady sat and faced to seaward.
Once again, the other glided down.
They lay together there in vain.

When the lady caressed him – yes! –
there was a frilly white sea-pickle there.
Then she wept. She wept. She wept.   210
Her women wept together with her.

And this one went back to the house
and continued splitting firewood.

Then evening came,
and the rest of them returned.
Instead of being cheerful,
her companions all had tearstains on their faces.

Then he asked them,
«Why are all of you so sad?
Have the Saw-whet songs turned all of you to witches?»   220
He chose those words, they say,
because it was the Snowy Owl
    who'd been the lady's lover.[35]

$\mathbf{A}$FTER he had lived there with the woman
      longer still,   [5]
someone said, «The headman's boat is coming in.»

At that moment, Plain Old Marten raced out back
and pulled up bracken ferns.
He held them close and kept them with him,
sitting on the door side, by the fire.

Five women of the Land Otter People
    sat there in a corner,
and one of them had Floating Overhead
    tucked down inside her clothes.   230

Then they trooped in from the beach and gathered round.
Big Man summoned one of the youngsters[36]
    out of the crowd around the door.
As soon as he had whispered in his ear,
the youngster went outside.

When that one had been gone a little while,
they spread a mat midway along the wall,
and five of those who never comb their hair
    came in and squatted down there.

As soon as they were seated there,
one of them got going
while the rest of them beat time on his behalf.[37]   240

After he'd been going for a while,
he pointed toward the one
who had Floating Overhead inside her clothes.

As they surrounded her,
that one over there started working with the ferns.
The house got dark at once,
and another of them hid him in her clothes.
They pulled the first one to her feet,
but there was nothing to be found.

Then another one got going,   250
and he pointed to the one
    who had him hidden in her clothes.
They started to go get her.

Plain Old Marten worked the ferns again.
While it was dark again,
another of them hid him in her clothes.
They pulled the one he fingered to her feet,
but there was nothing to be found.

And then another one got going.
He pointed to another.
There was nothing there.   260

And then another one got going.
When he pointed to the one
who had him hidden in her clothes,
they started to go get her.

Then Floating Overhead became a flake of ash
and wafted to the corner of the smokehole.

Then another one got going –
one sitting at one end
of the group that came with Big Man.

After they beat time for him awhile,   270
he pointed out exactly where he was,
and they started to go get him.

After that, he wafted down,
and yes, they caught him: they caught Floating Overhead.

They brought him up in front of Big Man.
That one tore off one of his two arms.
When he had torn off the other arm,
he handed each to one of those who sat there.
Then he yanked his legs off
and handed them to two of those who sat there.   280

Then he ripped his body into bits
and passed them out as well,
and then they ate them.
They ate every scrap there was.

After sitting there awhile,
they began to suffer stomach pains.
They died.
The others dragged their bodies out, they say.

And so it ends.   289

Daxhiigang (Charlie Edenshaw). *Waasghu (Seawolf) with human and two humpback whales.*

Graphite with ochre & turquoise colored pencil on paper, 20.5 × 27 cm. 1897.

(Boas Collection 1943, Dept. of Anthropology Archives,

American Museum of Natural History, New York.)

See the note on page 387.

The Qquuna Cycle §4

Spirit Being Going Naked[1]

Daxhiigang (Charlie Edenshaw). *Mask of the Lost Man (Gaagixiit Mask)*.
Alder; bluegreen, black & red paint; human hair, 30 cm tall. 1904.
(American Museum of Natural History, New York: 16.1/128, neg. 320575.)
See the note on page 388.

§4   Spirit Being Going Naked

THERE WERE TEN OF THEM, THEY SAY,   [1.1]
including both their mother and sister.
Things were going on within the eldest boy.
His younger brothers had become like killer whales.

Once upon a time, one of his brothers stood outside and yelled
    Huuuuuweee!
Then a cloud rolled in from out at sea.
It stopped in front of Guuhlgha.
Where it stopped, a person stood,
and they wrestled one another.

After they'd gone at it for a while,   10
that one pinned
    Spirit Being Going Naked's younger brother
and transported him away.
«Where the flint juts out, behind the fire
    in my father's house, go!»
He went up in a flurry making a noise.

Then another of them went out and shouted.
He went out and said what the other had said,
and once again a cloud rolled in and stopped,
and once again a person stood there,
and they wrestled.

After they'd gone at it for a while,   20
the other threw him down,
and that one said again,
«Where the flint juts out, behind the fire
    in my father's house, go!»
Then he went up in a flurry making a noise.

He disposed of all seven the same way.
After that, this one's mother was in tears.
She sobbed,
and then she blew her nose,
and then she started saying,

«It's as if my eldest boy   30
    did not exist, they say.
That's what I keep hearing in my mind.»

IN THE MEANTIME, her daughter took care of the fire.   [1.2]
    While the others went to bed,
Spirit Being Going Naked lay in the firepit.
He was weak.
He couldn't sit up.

Then he heard what his mother was saying,
and then he called his sister,
«Sister, bring out one of mother's stone chests.»   40

His sister filled one up,
and he inched himself toward it
and slumped in a heap
and lay there exhausted.

After lying there awhile,

he crept the rest of the way toward it
and hoisted himself in.

His butt was floating high,
and his sister took a kitchen stick
and poked it down.   50

After she had held it down awhile,
she took the stick away.
His butt stayed – yes! – beneath the water.

After floating there awhile,
he pressed his knees against the chest.
He broke it with his knees.

His sister filled another,
and he climbed inside.
When he had floated there
no longer than it takes to make a fist,   60
he cracked it open with his knees.

Then he got into another.
He broke it too, by pushing with his knees.

There was one more left,
and his sister filled it up.
As soon as he got into it,
he pressed it with his knees.
He shattered that one too.

THEN he went into the sea in front of Guuhlgha.   [1.3]
After he'd been floating there awhile,   70
something brushed against him.
He made a grab

and caught a flounder by the tail,
and he flung it up on shore.

After floating there some more,
he grabbed the tail of a halibut.
Then he got a harbor porpoise by the tailflukes,
    a Dall's porpoise also by the tail.

And after floating there some more,
he grabbed a humpback whale's tail.
«Cook this one, though, in water,»   80
he called out to his sister.

He floated there, he floated there, he floated there,
he floated there some more,
and something long and thin brushed past him.
He reached for it.
Nothing was there.

When he had floated there some more,
something touched him once again,
and he lunged out just ahead of it.

Something long and thin slithered in his hand.   90
It started slipping through his fingers.
He seized it with both hands.
Then it towed him off.

Offshore from Hlghaayxha he lay back and braced himself.
After he'd held steady there awhile,
something cracked at the base of the Islands.

Then he tied what he was holding in his hair
and swam back where he'd started.

He swam past the beach at Guuhlgha
and rested at the mouth of Xhaana Creek.   100

When he had floated there awhile,
something thundered down from the head of the creek.
He stayed where he was
and listened to it coming
as the thundering got closer.

Then he looked in that direction.
Uprooted trees were ricocheting down the streambed,
    heading toward him.
They got closer.
They were right there on top of him.
Then he jumped aside and ran ashore.   110

Everything that perches in the trees
and the creatures flying seaward of the trees
said he was a coward.
«Is this how he is trying to get powers for himself?
His powers are weak.»

Then he jumped back in the water
and they crashed and tumbled toward him.
When they struck him
he felt nothing.
They drifted off transformed to rotten logs.   120

And again when he had floated there
    and floated there and floated there,
ice hurtled down the streambed,
and again he jumped away.

Again they said he was a coward,
and he jumped back in the way again.
The ice crashed into him
and melted on the surface of the sea.

And again when he had floated there
    and floated there and floated there,
rocks came rolling, crashing down upon him,
and again he jumped away.   130

Again they said he was a coward,
and again he jumped back in.
They hurtled down upon him
and bounced off of him and sank,
    transformed to little chips of broken stone.

WHEN he had gone on floating there awhile,   [1.4]
    he heard loud footsteps coming toward him.
He looked in that direction.

A short, squat creature with red skin was headed toward him.
He was carrying a spruce knot and a bludgeon made of maple.
In the other hand, a rose-thorn club and seaweed.[2]   140

That one said, «Come up here, grandson.
Let me test you.»
He went up to him
and faced him.

That one clonked him with the knot.
He didn't feel it.
It shattered in his hands.
And then he bashed him with the maplewood.
He didn't feel that either.

204

Then he whipped his back with rose thorns.   150
He didn't feel a thing.
And then he whipped him with the seaweed.
He sagged until his forehead nearly touched the ground.

Then they laid their hands on one another.
He threw the Spirit Being of Strength.
That one smiled at him then
and walked across the ice to the edge of the trees.

He started tugging on a limb
sticking out seaward from a spruce
standing up at the top of the beach.   160
He couldn't pull it out.

Then this one went to it
and yanked it out of the tree.
And that one said to him,
«Go home now, grandson.
Your things have been there all along.»

Then he went back toward the mouth of the inlet.

HE SWAM and swam and swam,   [1.5]
and then he came ashore at Guuhlgha.
He stood for quite a time beside the door   170
and then went in
and dried himself.

He asked his mother, who was weaving near the wall,
«Mother, aren't there any here?»

«Yes, dear boy. When I knew that you were growing in my womb

I had some made for you.
They're here.»

His mother hunted in a chest
and brought a pair of skyblankets out
and gave them both to him.   180

Then he sat down on the bed
that belonged to one of his younger brothers.
He broke it.
Then he broke another.

After all of them had broken underneath him,
he made one for himself
and broke that too.

He built another one with yellowcedar corner posts,
and after it was finished,
even that broke.   190
Then he gave it up.

He made a lattice from the kitchen sticks
lying by the fire,
laid salmonberry canes across the top of it,
and laid a row of planks on top of that.

He sat there.
That was strong.
And then he went to bed.   198

Next day, he went out in fancy dress.[3]   221

         ▸   ▸   ▸

AFTER travelling a faint, faint trail for a long, long ways,   [2.1]
he saw a shrew who had a cranberry in her teeth
trying to cross a deadfall.
He put her across with his hand
and went on his way.

He came to where the mountain was covered with devil's club,[4]
and there he started eating.
He was only partway through when evening fell,
and he stayed there overnight.   230

Next day, he ate some more.
When evening fell,
he'd eaten all there was.

As he was chewing the last bite,
he spat it out and said,
«How could I cleanse myself enough
to catch a seawolf?»

Then up the inlet something said,
«Ooo-ooooo. Strutting Grouse can hear your words.»
Down the inlet, something said,   240
«Ooo-ooooo. Jumbled Wedges hears your words.»[5]
Then he went back to the house.

Next day he went inland once again.
The mouse was struggling the same way in the same place.[6]
He put her across with his hand again.

When he had travelled on a ways,
he reached the mountain thick with
    single-flowered wintergreen.[7]
He started eating,

spent the night there,
and kept eating the next day.   250

He spat out the last bite.
He said the same thing as before,
and voices answered him
the same way they had answered him before.

Then he went back to the house
and lay down.

As he was lying there in bed   [2.2]
and day was breaking,
he was thinking of the creature
he had lifted up and over with his hand.   260

Then he went back there.
Yet again – yes! – she was trying to cross over,
and he lifted her across.
Then he watched
which way she went.

She went behind the base of a cluster of sword fern.
And there he saw a house.
Then she spoke to him.
«Grandson, come inside.
The birds have been singing   270
that you would be borrowing something from me.»

He did go in,
and she seated him beside her.
Then she turned away.
She lifted a dish out of her purse.
A mouse's face was carved at either end.

She put a scrap of dried salmon on the tray
and set it there before him.
He was thinking,
«I've been fasting.   280
  This is all I get to eat?»

Then she said to him,
«Eat it.
  It stays as it is.
  No one ever eats it all.»

Then he took it.
After he had done that,
he still saw it sitting there.

He picked it up repeatedly.
He couldn't eat it all,   290
and she returned it to its place.

Then she turned away again.
She placed a cranberry in front of him.
He began to spoon it up.
He couldn't finish that off either.

Then she turned away again.
She took something blue out of her purse
and bit half of it off.
«In case you think of eating medicine for something,
  here it is.   300

«Go up to Guuhlgha Lake.
  Something that destroyed your younger brothers
  lives there, nesting in the Butcher Tree.

«When you come to where the ground is trampled down,
  whistle for him.
  Wait there and let him come up toward you.
  When he's right there on top of you,
  drop to the ground.

«As soon as you come to,
  you'll find you're in his belly.   310
  Put the medicine on yourself.
  After that, you can restore your younger brothers.

«After your brothers have vanished again,
  go down to Sealion Town.
  Climb the tree that stands to seaward
  at the head of the trail leading inland.

«When that one comes up to you out of the sea,
  stab him in the ears –
  you'll need to make something strong enough for that –
  and get yourself back up the tree   320
  while he staggers all around.

«There you give birth to your brothers again.
  When they've vanished one more time,
  and you've set out after them,
  you'll discover you're one of the spirit beings,
  going along on your own.»

Then he went home.   327

E ARLY NEXT DAY he went out to issue his challenge.   [2.3] 199
  As he started to wrestle   200
with the one who had destroyed his younger brothers,
he said to that one,

«If you throw me,
stand right there and wait for me.»

They laid hold of one another right away,
and that one threw him.
He went spinning through a daydream,
spinning toward the flint cliff.

He rubbed himself at once
with the medicine Mouse Woman had given him.   210

Now he slammed into the flint
and smashed it into pieces.
His younger brothers' bones came pouring out.

Then he lathered them with medicine as well.
When he flew back where he had started,
the other stood there waiting.

This time, this one threw him right away.
«Even the last people will see you.»
The other suddenly changed to chips of broken rock.

Right after that, his brothers disappeared again.   220

AFTER he had been in bed awhile   328
and the day was soon to break,   [2.4]
he went up through the woods   330
and came out in the open.

The place was trampled down.
Among the footprints, there were those of human beings.
Just before sunrise, he whistled.

When he'd announced himself this way,
something like a head with floating hair came toward him.

As soon as it got close to him,
he dropped down on the ground.
Then something happened.
He came to,   340
and there he was inside its belly.

He put the medicine on himself
and pushed against the other's belly.
His younger brother's bones spilled out,
and he slid out on top of them.

By then, the Butcher Tree was swirling.
This one grabbed it,
chopping it up fine,
like something ground to powder.

But then he set two limbs aside   350
and pulled two shorter branches off them.
He hurled one of them deep into a spruce.
Then he threw the other.
It buried itself in a hemlock.

He spat in the direction it had gone
and said, «Not even the last people in the world
will give up using you to get their food.»[8]

And then he lathered the medicine over his brothers.
They got up,
and then he said to them, «Go back   360
to where you used to be.»

He went back with them himself,
and after they'd enjoyed each other's company awhile,
one disappeared again.
One and then another and another, they were gone,
until all seven disappeared.

THEN he whittled down the Butcher Tree's limbs.   [2.5]
He sharpened the ends
and held them over the fire.

He took these in the middle of the night   370
and went to Sealion Town.
Then he climbed a tree
that stood beside the trailhead.

After he'd been sitting there awhile,
a pair of torches came up glowing from the ocean.
They came up glowing right beneath him.

A seawolf – yes! – was coming.
It stopped beneath the tree
that stood to seaward.

It was coming right up to him.   380
It had a humpback whale in its teeth.
It held another tightly in the curl of its tail.

When it was right there underneath him,
he dropped down on its head
and rammed the spikes of Butcher's Wood into both its ears
and pulled himself back up the tree.
It staggered back and forth below.

At daybreak, when the raven called,
it fell like any hunter's normal kill.[9]

Then he stretched it out   390
and prepared to slit it open.
Thunder crashed and lightning flashed.

Then he skinned and gutted it.
He found his brothers' bones in its entrails
and lathered them with medicine.

They got up,
and then he said to them, «Go back. Go back
to where you were before.»

The next day, one of them was gone again,
another the day after.   400
So it went
until all seven had disappeared again.

⸙   ⸙   ⸙

A FTER sitting, doing nothing for a while,   [3.1]
he started going nowhere in particular, they say.
He'd been travelling a ways
when he heard, in the middle of the island,
    something beating like a drum.

He headed toward it.
Yes! – a trail ran there.
There were fresh tracks.

He followed where they led,   410
and there a house stood –

but the door was off to one side of the housefront.
The sound of drumming was coming from there.

He peered inside.
There was a woman in the house,
    dressed in a red-fringed blanket,
spinning blanket-maker's yarn.
The drop-spindle made the drumming sound.

He sat there on the scuffed earth just outside the door
and glanced around.
There was a freshly broken salmonberry cane.   420
He pulled off a twig.

And as she worked there, facing toward the wall,
he poked her with it in the rear.
Then she turned around and looked at him.
She talked with him a long time pleasantly.

As they were talking,
he heard some other voices, going
Huk! huk! huk! huk! huk! huk! huk! huk!
He looked up.
Yes! It was his younger brothers brawling.   430

He went to them
and lathered them with medicine.
He put some on himself as well.
Then he tried to pull them apart from one another.
He couldn't.

He went through the same procedure again.
Even then, he couldn't do it.
That was Woman of the Lost, they say.[10]

A<small>FTER</small> failing at this,   [3.2]
   he headed home, they say.   440

And so he came to Guuhlgha.
He meant to go into his mother's house
but walked right past it.

Then he went toward it again,
and when he came close,
he grasped something sticking out from the housefront.
It came away in his hand.

When he was unable to enter the house,
he headed off nowhere in particular.
He tried in vain to find the summit of the island.   450
Wandering around there,
he stumbled on a meadow.

Then he sat down.
After sitting there awhile,
he looked at himself.
Yes! He was sitting there naked!
Both of his blankets were gone.

Then he turned his back to get some sunshine.
He bent forward
with his forehead in his hands.   460

As he was resting,
something touched him.
He looked for it.
Nothing was there.

Then he sat there poised to catch it,
and when it came again,
he grabbed out in front of it.

It was squirming in his hand.
It was soft. It was furry.
It resembled something brushed until it shines.   470

Then he skinned it
and stretched it on a frame
made from salmonberry stalks.
Still, believe it or not, it was slack in the middle.
So he stretched it on a bigger one.

Then he set it in the sun.
He did it just for something to wear, they say.
It started to get dry.
That made him happy.

When it was very nearly dry,   480
from the head and the toe of the islands they shouted,
«Oooooh! Spirit Being Going Naked is drying his skyblanket!»
They laughed at him.

Then he hung his head.
He sat like that awhile,
and then he went away and left the blanket.

T HEN he travelled on.   [3.3.1]
He made the whole place small with all his walking.
And one day, when he'd travelled for some time,
he heard a person singing a sad song.   490

Then he headed toward the sound.
There was a house there.
Going toward it, he kept tripping as he ran.

He looked inside.
Someone stood behind the fire.
His face was smudged with soot and streaked with tears.

He was wearing long earrings.
Small humans dangled from the earring tips,
heads down and mouths open,
wiggling their arms.   500

He was beating out a rhythm with his staff,
and singing on and on:

Thinking he'd revive his younger brothers
just as he'd revived them twice before,
a spirit being went to find them.
A spirit being went – and went forever.[11]

He listened to them – that one and his powers –
singing through their tears that song about himself.

ALL of that one's boxes were arranged   [3.3.2]
        so their ends were toward the fire.
They were stacked up four tiers high,   510
and this one wondered what was in them.

Then he scurried all around.
After poking here and there,
he found a big slab of rock.
He hoisted it up on his shoulder

and heaved it onto the roof of the house.
He hauled himself up after.

He made a hole there, just above the other,
and then he dropped the rock.
It cracked his skull.   520
He died at once.

This one jumped down off the roof
and went in through the door.
He opened one of the boxes
closest to hand.
It was completely filled with moosehides.

Then he went behind the fire.
He opened some there too.
He wrapped five hides around himself,
and then he headed off.   530

When he had gone some ways away,
he started hearing it again –
yes! – the beating of the staff.

Then it came up near him.
That one grabbed one of them back.
He put it on his own shoulder.
He took all five back
and went away.

When this one looked where he had been,
he'd disappeared.   540

Then he went back after him.   [3.3.3]
He was singing – yes he was! –
the very song he sang before.

This one scrounged around again.
He hoisted a rock onto his shoulder
even larger than the one he had before.
Then he heaved it onto the roof
and hauled himself up after.

Then he made a hole above the other's head.
He dropped the rock.   550
He knocked him flat.

He jumped down at once,
grabbed another five hides,
and ran away with them.

He hadn't gone far
when the other took them back.
This one stood and watched him disappear.
He couldn't kill him.
That was the Spirit Being of Tears, they say.

When he had gone on travelling awhile,   560
he came to a skunk cabbage swamp   [3.4.1]
and jumped across it.

When he had gone a little farther,
he reached an empty town.
Smoke was drifting up from the middle house.
He went there
and walked in.

An old man lay with his back to the fire.
When the old man saw him,
he got up   570
and offered him some food,
but he did not give him anything to drink.

A little later, this one said, «My, but I'm thirsty!
I'll go get myself some water.»

«Don't, sir. That's the way it happened
that my village was destroyed.
Go over there and sip,
as your father's father does, from the inside corner,
since it's all I have to offer.»

Then he went there.   580
It was a skunk cabbage swamp.
He turned and squatted over it,
and after he had crapped there, he said,
«Turds are floating in it.»

«Aaaaai!» said the other,
«What's in store for me in that case?»

T HEN he said again, «My, but I'm thirsty!»   [3.4.2]
    And the other said, «Don't go, sir.
That's how it came about
that my village was destroyed.»   590

Nonetheless, he took the bucket
and went to get some water.
When the spring had burbled four times,
he dipped some up.

He didn't notice what it was
that happened to him next.
When he came to himself,
he was there in its belly.

Then he pressed his hands and feet against its gut.   600
He stretched until it popped,
and bones spilled out of its belly.

He laid the bones in order.
Whenever a piece was missing,
he replaced it with a salmonberry stalk.

He lathered medicine all over them.
They sat up right away.
He revived all those who'd had their houses
    on the headman's right-hand side, they say.

After that, the water flowed.
He caught a bucketful
and went back in and said,   610
«Grandfather, have a sip.»

He reached out to take it.
After he looked at it for a time,
he turned away without tasting it.

A FTER he had sat there for a while,   [3.4.3]
    he said, «Well! Wherever they live,
they eat beach food.
Some octopus would hit the spot.
I'll go and get some octopus.»

«Don't, sir. That's the way it happened   620
that my village was destroyed.»

222

Then, in spite of what the old man said,
he headed out.

Two octopus spears were hanging up
    in one front corner of the house.
He took them both.
The other gave him some instructions.

«After it spits four times,
spear it.
That's the way to kill it.»
Then he went to get it.   630

What a thing was living there!
When the Octopus Spirit Being spat at him,
the spout went up to the clouds.

When it had spouted four times,
he speared it.
He found himself in its belly.

Then he smeared the medicine on himself
and started stretching out the belly.
He popped it open.
It gave birth to human bones.   640

Then he laid the bones in order,
and several of the pelvises were missing.
He replaced them with whatever he could find.
He fixed their faces the same way
and lathered them with medicine.

They all went off in a crowd.
He said to them, «After you get settled,
dress up and walk around.»

Then he dragged the octopus back by the tentacles
and tossed it through the door.   650

That one – Voicehandler – looked at him then[12]
as he entered the house and sat down.
    While he was looking, Spirit Being Going Naked said,
«Grandfather, go take a look at your town.»

Then he took his cane
and hobbled out with it.

He looked to the right,
and there it was!
They had started their parade,
wearing facepaint and feathers,   660
up and down in front of the town.

And he looked to the left.
The same kind of thing was going on.
He came inside.

As soon as he came in,   [3.5]
he went to get his urine box.

He took quartz pebbles from the chest
    that he'd been using as a pillow
and tossed them into the fire.
He kept an eye on them,
and after they were red hot,   670
he lifted them into the urinal with tongs.

He sharpened the red end of something long and thin –
    the other half of which was blue –
and dipped the sharpened end in boiling urine.

And he covered his nose
with the flap of the robe he was wearing.

Then he called him over.
«Come and sit beside me, grandson.»

This one went to him.
That one pressed the red end of his stick to this one's nose
and pulled it down.   680

Then he pulled the sea-urchin spines, the pine needles
    and greenling bones from his body.
After drawing out the needles, bones and spines,
he washed him off.

Then he brought out a comb
and raked it down from the top of his head over and over.
Then this one looked down at the floor.
Land otter fur – yes! – was lying there in piles.
Then he combed him on the other side too.

Spirit Being Going Naked had the stink of One of the Lost.
That's the reason Voicehandler
    had to hold his nose, they say.   690

Then he fixed his hair.
He combed it out long
and put it into two braids,
tying them with ribbon.
He used the blue end of the stick to make him attractive.

When he had worked him over for a time,
he poured water into a hand basin he owned

and said to Spirit Being Going Naked,
«Grandson, look at yourself.»

So he looked at himself.   700
His face was painted with scattered red clouds
flecked with black –
the kind of clouds that lie to seaward.

This one looked at it and said,
«It's awful.»
That one wiped it off and put it in his armpit.

Then he spent a while painting him again
and this one took another look.
His face was painted with a broad red cloud –
the kind that forms to northward.   710
He didn't like that either.

Then he painted him again.
He painted his face like the breast of a mallard
at rest on the water.
This one said he liked it very well.

That one painted this one's face
because he'd brought his people back to life again.
He gave him two skyblankets too.

Then Voicehandler said to Spirit Being Going Naked,
«Soon you ought to leave.   720
The one who's always causing trouble in your mind
is living right close by.

«When her servants go for water,
bathe in the waterhole

and make it seem that things
are coming through you.

«The ones who come there first
will not want anything to do with you,
but the last will take good care of you.»

          ➤   ➤   ➤

THEN he headed off.   730
  He perched beside a waterhole   [4.1]
        over on the west coast, just outside of Qaysun.
After he'd been waiting there awhile,
they came for water.

They brought their boat ashore
and carried up the buckets.
He made himself a skinny little thing.

Then, as they came nearer,
he made himself resemble
one of those whose visions throw them in the water,
and in he plunged.   740
He and his visions were floating there limply.

The first to arrive drew back with a start.
«Phyuu! There's something sprawled across the surface
    of her waterhole!»
«Fish it out with a stick,»
the middle one said.

And the last one, who was lame, said,
«Handle him with care!
He'll be stronger
once he's drunk some whale broth.»

Then they broke a stalk from a salmonberry bush   750
and gently fished him out.
After that, they got their water,
and after they had loaded it aboard,
they remembered he was there.

The lame one put him aboard with the stick
and set him in the bailing hole.

After they had landed,
they carried up their water,
and they boiled up their whale.
They forgot about him again.   760

It was the lame one who remembered him
and said, «We've forgotten about something
that was sprawled across the surface of the water
that the headwoman drinks.»

Then Sea Dweller's Daughter said,[13]
«Come on! come on! come on! come on!
Let's have it!»

The lame one went to get him
and came back with something dangling from a stick.
He was drooped across the salmonberry stalk.   770
They had him sit toward the door,
and he warmed his hands by the fire.

Then they offered him some whale broth.
As soon as he took it,
as he was lifting it to his mouth,
he spilled it all down the front of himself.

They laughed at him,
but still they gave him some more.
He spilled that too.

The headwoman lived at Skate Island, they say.[14]   780

O N THE FOLLOWING DAY, the people   [4.2]
     went out with a handnet.
They pulled in a whale,
and they flensed it.

Meanwhile, after he had warmed himself
     there on the door side for a while,
he said, «A little something for your ladyship?
     Eh? A little something?»

Then she said to him,
«Well, kiddykins, whatever you are thinking of, go get it.»
Then he dragged himself over.
He touched the headwoman.

She grabbed him by both ears   790
and bashed his head against the floorplanks.
Then she said,
«The shit stays over toward the door.»
He dragged himself back
and sat there toward the door.

When he'd been sitting there awhile,
the headwoman called to him,
twiddling her lips at him.
«Kiddykins, slave they say I haven't even got, go out
     and get some firewood.»

Then he dragged himself away,   800
and there outside the house he shed his skin.

He wrapped both hands around a dying spruce
    with dry limbs
standing alone at the top of a slope with rocks below.
He and his powers lifted it out, roots and all,
and hurled it down from the top of the slope.
At the base of the slope, it shattered.

Then he gathered up the pieces
and carried the bark back on his shoulder.
Then he dragged himself inside,
and put a little bark into the fire.   810
He crouched there near the flames.

Fishing with a handnet, the headwoman's companions
    had taken a whale.
They were happy.

When he had thought about the lame one for a time,
he told her who he was.

«Help yourself to the firewood
I stacked there for all of you.
I am Spirit Being Going Naked.
Don't tell anyone about me.»

Then the lady told her servants to get firewood,   820
and then they brought it in.
She twiddled her lips again.
«Kiddykins, my latest acquisition,
split that firewood,» she said.

O NE DAY he and all his powers crept outside.   [4.3]
  They shed his skin.
They'd had enough of acting weak and old.
They decided to marry the headwoman.

Then he painted his face
with the painting that Voicehandler gave him.   830
He put his two skyblankets on.

When he'd been standing there awhile,
one of the lady's companions came out.
As soon as she caught sight of him, from far off,
she started running toward him, arms wide open.
«Unnnh-unnnnnh,» he said,
and then she went boo-hooing back inside.

Then she said, «Come look at Spirit Being Going Naked,
who is standing just outside.»
Another one came out.   840
He turned her down the same.
He turned down ten in all.

Then the lame one came to him.
He stood still
while she came up and embraced him.

A little later on, he came inside
and married the headwoman.

H E WENT ON living as her husband.   [4.4]
  Every evening, in the house, behind the fire,
        stars came out and gleamed.
He never gave it any thought.   850

One day something passed beneath his pillow saying,
«Spirit Being Going Naked, are you trapped here
   by the savor of black cod?»[15]
For a time, he gave no thought to what it said,
and then it said the same again.

Then one day, lying there in bed beside his wife,
he said he wanted to go fishing with the net, they say.

His wife said, «Let me tell you something first.
You shouldn't let out any more
than you have strength for.
They let out only one mesh.»   860

Then he took the net
that was hanging in one corner
and went out on the point.

There were lobtailing whales on the ocean.
Then he let two meshes out.
He tried to go that far.

He couldn't haul it in.
The other meshes went out too.
All five went out.

Then he left the place.   870
He came in and flopped down,
   gasping for breath.

«Did you lose the net?» his wife asked.
«Yes,» he said.
  She only laughed.
«Alright. I'll go and get it from my father.»

232

FIRST THING NEXT DAY, they paddled off   [4.5]
    to see her father.
All of her companions went.
The lady went,
and Spirit Being Going Naked came aboard.   880
They headed out to sea.

They travelled over water for a time,
and the town came into view.
Then they beached the boat,
and her father came to meet her.

He asked his daughter,
«What brings you here, my princess?»
«Father, we came to get the net.»
«It's here in the house, my princess.»
And he smiled with his eyes at Spirit Being Going Naked.   890

Then they went inside,
and he put four quartz pebbles in the fire.
When these were glowing with the heat,
he brought a white stone platter from the corner.
He put the pebbles into it with tongs
and set the platter there in front of this one.

Then his wife moaned,
«Aaa, aaa, aaa.
Anytime I find a man who pleases me,
no matter what, he always kills him.»   900

Then he asked his wife not to say a word.
And then, after sucking on the medicine,
he swallowed the first stone.

It went right down and out, right through the floorplanks.
He did the same thing with all four of them.

They brought him a hand basin next.
When his wife began to wash her hands as well,
they brought out five black cod.

She told her husband not to eat them.
«It isn't what it seems,»   910
she said to him.

They set the fish in front of him,
and after they had sat there for a time,
she said, «He says they needn't stay there any longer.»
Then they took them away
and tossed them outside.

But then they brought another helping.
He didn't eat those either.
And she said, «He says
it is not what it seems to be, father.»   920

Then they took away the cooking box
and brought another out,
and then they brought another five black cod.
«These,» she told her husband,
«are black cod.»

Then they scored them
and they steamed them.
When they were cooked,
they served them.

Before they could take them away,   930

234

she picked one up.
«Keep the heads and bones from these,» she said,
and she handed him another.
She gave him those parts of all five black cod.

Then she said to her husband,
«Don't let loose of them.
He can take them out from right inside your clothing
without your feeling anything.»

And then she kept on asking,
«Are the heads and bones still there?»   940
«Yes, right here.»

Then on the following day they got ready to leave.
Again she asked her husband,
«Are the heads and bones still there?»
«Yes, right here.»
«Are the heads and bones still there?»
«Yes, right here.»
«Are the heads and bones still there?»
«Yes, right here.»
«Are the heads and bones still there?»   950
«Nnn-no. Is that why Spines for Earrings[16]
      smiled as he passed?»

Hu! hu! hu! hu! hu!
They put huge piles of black cod aboard the boat.

Then they came ashore at home
and they unloaded the black cod.
And then the evening came,
and then they slept.

              ➤   ➤   ➤

A<small>FTER</small> many nights had passed,   **[5.1]**
he heard the thing that spoke beneath his pillow
passing by again and speaking.   960

Spirit Being Going Naked, are you trapped here
    by the savor of black cod?
To repay you for replenishing his town,
Voicehandler brought your younger brothers back
and caused himself to come
    through the womb of your own mother.

He sits up high between white banded cloud
    and black banded cloud.
By making love right next to you,
he's slithered up inside you.

Then he looked up. Yes!
He saw a marten's tail curling up inside a shining star.

He tracked it.   970
It was true! With the covers pulled away
    from the upper part of her body,
she was sleeping there at Voicehandler's side.

This one reached down and touched her,
and she said, «I wasn't expecting you.
But yes, it's true, he comes around quite often.»[17]

And then he went back by the fire,
very unhappy.
Then his wife asked, «Why are you so sad?»

«The problem is» – he told her a lie –
«I miss my mother.»   980

THEN they got ready to leave.   [5.2.1]
    They loaded up with black cod,
and they headed off.

He steered into the Inlet[18]
and brought his boat ashore at what was now
    his elder brother's town.
His younger brothers and his sister – the eight of them, yes! –
    came out to meet him.

Then they went into the house.
Voicehandler, though, was the only elder brother
    that it pleased his younger brothers to look up to.
They had no time for Spirit Being Going Naked.

Even before they had offered him food,   990
he started giving food to them.
Up behind the fire, Voicehandler cleared his throat repeatedly.
A thundercloud was clinging to his head.
His face could not be seen.

They scored the black cod,
and they steamed it.

They invited Voicehandler to come and sit next to the fire,
and brought out a hand basin for him.
The cloud never lifted from his face.

He washed his hands   1000
as they were serving the black cod.
Nothing could be seen except his hands.

The younger brothers did as he did,

but Spirit Being Going Naked and his wife
    were seated elsewhere, over toward the door.

Voicehandler didn't bother walking when he came down.
The cloud moved on its own.
He was lifted up and carried.
The cloud drifted down and brought him with it,
stopping behind where the hand basin lay.

Now, when they had eaten,   1010
the cloud drifted back with him.
Once again, nothing could be seen on the bed
    except his body.

T HEN that one called his sister.   [5.2.2]
  She went to him,
and after he had told her what he wanted,
she went out.

She brought cranberries back.
The tray bore the image of One of the Lost.
After eating a bit,
he was through,   1020
and the younger brothers ate what remained.

Then they put more cooking stones in the fire
and brought the hand basin out again,
and the cloud carried him down.

When he was sitting there again,
this one's wife set more black cod in front of him.
He and all his younger brothers ate.
Still, his face could not be seen.
Then Spirit Being Going Naked's wife was sad, they say.

238

Voicehandler slept with the Woman of the Lost   1030
to bring Spirit Being Going Naked's younger brothers
    back to life again, they say.

And because Spirit Being Going Naked
    brought his town back to life for him,
he also made arrangements to be born
    from Spirit Being Going Naked's mother.

Then the cloud lifted itself.
He was sitting up above again.

THEN that one called his sister again.   [5.2.3]
    «Sister, come to me.»
And then his sister said,
«Huuuuu, huuu! Anytime he and all his powers
    have a chore for me to do,
he promises me something.   1040
Later on, he always takes it back again.»

Then and there, he tossed something down to her.
It landed with a sound that echoed up and down the house.
She grabbed it right away.

She wrapped it in her blanket.
But in that moment, Spirit Being Going Naked's wife saw
that it was something she had given to her daughter.

«Aaa, aaa, aaa,» she groaned,
«I thought I and no one else
    bestowed that on my daughter.»   1050

Her husband's mother answered her.
«Your ladyship, everywhere killer whales settle,

they employ it as a killer whale crest.
It already belonged to the lady your sister-in-law
as well as to her brother.
Are you saying they learned it from you?»

Then she quit complaining.
Even though she saw it clearly,
she believed what her mother-in-law said.

NEXT DAY, Voicehandler's sister-in-law served   [5.3.1]
    another meal of black cod.   1060
Afterward, when that one and his powers
    were sitting back up on the throne,
he called his sister.

After he had told her what he wanted,
she came down and sat
where Spirit Being Going Naked and his wife sat.

Then she said,
«That one and his powers want something
that he says your husband owns.»
He couldn't figure out
what she was speaking of.   1070

Later he remembered
the seawolf he had killed.
Then he started down the inlet.

He shinnied up the big two-headed cedar
where he'd put it for safekeeping
and pulled the seawolf's tail off.
Then he started back with it.
He went directly home.

Then he told his wife,
«This has to be the thing   1080
that she was speaking of.»
And then she called her husband's sister,
who put the tail of the seawolf into Voicehandler's hands.

After he had gazed at it awhile,
he fastened it onto the brim of his hat.
There it rested.
Ooooooooooh my!

A s soon as that was done, they steamed   [5.3.2]
        black cod again.
And yes, the cloud began to stir again.
His younger brothers gorged themselves on black cod.   1090

This one's wife was just appalled.
She faced away
and started plaiting cedarbark.

When she'd been doing this awhile,
suddenly her husband's brother – yes! his brother! –
        wrapped himself around her.
He peeped at her from right inside her clothes.

She also saw her husband's brother there behind the fire.
His image was still sitting up in Voicehandler's place.
Then, right there, they lay together.

E ven so, she told her husband,   [5.3.3]
        Spirit Being Going Naked,   1100
he was not to mess around.
«No messing around – or else!
I'll cross the ocean to my father.»

Then her husband started going out himself to get their water,
with a falcon's feather floating in the basket.

Every time he came back in,
she lifted out the feather.
The water streamed off freely,
and she sipped it.

T HEN one day he went to bed   1110
   with one he was in love with.   [5.4]
When he came back to the house,
his wife tugged at the feather.
It wouldn't come loose from the water.

She flew into a rage.
Her labret was going like something they shake
     when they're shaking out blankets and mats.
Then she poked through her purse.
At the same time, the tears were streaming out
     as if someone were pouring them from a jug.

She licked from her hand
what she took from her purse.   1120
It was powdery white.
She spat it back into her palm
and rubbed it into the soles of her feet.

Her husband, who was sitting right there,
took some that she spilled.
He rubbed the soles of his feet with it too.

She was doing this, they say,
because she was getting ready to leave him.

Then she went down to the water,
and he stayed close by her,   1130
walking right out with her on the surface of the sea.

She wouldn't look at him.
She said to Spirit Being Going Naked,
«Let me alone and go back where you were,
or else I'll look at you.»

Then he said to her, «Being looked at
would be something.»

He went through the surface
as soon as she glanced at him.
There wasn't a sign of him left.   1140

Then she came into her father's house
and said to her father,
«Daddy, I stared at him
and sank him.
Now fish him out.»

Then her father pulled apart the stone floorplanks.
He trolled for him between them,
and he pulled him in,
with nothing but the ligaments still linking up his bones.

When he lathered him with medicine,   1150
his form came back to him again,
and he went back where he was from.

As soon as he arrived,   [5.5]
    they sent for Master Carver.
That one built them a white mountain all their own,
    on top of ten canoes,
and this one's younger brothers settled there together
    in that mountain.

He also wrapped a skyblanket round his sister's shoulders.
She went to stay among the people out to seaward.
His mother, though, remained
    among the people here to landward.

This one dressed up too, in dancing blankets
    and in dancing leggings,   1160
and went up near his younger brothers.
He ran out stooping, stretching out his arms,
and stood up singing farther off.
He took the Varied Thrush's form,
    Spirit Being Going Naked did.

His younger brothers floated out to sea, they say.
Out of what is floating there, they keep on getting powers,
    I can tell you.

So it ends.   1167

The Qquuna Cycle §5

Born through Her Wound[1]

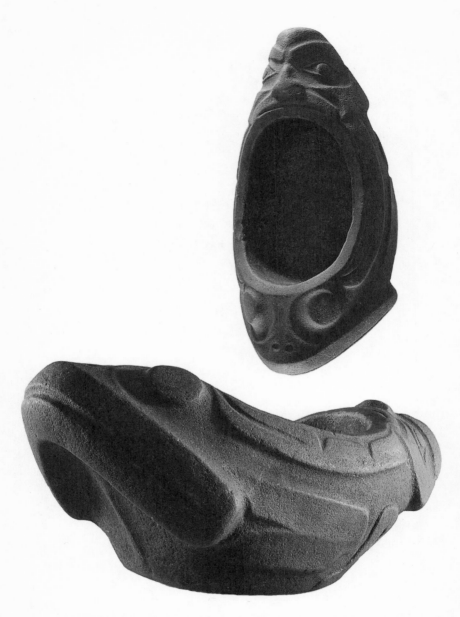

Anonymous Haida or Tlingit artist. *Tobacco mortar in the form of a frog.*
Stone, 43 × 21 × 18 cm. ca 1800?
(McCord Museum of Canadian History, Montreal: ACC1205a.)
See the note on page 388.

§5 Born through Her Wound

THERE WAS ONE OF GOOD FAMILY, THEY SAY.   [1.1]
She was a woman.
Whenever she went out,
they propped the doorflap up on her behalf,
and she was always going out.

Once, as she was coming back inside,
she was cut on the hip
when the doorflap slipped,
and then the cut became infected.

By and by, she had a suppurating wound,   10
and when the people of the town found out,
her father gave the order to abandon her.
They left her the next day.

Then she kept going into the surf
to cleanse the wound.
She treated it with healing leaves as well.

Then one day, as she was washing out the wound,
she saw something blood-red moving there inside.
She tried to pull it out and failed.
Then she used the medicine again   20
and crawled back up the beach.

Again the next day, there was something creeping
    underneath the blood.
When she had washed herself again,
she plucked at it again,
and – yes! – she pulled it out.

She set it lightly on a beach rock,
and after she had used the healing leaves again,
she picked it up
and went back up the beach.

She made a folded cedarbark container   30
and put it into that
and set it out beside the house.

Then she went to bed.
Just as she turned her back to the fire,
she heard a child start to cry.

She raced outside,
though she was not then even capable of standing.
The sound of something crying
was coming from her cedarbark container.
She peeked inside.   40

A baby lay there.
Then she picked him up
and bathed him.
Then she started taking care of him.
She thought of him as hers.

He started crawling very quickly.
Before he had started to eat,
he started walking.

Then one day he started crying.
«B-b-b-b-b,» he kept saying.   50
And then she made him a bow.

She used a limb from a hemlock sapling.
As soon as she had finished it,
she gave it to him.

After he had looked at it awhile,
he put it into the fire.
She made him others out of one thing and another.
He did the same each time.

After awhile, she made him a bow from genuine yew.[2]
Oooooooooh yes! It glowed in his hands.   60
It was good.

But after he had looked at it awhile,
he threw it away,
and the blunt-tipped arrows with it.[3]

Then she hammered copper for him.
She spoiled him as though he were her own.
And right away, she hammered out a pair of copper arrows.
One bore the image of an ermine.
The other bore the image of a mouse.

When she handed him these,   70
he didn't look at them at all.
He headed outside right away.

AFTER he'd been gone a little while,   [1.2]
he brought in some wrens
and said to his mother,

«When you've plucked these,
eat them.»

His mother plucked them
and then boiled them.
When they were cooked,   80
she ate them.

His mother offered some to him.
He only shook his head.
He wouldn't touch a thing.

After that, he headed out again.
He came back in.
He'd shot a lot of sparrows,
and his mother boiled them as well, and ate them.
He however would eat nothing.

Again the next day he went out.   90
He bagged a lot of mallards,
and then his mother plucked them,
and she cooked them to perfection.
She took them from the cooking box
and ate one.

Again the next day he went out.
He bagged a lot of geese.
And he went again the next day,
and then he got a porpoise and a seal.
Day after that, he got a humpback whale.   100
His days of shooting birds for his mother were over.

THEN he headed out again.   [1.3]
    When he'd been gone twice as long as he was before,
he brought a lot of flickers in.
He said to his mother,
«Skin these for me
and take out all the sinews.»

Then his mother skinned them
and took out all the sinews.
After she had done that,   110
she arranged the skins together.

She put them into five rows,
stitching them together with their sinews.
After it was made,
she held it out to him.
The flock of flickers flew.

Then he stretched his mother's house.
He set a pair of planks behind the fire.
He hung the blanket up between them.

He was out a long time again the next day.   120
Sapsuckers.
Then she did the same thing again:
made another blanket.

After it was done,
he came to her
and then she held it out to him.
The flock flew up just like the other,
⟨and he hung the blanket up behind the fire.⟩   127a

At that point he lay down.
It was then that he first ate, they always say.
He was fasting up till then, they say.   .   130

Then he headed out again.
When he'd been gone twice as long as he was before,
he brought a bag of tanagers in.

Then his mother made him yet another,
and as soon as it was finished,
he came over.

She held it out.
The flock flew up again.
He draped it up behind the fire too.

Again the next day he went out.   140
He brought a bag of siskins back.
His mother made him yet another blanket.

When it was done,
she held it out.
It flew up in a flock.
He draped it up as well.

Again the next day he went out.
Kinglets it was this time,
and his mother sewed them up for him the same.

Then he headed farther off.   150
When he had been away awhile,
he came back to her together with the daughter
    of the One Who Wanders Inland,[4]
his new bride.

Aᶠᵗᵉʳ he had lived there as a married man awhile,   [2.1]
        a day came when he didn't get out of his bed.

As he lay there,
something passed behind his pillow,
        and it swayed him with its words.
«Born through Her Wound, are you awake?

«Doesn't it seem to you
        that spirit beings you haven't so much as imagined   160
        might be gathering against you?»

He dashed outside,
but there was nothing to be seen.
Then he went back out again
and pulled an elder along with him.
He perched him out on a point not far from town.
That, they say, was the Great Blue Heron.

Lᵃᵗᵉʳ ᵒⁿ, he stayed in bed another morning,   [2.2]
        and something drifted by and whispered,
                deep below his cheekbones,
saying the same words it said before.   170
Then he grabbed his bow,
and went outside.

When he had peered throughout the ocean depths,
he happened to glance upward.
A thunderbird was flying above the village,
clutching a village in its claws.

Then he started walking toward the old one.
He said to him,
«Grandfather, they're after me.»

«How are the prows of their canoes?»

«A thunderbird keeps flying over the village,
  clutching a village in its claws.»

Then the old one said to him,
«Well, hero, take it with an arrow.»

He aimed at it with the one that bore the image of a mouse
and then – surprise! – the village it was clutching
split wide open so that everything poured out.

He put the skeletons together.
Wherever any bone was missing,
he replaced it with a salmonberry stem.   190
Then they all got up and headed home.
It was his grandfather's town that he restored.

A GAIN he stayed in bed one morning.   [2.3.1]
  Something drifted by again,
        beneath his cheekbone, saying,
«Born through Her Wound, are you awake?

«Doesn't it seem to you that spirit beings –
  spirit beings you haven't so much as imagined –
  might be gathering against you?»

Then he seized his bow
and dashed outside.   200
Ten canoes whose prows were red
    were coming round a point at the edge of town.

Then he started toward his grandfather again.
«Grandfather, they're coming to hunt me down.»

His grandfather asked him
how exactly were the prows of their canoes.
«The prows of their canoes are red,» he said.

«Well, hero, have the people of the town
    pull rice lilies out of the ground[5]
and scatter the bulbs in front of them.»

He did what that one said.
Their eyes were rolling upward not much later.   210
Those, they say, were coho.

A GAIN while he was lying in his bed,   [2.3.2]
    something down beneath his cheekbone
    said the same thing as before.

Then he grabbed his bow
and dashed outside.
He stared out at the creatures on the water.
There were streaks down the prows of their canoes.

He went to his grandfather again.
«They're after me, grandfather.»
«Well, hero,» he said,   220
«How are the prows of their canoes?»

«There are streaks down the prows of their canoes.»

«Well, hero, have the town pull the rice lilies out of the ground
    and scatter the bulbs in front of them.»
He did that very thing again,
    and their eyes rolled upward in their heads.

Those were the chum salmon, they say.[6]
They were frightened, they say,
    of Born through Her Wound,
because he put rice lily teeth in their mouths.

AFTER more time had passed,   230
    some speaking creature said again,   [2.4.1]
«Born through Her Wound, are you awake?

«Doesn't it seem to you that spirit beings –
    spirit beings you haven't so much as imagined –
    might be gathering against you?»

Then he lunged for his bow
and ran outside.
There were ten canoes again, with red
        formline paintings on their prows.

Then he went to his grandfather.
«They're after me, grandfather.»   240

«So, hero, how are the prows of their canoes?»

«Red formline paintings.»

Then he said to him,
«Gather all the urine you can get, from everyone in town,
    and cook it,
    and then scatter it in front of them.»
He did so.
Those were sand fleas, they say.

AWHILE LATER some speaking creature passed again   [2.4.2]
        beneath his cheekbone, saying the same thing.
He ran out carrying his bow.   250
Another ten canoes with red paintings on their prows
    were coming toward him.

He started toward his grandfather again.
«They're coming after me.»

«How, hero, tell me, how are the prows of their canoes?»

«The prows of their canoes are painted in red.»

«Well, hero, do as you did
    when you killed them before.»

Then he scattered urine in front of them again.
The corpses piled up again.
Those, they say, were beach fleas.   260

THEN he stayed in bed again.   [2.5]
    Something started shuddering underneath his pillow.
«Born through Her Wound, are you awake?

«Doesn't it seem to you
    that spirit beings you haven't so much as imagined
    might be gathering against you?»

He ran out with his bow.
He looked out where he'd seen them several times before.
Nothing to be seen.
He also looked up overhead.   270
Nothing to be seen.

And then he glanced toward the edges of the sky.
Yes! Across the surface of the sea,
    roaring flames were raging toward him.

Then he went to the old man.
«Grandfather, they're coming to hunt me down.»

«How are the prows of their canoes?»

«The horizon is on fire.»

«Uh-oh. Uh-oh. Now what's in store?
  Well, hero, take the facings off the coffins.
  Strew the bones across the beach in front of town,   280
  and prop the coffin facings up on edge
      just seaward of the houses.
  That's the custom in such cases, hero.»

Then the fire came up closer,
and still closer, and then closer still it came,
burning right up to the bones.

Things were at a standstill for a while.
Then in one place it burned through,
and then in another,
and then in another.
Then the bones no longer slowed it down.   290

As soon as it got to the coffin facings,
it stopped again.

He put on all five blankets,
and then he tucked his mother under his arm.

258

He put his wife in the knot of his hair
and started walking back and forth behind the barrier.

Things were poised that way awhile.
Then it burned through there in one place too.
As soon as he saw that, he headed off.

WHEN he'd been moving for a while   300
    toward the highest part of the island,   [3]
something called out,
«Grandson, there's a strong one over here.»
He veered at once in that direction.

He went inside and sat.
As he was sitting in the house,
the fire roared across the roof.

It was a tie there for a while.
Then a glowing hole appeared just overhead,
and then they yanked him to his feet.

They slugged him from behind to drive him out.   310
When he ducked,
one of his blankets burned away.
Toppled Over in the Water owned the house
    that he was in, they say.

And then, when he had travelled on a ways:
«Grandson, over here, my house is strong.»
He went inside.

A hole burned through the roof of that one too,
and then they pushed him out.

And when he ducked, another one burned off.
That was the Yellowcedar's house, they say.   320

When he had gone on running for a while,
something else called out,
«Grandson, over here, this is a strong house.»
In he went.
Fire roared and crackled on the roof a little while
and then another glowing puncture formed.

Then they drove him out.
Another one burned off.
That was the Yew's house, they say.

When he had run a little further,   330
something hailed him in.
«Grandson, over here, this house is strong.»

Then in he went.
When he had sat there for a while,
fire pierced the house.

Then they pummeled him again.
Another one burned off.
That was the Spruce's house, they say.

Then, when he had gone a little further,
something else invited him in.   340
«Grandson, over here, my house is strong.»

He went inside.
He sat awhile,
and the glowing hole appeared.

Then they beat him up and drove him out,
and when he ducked,
that blanket burned away.
His mother also burned away.
That, they say, was Rock's house.

When he had gone a little farther,   350
something else invited him in.
«Grandson, over here, my house is very strong.»

Then he went inside.
The fire raged across the roof of that house also for a while
and then died.
And when it did, he went back out.
That was the Marshland's house, they say.

W HEN he had wandered back and forth   [4.1]
        among these islands for a time,
he heard the sound of something tapping.
He headed for it.   360
Yes! It was the old man, patching a canoe.

Wherever it was sound,
he continuously split it with his wedge.
Then he drilled it with a gimlet
and then he stitched it shut.

After watching him awhile,
this one filched the gimlet
and took it with him under a clump of fern.

The elder hunted for his gimlet high and low.
Then he sucked his fingernails.   370
A moment after that, he said,

«Grandson, if that's you,
   come out and see me.

«The birds continue singing
   of five blankets that you own
   that led the Fire in the Sky to chase you down.»

Then he went to him.
He gave him back his gimlet,
but the point was broken off the one he had,
so he made a new one for him   380
and offered him a whetstone to go with it.

Then he reached out and picked up the two creeks
flowing there on either side
and asked him to come closer.

«Now, grandfather, think what you're going to do
   when ordinary surface birds come out to get their food.
   Do the same thing now.»

Then, from those two creeks, he made a beak for him.
Along with that, he handed him a skin.
Then he said, «Now, grandfather, give it a try.»   390

That one flew off.
He perched among the kelp beds
seaward of the ruins of the town.

After holding himself motionless awhile,
he made a sudden jab.
A prickleback wriggled in his mouth.
He swallowed it.

Then he flew again
and landed close to the canoe.

Then he said to this one,   400
«Now then, grandson, come with me.
You'll see your high-class blankets once again.
At this moment they are raising someone's status
    over on the other side.

«So, grandson, bring that boat down to the water.
We'll go and see your highfalutin blankets.»

The elder got aboard astern,
and so did this one,
and they paddled out to sea.

A꜀ᴛᴇʀ they paddled and paddled and paddled,   [4.2]
    they came to his town –   410
the town of Fire in the Sky.

People gathered there to greet him.
The rest of them poured into that one's house
like a cascading mountain stream.

They said to one another,
«He's brought his sister's son to dance, they say –
the Sandhill Crane has.»

Then the Heron gave him his instructions.
«As I go in,
you look behind the fire.   420
Once your good-for-nothing nephew
    has done his little dance,

go get your blankets.
Get your mother out of there as well.»

Then this one brought the boat ashore.
He walked up to the house,
and he was carrying his bentwood box.
⟨He also had a cane.⟩⁷   426a

He kept himself hunched up,
but once he got inside,
he stretched up tall.
Behind the fire – yes! – the blankets
    flapped their wings at him.   430
His mother sat beneath them too.

He took his place there, just midway along the side.
The firepit was ten tiers deep.

Then he poked around inside his bentwood box.
He took his nephew out of it.
Oooooooooh my!

And then he stood him up.
That one struck a pose.
He held his wingtip in his beak.

When he had pranced around the box a little while,   440
the people in the house went *Ssssssssss*.
All those in the first row fell asleep.

When he had danced a while longer,
this one lifted up the cane
and then he picked his nephew up
and tossed him up, together with the cane.

That one, in an instant, took a weasel's form
    and scampered up the cane.
They sighed again, *Sssssssss.*
The next row went to sleep.

He scooped him up again   450
and tossed him up again together with the cane.
He took a sapsucker's shape and clutched the cane
    and rapped it with his beak.
The whole house sighed another sigh, *Sssssssss.*
The next row fell asleep.

A moment after that, he picked him up again.
He tossed him up together with the cane.
He spiralled up the cane in the form of a brown creeper.[8]
Another *Sssssssss.*
They also went to sleep.

Then he went and got his cane.   460
    Right after that, he put his nephew back inside the box.
«That's all for now.
Better keep a treasure for a long time
than dance it all away at once.»
He tucked him out of sight.

Born through Her Wound went back behind the fire then
and put his blankets on
and grabbed his mother too.

The old man made his own way out.
Then they went aboard the boat   470
and paddled off.

THEY were halfway back   [4.3]
   when he saw the fire raging up behind them.
As it came close,
he showed that he was frightened.
Right there is where it stopped.

They came to shore then,
and they walked back up the beach.
All five blankets had been burned away again,
his mother too.   480

He reached up for his wife,
but she was also gone.
She had married on the other side, they say.

After that, he wandered here and there
     and everywhere, they say,
and after wandering awhile,
he went behind a tree
and wept.

He looked up inland.
All the trees and all the creatures of the trees
     were weeping with him.
Then he looked to seaward.   490
All the ocean creatures wept with him as well.

Then he tried to stop his crying,
and then he went on walking.

                    ➤   ➤   ➤

AFTER he had gone on walking for a while,   [5]
he heard creatures chattering and laughing
          as the birds do in the morning.
So he went there.

They were shooting at the leaves of a big tree.
As soon as they had shot one down,
they ate it.

When he got there,   500
they began to step aside.
«Born through Her Wound is going to shoot,» they said.

Then he took aim.
He shot at the base of the trunk.
It started to fall.
His shot was greeted with cheers by those
          who are spirit beings from birth.

Then he said to them,
«Be careful with the seeds.
I intend to give the seedhead to my father's sister,
          Woman of the Clouds.»
They were tobacco seeds, they say.   510

They sent a messenger to get her,
and she came there by canoe, they say.
She took all the seeds,
and then she started planting.
The seeds, they say, went all throughout the islands.

So it ends.   516

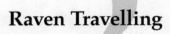

Raven Travelling

Anonymous Nishga (Nisg̲a'a) artist. *Raven rattle.*

Alder, stones & pigments, 30 cm long. ca 1800?

(Glenbow Museum, Calgary, Alberta: AA 552)

Raven Travelling

Prologue: Skaay's Flyting with
the Southeast Wind

Anonymous Haida artist. *Three black spoons.*

Mountain goat horn. Each approx. 26 cm long and approx. 6.5 cm wide in the bowl. ca 1850.
(American Museum of Natural History, New York: *left to right:* 16/8464, 16/8465, 16/8463.
Photos by R. Mickens.) *See the note on page 388.*

A

... ᴀꜰᴛᴇʀ ᴛʜᴀᴛ, ᴀꜱ ʜᴇ ᴡᴀꜱ ᴛʀᴀᴠᴇʟʟɪɴɢ ᴀʟᴏɴɢ,[1] [1]
he called out for a crew, they say.
He asked a lot of different birds to join his crew.
The Steller's Jay said that he was ready.
«No,» he told him.
«You're too old.»

That one said again that he was definitely coming.
Then this one grabbed him by the topknot
and gave it a good yank, they say.
And that one's head got long and thin on top, they say.   10
And then he gave up calling for a crew.

Then everybody went aboard the boat,
and then they headed off.
They travelled and travelled and travelled.

They came in front of the Halibut people's town.
Hu hu hu hu hu! They crowded down.
«The Raven is going to fight, they say.»
They said that sort of thing as they crowded down.

And then he asked them to come too,
and they agreed.   20

They stuck themselves like lapstrakes
    to the hull of the canoe,
and then they started off.
They travelled and travelled.

At dawn they landed there in front of that one's town.
The Halibut people lay with their heads facing out
flanking the path going up to the house.
Birds flanked the path as well.
They hid behind the halibut.

They waited quite a while.
Then, dressed up in his fancy hat,   30
that one stepped outside.

One of the halibut flipped its tail,
and down he went.
Then the next one flipped its tail.
One by one they flipped their tails
until they'd rolled him down right into the canoe.

Then he asked them why they treated him this way.
They said, because he blew too hard and long.
Then they let him go, they say.
And then they headed back.   40
That was Xhyuu, the Southeast Wind, they say.

After travelling awhile,
they dropped the halibut off where the halibut live.
The birds flew off then too.

And after travelling awhile
he came upon some children
who were playing,
and he asked if he could join them.

«Hey! You kids!
  I want to play with you!»   50

«Yikes! You'll gobble all our seal meat!»

  Then he said,
«My grandfather's just gone out to get me some!
  My father's gone to get some for me too!»

So they let him join their game,
  and then he swallowed all the children's seal,
  and they cried for what they'd lost.

T HEN he headed off.   [2.1]
    When he had travelled for a while,
he found a flicker feather floating on the water.   60
«Be a flicker!» he insisted.
  Right away, it flapped its wings.

When he had gone on further for a while,
  he came to the place
  where Fishing God lives with his wife.
  That one wanted this one's flicker.
  This one placed it in his hand.

«Creatures such as this are often found
  on the island that I own.»
  So that one asked to see the place,   70
  and this one said that he would show him.

Then ⟨they drank salt water,   71a
  and after they'd been drinking it awhile,⟩   71b
Fishing God baited one of the halibut hooks
  that hung there in a cluster.

He dropped it in the vomit box^2
and lifted out a halibut.

His wife cleaned it
and steamed it,
and as soon as it was done,
the three of them consumed it.
Then they slept.   80

He took him out next morning
    to show him Flicker Island.
They paddled close,
and then he said to Fishing God,
«Don't come ashore just yet!»

He went ashore alone.
He broke some twigs.
Then he shoved them up his nose
and let the blood spill over his hands.
Then he scattered all the blood-spattered twigs.

«Turn to flickers! Turn to flickers!»   90

A flock of them hopped up and down.
Then he brought some to the beach.
«Come ashore now. There are lots.»
Then the other went ashore.

THEN the one we speak about lay down in the canoe,   [2.2]
    and then the wind began to take him out to sea.
The other hollered,
«Hey! You're drifting away! You're drifting away!
    You're drifting away!...»^{3} 98

276

XHYUU (THE SOUTHEAST WIND):

B

UT THIS ONE PAID HIM NO ATTENTION.
He drifted way, way out,
and then he paddled off, they say.
He changed himself to look the same as Fishing God
and came ashore where that one's wife was waiting.

«It was, if you can believe it,
    the one that it usually is,» he said.
«The creatures he took me to see
    were nowhere around.»

When he had been there with the woman for a while,   10
he said, «My child's mother,
things are different now with me,
and I am feeling rather hungry.»

She steamed him a fat halibut.
He ate it.

After sitting there a moment more,
he spoke to her again.
«My child's mother,
things are different now with me.
I'm feeling warm, very warm....»[4]   20

After that, he drank some more salt water.

When he had drunk salt water for a while,
he baited a halibut hook
and dropped it in the vomit box.
It worked the way it did before.
He hoisted up his catch.

T HEN his wife went out to get fresh water.   [2.3]
    Her husband, if you can believe it, sat by the creek,
and what he said to her was this:
«It's the one that it usually is.   30
Close every crack in the house.»

As soon as this one's boat blew out to sea,
⟨the one he left behind had started thinking,⟩   32a
«Suppose my harbor-seal club
        swam out here from the house.»
{ And so it did swim out to him,
    and then it brought him home again, they say. }⁵

And now he raced inside with his harbor-seal club.
While that one chased him through the house,
this one squawked and squawked and went on squawking.
After a while, he clubbed him, they say.
Then he threw him into the latrine.   40

Later, they say, his voice came out of the hole.
He pulled him out
and hammered him again.
He even pounded up his bones.
Then he went down on the beach while the tide was out
and rolled a boulder over top of him.

THE WATER started lapping at his head.   [3]
He tried out lots of different forms.
Nothing but his beak could still be seen
when his ten spirit powers finally came to him, they say.   50

They rolled away the boulder,
and he floated up, they say.
A Tlingit spirit with a bone stuck in his nose
was the one of the ten who smelled him first, they say.

When he had floated there awhile,
a canoe came by, they say.
«What would cause a headman to be floating on the sea?»
«Sleeping around» is what he said, they say,
when they had gone a little farther.

When he'd been floating there awhile,   60
a humpback whale spouted not far off.
«Suppose he swallowed me,» he thought.
The whale did that very thing, they say,
and this one gobbled up his guts from the inside.

When he had utterly destroyed him,
he had another thought.
«Suppose we washed up on the beach in front of a village.»
So they washed up on the beach in front of a village.

When they'd been carving at the carcass for some time,
the villagers cut through to where he was.   70
Out he flew, they say.

Then he soared way up
and came back down at the edge of town,
where an old man lived.

He pulled off that one's skin
and threw his bones away
and got inside his skin
and took his place.

And then they came to him and asked
what sort of thing it could have been   80
that had escaped from the whale's belly.

He answered,
«Long, long ago, they say, when something like this happened,
everyone dropped everything and ran.»
And just like that, they say,
    they all dropped everything and ran.

Then he went on eating
all the whale meat and blubber they were storing.
That's why he'd taken on that shape, they say.

And after he had travelled on awhile....   89

Raven Travelling

The Old People's Poem

Bill Reid. *Haida housepole (detail)*.

Redcedar & paint, 15 m tall. 1959.

(Museum of Anthropology, University of British Columbia, Vancouver.)

See the note on pp 388–389.

H̲EREABOUTS WAS ALL SALT WATER, THEY SAY.[1]   [1.1]
He was flying all around, the Raven was,
looking for land that he could stand on.
After a time, at the toe of the Islands, there was one rock awash.
He flew there to sit.

Like sea-cucumbers, gods lay across it,[2]
putting their mouths against it side by side.
The newborn gods were sleeping, out along the reef,
heads and tails in all directions.
It was light then, and it turned to night, they say.   10

T̲HEN, when he had flown a while longer,   [1.2]
something brightened toward the north.
It caught his eye, they say.
And then he flew right up against it.

He pushed his mind through
and pulled his body after.

There were five villages strung out in a line.
In the one that was farthest to seaward,
the headman's daughter had just given birth to a child.

Then evening fell.   20

They went to sleep.
Then he skinned the child, starting at the feet,
and crawled inside the skin.
He took the baby's place.

Next day, his grandfather asked for the child,
and they passed him along.
Then his grandfather washed him
and pressed the baby's feet against the ground.
He stretched him up to a standing position.
Then he handed him back.   30

Next day he stretched him again
and handed him back to his mother.

He was hungry after that.
They had not yet started feeding him chewed-up food.

Then evening came again,
and they lay down.
As soon as they were sleeping,
he craned his head around.

He listened throughout the house.
They were sleeping, one and all.   40
Then he unlaced himself from the cradle.
He wiggled his way free
and went outside.

Someone who was half rock, living in the back corner, saw him.
While he was gone, she continued to sit there.
He brought something in in the fold of his robe.
In front of his mother, where the fire smoldered,
he poked at the coals.

He scooped out a cooking spot with a stick,
and there he put what he was carrying.   50
As soon as the embers had cooked them,
he ate them.
They slithered.

He laughed to himself.
Because of that, he was seen from the corner.

Then evening came again,
and they lay down,
and once again he went outside.

He was gone for a while.
He brought things in again in the fold of his robe,   60
and then he took them out
and cooked them in the coals.
Then he pulled them out and ate them, laughing to himself.

The one that was half rock watched him from the corner.
He gobbled his food,
and then he lay down in the cradle.

Morning came,
and all five villages were wailing.
He listened to them talking.
There were five towns.   70
In four of them each of the people was missing an eye.

THEN, they say, one of the old people spoke.   [1.3]
«The headman's daughter's baby is to blame.
I've seen him.
As soon as the others are sleeping,
he takes off his skin.»

Then his grandfather gave him a marten-skin blanket.
They wrapped it around him.
His grandfather whispered,
and someone went out.   80
«Bring the headman's daughter's chi-i-i-i-ild outsi-i-i-i-ide.»

As soon as the people had gathered,
they stood in a circle,
bouncing him up as they sang him a song.
And after a while they dropped him
and watched him go down.

Turning round to the right, he went down through the clouds
and struck water.
He cried and cried as he drifted around,
and after his voice grew tired, he slept.   90

WHILE he was sleeping, something spoke.   [1.4]
     «Your father's father asks you in.»[3]
He looked around.
Nothing was there.
Again, when he had floated there awhile,
something said the same thing.

Again he looked around.
Nothing was there.
Then he looked through the eye of his marten-skin blanket.

A pied-bill grebe appeared.[4]   100
«Your father's father asks you in.»
As he said this, he submerged.

Then the one we are speaking of sat up.

He had drifted close to a two-headed kelp.
He stood up and stepped onto it.

He was standing, in fact, on a two-headed stone housepole.
Then he started climbing down.
It was the same to him in the sea as it was to him above.
Then he came down in front of a house,
and someone invited him in.   110

«Come inside, my grandson.
The birds have been singing
    that you would be borrowing something of mine.»
Then he went in.
An old man, white as a gull, was sitting in back of the fire.
He asked him to bring him a box that hung in the corner.

When the old man had it in his hands,
he took out five boxes, one inside the other.
In the innermost box were cylindrical things:
one that glittered
and one that was black.   120

As he handed him these, he said to him,
«You are me.
You are that, too.»

On top of the screens forming a point behind the fire,
sleek blue beings were preening themselves.
Those are the things of which he was speaking.

Then he said to him,
«Set this one into the water, round end up,
and bite off part of that one.
Spit it at this.»   130

Now when the one that we are speaking of came up, [1.5]
he set the black one into the water
and bit off a piece of the one that glittered.
When he spat that at the other,
it bounced away.

He did it the other way round from the way he was told,
and that is the reason it bounced away.

Now he went back to the black one
and bit off a piece of it,
and spat that piece at this one.   140

Then it stuck.
And he bit off a piece of the one that glittered
and spat this piece at that one.
It stuck too.
Trees came into being then, they say.

When he laid this place into the water,
it stretched itself out.
The gods swam to it, taking their places.
The same thing happened with the mainland
when he set it in the water round end up.   150

T HEN HE SAT OFFSHORE FROM HERE, THEY SAY.   [2.1]
He called toward shore from the canoe,
«*Goosga sagaytweel txa'nii gya'wn!*»[5]
And then, «Hey! Get a move on!»
Someone came down to the beach.

*The Raven
speaks in
Tsimshian
first, and
then in
Haida.*

Then he paddled to the towns along the mainland.
He gave the same command:
«Hey! Get a move on!»
There was no one to be seen.

Then he spoke again in the Tsimshian language.   160
Someone came down to the beach with a cape and a paddle.
That's how he made the mainland people ambitious.

Crossing over this way again,
he stepped ashore at the toe of the Islands.
Someone walked along the beach rocks.
Someone else was walking inland,
    among the windfall trees.

He slugged the person on the beach and knocked him
    into the water.
The one he clobbered floated on his back.
He hit him once again,
and still he floated there.   170

He wouldn't sink.
That's how the Southern People got their sorcery, they say.

But that one walking inland had a scratched-up face.
He didn't even try pushing that one under water!
That was Crazy God, they say.

T HEN he paddled seaward, [2.2]
heading for the Distant Coast, they say.

After he had travelled there awhile,
a spring salmon leaped.
«Spring salmon!» he said to it. 180
«Hit me in the heart!»

It headed inshore, toward him.
It rammed right into him.
After he had lain there senseless for a while,
just as he was getting up,
it went back out to sea.

Then he built a low wall of stones near shore
and a second one behind it.
After he called it to hit him again,
it rammed right into him. 190

Then, as he was lying there again,
the spring salmon thrashed against the trap,
breaking free of the upper pool.

While it was still thrashing around in the lower pool,
he got back on his feet,
and then he clubbed it,
and he carried it away.

He invited the crows to join him.
Then they made a fire
and they cooked it in a pit.   200

He lay down with his back to the fire.
Then he told them to wake him
as soon as it was done,
and then he slept.

So they opened up the pit
and ate it.
They ate everything there was.
Then they used a twig to stuff some scraps between his teeth.

After sleeping for a while,
he woke up.   210
He told them to open the pit and take out the food.
Then they said to him,
«You've eaten it already!
After that you went to sleep!»

«No! You haven't opened up the pit yet!»

«You should check between your teeth!»

Then he poked between his teeth.
He found what was stuck between his teeth
and spat it in the faces of the crows.

Then he said to them,   220
«Not even the last people in the world
will see you fly the way you did before.»
They were white, they say.
Since then they have been black.

WHEN he had gone some distance farther,   [2.3.1]
    he stopped on the beach at the mouth of a trail.
When he'd been sitting there blubbering awhile,
beings sprinkled with eagle down arrived,
    carrying gambling sticks on their backs.
They asked him who he was.

«My mothers and fathers are dead.   230
 People tell me that your family
 and mine are from the same place,
 and so I came to find you.»
 They told him to come home with them, they say.

 And what a place they came to!
 And they asked him to sit down.
 One of the men went back of the housescreen.
 He was absent for a while
 and wet from the knees down when he returned.

 He had just killed a salmon,   240
 and he had it in his hands.
 Then they rubbed quartz pebbles back and forth,
 and the fire started to burn.

 They dressed the salmon then and there.
 They heated cooking stones,
 and then they broiled the fish.
 When it was cooked,
 they sat him down between them.

 These people were beavers, they say.
 And they were going out to gamble.   250
 They went home again because of him, they say.

Then one of them went to the back.
He brought some cranberries out in a dish.
They ate those too.

One of them went to the back again.
He brought out some mountain goat tripes
and they cut three portions off.
They served the largest of these to their guest,
and they said, «Don't go away.
Make yourself at home here.»   260

T HEN they put bags of gambling sticks on their backs,   [2.3.2]
  and off they went.
When evening came,
and they returned,
he was still there, sitting where they left him.

One of them went to the back again,
and again he came in with a salmon.
They broiled it.
Then they brought in a platter of cranberries,
then mountain goat tripes,   270
and when they had eaten,
they went to bed.

N EXT DAY at dawn,   [2.3.3]
  they ate another three-course meal,
slung their sacks of gambling sticks on their backs
and went away again.

Then he went behind the screen.
There – yes! – he found a lake.
The salmon trap sat in the outflowing stream.

The trap was shaking   280
like a person who is standing in the cold.
It was that full of salmon.

Small canoes were going here and there across the lake.
The points were glowing with ripening cranberries.
Spring songs and women's songs were sounding on the water.

He pulled out the salmon trap
and folded it flat
and set it on the lakeshore.

Then he rolled it up together with the lake
and rolled the house up too,   290
and put the bundle under his arm.
He climbed into a tree that stood nearby.
He could hold it all in one arm.

Then he came down from the tree
and unrolled them again.
He lit the fire,
and he went behind the screen.

He brought out a salmon
and cooked it and ate it at once.
Then he put out the fire   300
and sat there beside it and sobbed and sobbed.

He was sitting there with tear stains on his face
 when they returned.
«Hey, why are you crying?»

«The fire went out. That's why I'm crying.»
 They spoke to one another.

Then they said to him,
«That's how it goes.»

They started the fire,
and one of them went behind the screen   310
and brought out a salmon.
They split it and cooked it and ate it.
Then they ate berries and mountain goat tripes,
and then they lay down.

E ARLY next day,   [2.3.4]
    after they had eaten yet another three-course meal,
they put their bags of gambling sticks on their backs
and went away.

Then the one whom we are speaking of ran back of the screen.
He brought out a salmon.   320
He cooked it and ate it.
Then he ate berries and mountain goat tripes.

Then he went behind the screen again,
and he pulled up the trap and folded it flat.
The same with the house.
Then he set them by the lakeside
and rolled them up together with the lake
and put the bundle under his arm.

He climbed a tree that used to stand beside the lake,
and halfway up the tree he sat and waited.   330

After he'd been sitting there awhile,
someone came.
The house and lake had disappeared.
After looking all around,

Daxhiigang
(Charlie Edenshaw).
Model housepole
(*detail*).
Argillite,
53 × 8 × 6 cm.
ca 1895.
(Collection of
Bill & Marty Holm)

296

that one suddenly looked upward.
Yes! The guest was sitting there
with all his hosts' possessions.

The beaver went away then,
and two of them returned.
They went directly to the tree.   340
They started chewing on the trunk.

When it started to fall,
the one we are speaking of jumped to another.
When that one started to fall,
he jumped to the next with his bundle under his arm.
When he had leaped and leaped and leaped from tree to tree,
they let him go.

They wandered all around, they say.
After they had wandered for a time,
they found another lake.   350
They settled there, they say.

WHEN he had travelled the high country for a while,   [2.3.5]
    a big meadow opened up before him.
There he unrolled the lake, they say.
It sprang into being before him.

But he didn't let loose of the house or fishtrap.
He held on to those, they say,
so he could show them to the people out to seaward
    and the people here to landward later on.[6]

THEN, when he had walked along the tideline   [2.4.1]
    for a while in the Nuxalk country,[7]
something like a woman stood before him half submerged.   360

He looked at her in wonder.
Then he made a canoe
and paddled out to her.
When he came up close to her,
she vanished right before his eyes.

He made a canoe from something else
and headed toward her again.
When he came up near her,
she went under.

He made one out of something else again.   370
She sank just in front of him again.

After searching through the shoregrass for a while,
he put spreaders in a vetch pod.[8]
Then he headed out to her in that.
When he came near her,
she did not go under water.

When he came up alongside her,
he lifted her aboard.
She was dressed in a dancing skirt and leggings.

When he brought her to the shore   380
he unlaced her dancing leggings and her skirt
and dried her off.
Then he went inland
and got her a ground squirrel skin for a robe.

Then he launched the canoe
and put her back aboard,
and headed off, they say.

He brought her ashore at Big Bay[9]
and set up the house for her,
but still he kept the fishtrap under his arm.   390
He did so, they say,
so he could show it to her later.

Then he paddled back again.

A FTER he had paddled down the mainland coast a ways, [2.4.2]
there was – yes! – someone else in a canoe.
His hair stuck out in sharpened tufts.[10]
The one we are speaking of came alongside,
     holding the other one's boat by the gunwale, they say.

That one's boat was full of harbor seal.
And this one asked,
«Where'd you get this load of game?»   400

«They're everywhere.»

That one picked up his harpoon.
He looked down between the two canoes.
He thrust at something.
Then he lifted out another seal.

«Look into the water!»

So this one looked into the water.
Nothing showed itself.

«Well, that's how it is with me lately.
I haven't been able to see a thing   410
since a butter clam spat at me.»

«Lean over this way,» said the other.
This one leaned toward that one.
That one plucked the bloodclots out of this one's eyes
and put them right back in again.

This one spoke to that one rudely.
That's why that one wouldn't clean his eyes, they say.
Now, all at once, he was very respectful.
He tried all kinds of things,
but nothing changed,   420
and so he paddled off, they say.

W HEN he had paddled for a while –   [2.4.3]
yes! – Stlgham was passing by,[11]
and this one said to him,
«Friend, I've been taking salt water.
You should take salt water too.»

Right before his eyes, the one we speak of drank some.
It spurted out of his bum as he travelled along.

Stlgham then drank some too.
It went right through him, just the same.   430
And then the one we speak of said,
«Cousin, we ought to build a fire!»

«Not so fast! The signs must come together.»

Stlgham took a spruceroot waterjug out from under his arm.
He rinsed his mouth
and spat as he went along.

After they had travelled for a while,
they came to Flatrock.

Then the Raven went ashore
and lit a fire.   440

Once again the other took his spruceroot waterjug
and sipped fresh water.
The one we speak of wanted it.
The other held it fast.

What was left in this one's guts spurted out
and ran along the ground.
He deftly stepped aside.

«I'm going for a drink,» he said,
and walked into the woods.

Then he dug some spruce roots.   450
He wrung some juice out of the roots
into the woman's hat, which he happened to be wearing.
Sauntering back,
he pretended to be drinking.

That one asked if it was tasty.
This one offered him a sip.
He peered at it.
He sniffed it.
«Cousin, why does your water smell like spruce gum?»
«Cousin, I'll tell you: it came from a tap in an alder.»[12]   460

Then this one broke some twigs
        from the overhanging branches right nearby.
«Cousin, put these in the fire.»

So he put them in the fire.
Ooooooooooh yes! How it roared.

Soon after he had done this,
that one – yes! – started reaching for his waterjug.

As soon as this one saw it,
he climbed the biggest overhanging branch
and started stomping up and down.
«Fall! You widowmaker, fall!»   470

And then it cracked,
and then it broke right through.
This one hollered
Timmmberrrrr!
And that one jumped away and left his jug.

This one entered his own skin
and seized the waterjug and flew.
And then Stlgham put on his skin.
He also flew.

As that one grabbed for this one with his talons,   480
the water splattered out.
It kept on forming streams and rivers.

That one let him go,
and this one kept on tipping out the water with his beak.
Finally, they say, he brought the flowing water
all the way up to the lake he had put there before.

He did the same thing on the Islands here, they say.
And he poured out the last of the water he had
    up at the head of the Skeena, they say.[13]

Another of the Eagle's names is Hlaaghahlam.[14]

THE ONE we speak of finished all of this,   490
and then he headed north, they say.   [2.5.1]

After he had travelled for a while,
he came to where a village stood.
He became a little feather
    in the waterhole behind the headman's house.
And then he lay there, floating,
waiting for the headman's daughter.

Now the one of good family was standing beside him,
and he floated as a feather
in the water she dipped up.

She poured it out, they say.   500
Then she scooped some up again,
and there he was.
And then he whispered to her,
«Drink me.»

Not long after that
she was pregnant, they say.
Then she gave birth to a child, they say.

His grandfather washed him
and stepped on his feet,[15]
and he started to crawl.   510

When he'd been crawling for a while
he started wailing steadily, they say.
«M-m-mooooon!» he kept yelling.

When they just couldn't bear it any longer,
they closed off the smokehole.

Then they opened a box – and one after another
    pulled out the four inner boxes
and gave him something round.
Light spread throughout the house.

After he had played with it awhile,
he let it go,   520
and then he started bawling once again.
«S-s-smooooookehooooole!» he wailed,
and they opened the smokehole.

He wailed again.
«M-m-morrrrre!» he bellowed.
They opened it further.

Then he flew out with it.
Plain Old Marten chased him down below.
The One Who Outruns Trout flew after him above.[16]
When neither one could catch him,   530
both came back.

Then he put the moon in his armpit, they say.

WHEN he had travelled for a while,   [2.5.2]
    he met a gull and a cormorant together.
He got the two of them to quarrel.

Then he said to the cormorant,
«Whenever people speak to me that way,
    I make myself look dangerous by sticking out my tongue.»

The one he spoke to did as he suggested.
Then the one we speak of seized his tongue.   540
He bit it off.

He changed it into an eulachon.
Then he dressed in a cedarbark cape
and smeared the eulachon all over it.

He also smeared it on the hull of his canoe,
and then he put some rocks aboard
and paddled out offshore from Qadajaan.[17]

Then he entered that one's house.
«Brrrrr! I got quite chilly coming over.»

Qadajaan lay still, with his back to the fire.   550
Then, looking up at this one,
he saw the oily sheen on his canoe
and saw how low it was riding in the water.

That one flew into a rage
and toppled the screen in his house.[18]
Then they poured out in a stream.

The one we are speaking of dumped out his cargo of stones
and moved in close with his canoe.
It filled to the gunwales, they say,
and he paddled away with his catch.   560

Then he went along the mainland
leaving eulachons where eulachons are now.
He dumped out half of all he had at the mouth of the Nass.
He also kept a few in the canoe.

THEN he got ten extra paddles,   [2.5.3]
one with a knothole in the blade.
Then he called ashore
to someone who was living there.

She came down to the tideline with a creel,
    and he said to her,   570
«Help yourself, my lady.»

When she had packed them in her basket,
    and it was nearly full,
    he tromped on a stipe of bull kelp
    he had lying in the bilge.
«Aaaaah! My canoe is cracking, it seems.»

Then he nudged the boat to seaward.
As she reached out to take a little more,
he plucked out her armpit hair, they say.

Swordfern Woman called her sons at once.   580
Her sons were both good shots with rocks, they say.

He pushed right off,
and they shot rocks at him with throwing sticks.
They broke his paddle.
After they had broken ten,
he used the one that had the knothole.

  They kept on shooting.
«Through the knothole!» he kept saying,
and their rocks went through the knothole.
He got away, they say.   590
He got her armpit hair.[19]

THEN he abandoned the canoe, they say.   [2.5.4]
He came to where they fish with fishrakes in Nass Inlet.
Then he spoke to the fishermen, they say.
«Hey there! Throw me some!
    I can give you daylight!»

They answered right away, they say.
«Ohooo! Here's this one,
who as usual is talking!»

Then he let a little of it shine,   600
and then he closed it up again.
They poured out fish in front of him, they say.

T HEN he called to something else – a dog –   [2.5.5]
and told it what to do.
«Say that the number of months should be four.»

The dog wouldn't say it.
The dog was hoping for six.
He said to it,
«Why do you want to die?»

«When spring arrives,   610
and I'm hungry,
I'll rub my forepaws over my eyes.»

He let it be
the way he said, they say.[20]

Then he took a bite out of the moon.
He chewed it for a while
and flung it upward into place.
«Not even the last people in the world
will see how you are stuck there.»

And then he dropped the moon and shattered it   620
and threw the pieces upward into place –
the one that lives inside the daylight too.

Anonymous Haida artist. *Pipe: The Raven in action.*

Argillite, 19 × 5.5 × 2.5 cm. Early 19th century.

(Burke Museum, University of Washington, Seattle. Gerber Collection: 25.0/280)

3

T HEN HE CAME FROM UP NORTH.   [3.1]
The smoke from House Point village was nearby.
He pulled his headband off
and threw one end of it this way
and walked across it quickly.

He looked through the cracks into the houses of the town.
The House Point headman's wife had a newborn child.
He waited until evening.   630

As soon as they were sleeping,
he climbed inside the child's skin
so that he too was newborn.

Morning came, and they gave him a bath,
and his father held him.
Later on, his father's sister came to the fire.
They let her take him.

After she had held him for a while,
he grabbed her by the breasts.
«Owhooo!» she said.   640
«What made you say that, dear?»
«Well! He nearly wiggled out of my lap.»

The headman of the town, they say, was Pierced Fin.
His nephew's name was Rippled Fin, they say.

Soon after that, he had a thought, they say:
«Suppose they took the children of the headmen of the village
    on an outing!»
Next day, the village children were taken on an outing.
They brought along their favorite foods.
The one in charge of him that day was his father's sister.

The children played together for a time,   650
and then the others left.
After they had gone,
his father's sister sat there all alone.

He looked around.
Then he dressed in his own skin,
and then he threw his arms around his father's sister.

«Don't touch me!» his father's sister said to him.
«Your father wants to keep my dowry.
  Why else would I be single?»

Then he went away and changed himself again.   660
His father's sister cried,
and she was thinking about how she would explain it.
He had a thought himself: she should forget it
as soon as she went home.

Then she went inside,
and her brother looked at her awhile.
«Why do I see tear stains on your face?» he said.
«I caught him eating sand.
  That's why I was crying.»

310

THEN he headed out along the sleeping sea.   670
    He strung some keyhole limpet shells   [3.2.1]
        he found along the beach
and made a pair of ring-shaped rattles.

Then he veered up toward the trees.
He pulled the mat away from someone's grave[21]
and pulled the weft out at one side to make some fringe.
He tied a row of shells along the hem
to make a dancing apron from the mat.

Then he called out to the ghost,
«Are you awake?»
The ghost stood up for him.   680
He tied the dancing apron to its waist.
Then he put the rattles in its hands.

«Walk right along in front of town,» he said.
«Midway along, shake the rattles toward the houses.
That will shower them with nightmares.»

It started dancing like a shaman then, they say.
And when it shook the rattles toward the town
the way he told it to,
the people squirmed and mumbled in their sleep.
They all had nightmares.   690

He went into the house at the edge of the village,
yanked the finest-looking woman out of bed
and lay down with her right there.[22]
Then he entered the next house
and lay down with another woman there.

He did it again and again,
and when he reached his father's house
he went to where his father's sister slept
and then he went to bed with her.

There was an old person living in the corner   700
whose mind was free of nightmares.
She knew him when she saw him.
She knew the headman's son had slipped outside
and left his skin behind.

Later on he came back in   [3.2.2]
and lay down again in the cradle.
He gave the ghost its own bed too, they say.

It seems that he had slept with his father's sister
and his own mother, Floodtide Woman, too.[23]
This is what they whispered to each other in the town.   710
Some time passed,
and then they knew.

Then they chased his mother out of town.
They chased her son away as well.
She was Big Surf's sister,
married among the People of the Strait, they say.[24]

They started out walking then,   [3.2.3]
the two of them, they say,
and after travelling awhile,
they came to the foot of the trail across the point.   720
They saw a silver otter there, they say.

His mother skinned it.
Then she laced the skin into a frame.

She stretched it first of all,
and then she scraped it.
Then she hung it up to dry.

As soon as it was cured,
she dressed her son in it.
He was Voicehandler's Heir, they say.

AFTER travelling awhile,   730
she arrived with her son at her brother's door.   [3.2.4]
A little while later,
someone stuck his head out.
«Floodtide Woman is standing outside.»

«Mmmmm.
Then she's been up to her old tricks again,»
her brother said.
«A young boy is with her,» said the other.
«Is that so! Then ask her in!»

Then he invited the two of them in.   740
Her brother's wife offered them food.
Later on, her brother said,
«Floodtide Woman, what are you going to call the child?»

She put her hand on the back of her neck then
and rubbed it up and down.
«I'm naming your nephew Voicehandler's Heir.»
She spoke the words slowly, pausing between them.

«Well, name him something else!
Word would surely get around
that someone named her child   750
for a god too dangerous to think of!»

All the while they lived with her brother,
the child slammed the doorflap, going out and coming in.[25]
«Floodtide Woman, stop that boy
  from doing that so often.»
«Sorry, sir, I can't control him.»

«Ahhh! Listen to what she says!
  She lets her own child do
  what the gods would be afraid to.»

Another day he slammed the door again   760
  while his uncle was still sleeping.
«Floodtide Woman,» said his uncle,
«stop that shit-assed kid
  from doing that so often!»

«Sorry, sir, I can't control your darling nephew.»

Then he pooped right there, where he was sitting,
  by the fire, near his mother,
  on the side that was closest to the door.
  His uncle's wife twiddled her lips at him.
«Isn't he sweet! I'm certain to sleep
    with my husband's nephew!»   770

He heard what his uncle's wife said about him.

Early the next morning he went out.
  When he had walked some distance inland,
  he met some people singing songs and dancing.
«Hey,» they said to him,
«what are you doing?»

«I'm looking for women's medicine.»
«What does that mean?
   Women's medicine? Medicine for women?
   Medicine for love, you mean?»   780
«That's it. Medicine for love.»

The singers kept on singing.
   As they sang, they sucked the spruce gum in their mouths.
   Then one of them broke off a piece for him.
«This is women's medicine.»
   She told him what to do.

«Go around to the right when you enter the house.
   Have the gum in your mouth.
   When your uncle's wife asks for it,
   don't let her have it.   790
   Ignore her! Ignore her!

«Tell her you want what belongs to her husband.
   After you get it,
   give her the gum.»

Then he left the singers.

He went back to the house,
   and when he came in,
   there was something red sticking out of his mouth.

His uncle's wife said to him,
«Voicehandler's Heir, give me some gum, please.»   800
   He paid her no attention.

He sat with his mother
   and said to his mother,

«Tell her I want what belongs to my uncle.
After I have it, I'll give her the gum.»

His mother went up to his uncle's wife
and delivered the message.
His uncle's wife gave him something white and round.
Then he let her have the gum.
She chewed it.   810

As soon as she swallowed the juice,
the way she felt about him changed,
and he could see that this was so.

L ATER, when his father and his father's people   [3.2.5]
        passed in their canoes,
he called out to a dog
who was lying near the doorway,
«Voicehandler's Heir would like the tide to fall
and leave his father and his father's people stranded.»

The dog repeated his instructions.
Then the ebb tide left the creatures high and dry.   820
They spouted there.
Then he said to his mother,
«Give them water.»

Out she went, but not to her own husband.
She poured the water over Rippled Fin alone.
Then the one we are speaking of went to his mother
and told her to pour water on his father.
She pretended not to hear him.

They were going out to buy some humpback whales
from the gods along the outer coast, they say.   830

After that he came back in
and talked to the dog a second time.
«Now Voicehandler's Heir wants the tide to rise
to where his father and his father's brother are.
Go out and say that.»

The dog ran out and said what he had said.
Xuuuuuw!
They were floating again on the ocean.

They were gone for quite a while.
Then they reappeared in their canoes.   840
He talked to the dog again.
«Voicehandler's Heir wants a share of what they have.
Go out and say that.»

The dog ran out and said what he had said.
Something black was pushed across the sea
and up to the edge of the village.
He went out to see what it was,
and what he found was a humpback whale.

O N the beach, beside the whale,   [3.3]
  he built himself a blind out of evergreen boughs   850
and shot many different kinds of birds.

Later, a bufflehead came there to feed.[26]
He wanted it.
He shot it, taking aim above its head,
and then it flew.
Square in the head is where he hit it.

He took its skin and put it on.
Then he thought of waves coming ashore.

317

The waves began to come ashore then,
and he glided down to the water.   860
He dived under a wave as it came toward him.

When he had done this many times,
he flapped up on the shore
and came out of the skin.

He hung it to dry in the blind.
He made it his, they say.
He put it into a two-headed spruce for safekeeping.

After he had shot many different kinds of birds,
a sleek blue being came to the whale to feed.
It flew down from above.   870
It ate from the back of the whale.

He took a shot at it.
His arrow passed between its wings.
That made him sad.

He returned to the blind
early the following morning.
After he had sat there for a while,
it flew down out of the sky again.
It was calling.

As soon as it started to eat from the back of the whale,   880
he took another shot at it.
Again the arrow slipped between its wings.
That made him sad.

He returned to the blind early again

on the following morning.
Soon it came again to feed.

He aimed above it this time,
just as it was lifting off,
and hit it in the head.
Then he went down to the water to get it   890
and brought it up to the blind.

He skinned it.
Then he wrapped the skin around himself, they say.
And then he flew, way up.
He flew around for quite a while.
Then he dived.

He rammed his beak into the rock
out on the point at the edge of town.
He cried as he struck it.
«Ghaaaaaw!»   900
It was solid, that rock,
and yet he splintered it by speaking.

Then he hung the skin in the blind to dry,
and then he stored it,
side by side with the skin of the bufflehead.

Then he left the place, they say.
He went back to the house
and sat with his mother.

A FTER a time, his uncle's wife said to her husband,   [3.4]
    «Why are you sitting here day after day?   910
Go out and hunt something.»
That's how she spoke to him.

Then someone brought him his spear and his quiver.
He put pitch on his spearhead and arrowhead bindings.
When midnight arrived
he set off,
and his seat was empty next morning.

Then the one we are speaking of went through the door
and stepped out of himself.
He put paint on his face   920
and a pair of skyblankets over his shoulders.

The moment he came back inside
his uncle's wife began to cast her eyes around.
They went behind the screen.
A little while later came the sound
of bedrock cracking deep beneath the island.

Then her husband came ashore.
«Mother of my child,» he said to his wife,
«why was there that sound
we only hear when we make love?»   930

She laughed,
and then she said,
«Perhaps I was together with your nephew,
Voicehandler's Heir.»

At daybreak next day,
Big Surf was sitting in the firepit.
Feast-rings were stacked on the top of his hat,
a globe of seafoam spinning at the crown.

Voicehandler's Heir began to cast his eyes around,
and then he went outside.   940

He retrieved his pair of birdskins
and dressed himself in two skyblankets.
After that he came back in.

There were two knots tied in this one's hair
and a globe of seafoam crowning that one's hat.
It started spinning very fast.

Streams began to flow from the corners of the house.
He put his mother under his arm
and dressed in the skin of the bufflehead
and bobbed around in the swirling water.   950
He dived and surfaced here and there.

When the water came up to the roof,
he swam out through the smokehole.
Then he dressed in his raven skin and flew.

He rammed his beak into the bottom of the cloud.
The water lapped against his tail.
He smacked it with his feet.
«Stop! I'm the one who owns you!»

That was where it ended.
The big waves started to recede.   960

Then he looked below him.
Smoke rose peacefully from his uncle's place.
Seeing this displeased him.
He flew down.

After flying for a time,
he rammed his beak into the housepole,
calling as he did so.

«Ghaaaaaw!» he said.

«The foremost headman! Yes, it's you!
  You'll be in charge.»   970

Then he was a child of good family   [3.5]
  just as if a child of good family were what he really was.
He came into the house with his mother.
Right after that, he actually did begin to shoot birds.

  One day he came into the house
  and said to his mother,
«Mother, Qinggi says he is adopting me, they say.»

  Then his uncle said,
«Fools open their yawps! Floodtide Woman,
  stop that boy from talking as he does!   980
  That's one thing we're prepared for, an adoption!»

  When he had said it several times, they looked outside,
  and their hearts started hammering, they say.
  Ten canoes of people dancing!
  Voicehandler's Heir put his two skyblankets on
  and pranced back and forth on the rim of the housepit.

  His uncle said,
«His talk has brought it to be.
  It is just as he described it.
  Well, we have plenty of people and food!»   990

  After Voicehandler's Heir had walked back and forth,
  he stamped on the ground to the right of the doorway,
  and the earth split open at his feet.

Someone held a drum up from under the ground,
and people formed a line behind it.

He went to the opposite side.
He stamped there too.
«Even dirt can turn to human beings!»
Someone lifted up a drum in that place too.

He did it again in the back of the house at one side.　　　　1000
Someone lifted a drum in that place too.
He did it again on the opposite side.
Then there were four lines streaming.

Tsimshian, Haida, People from the Distant Coast, and Tlingit
were singing their songs from his uncle's house.
And while they were singing, his uncle was saying,
«Well, we have plenty of food!»

They arranged themselves in the house,
and a crowd of people gathered near the door
to serve the meal.　　　　1010

Then, they say, Voicehandler's Heir said,
«Go to my sister Sniffing the Wind.[27]
Ask for food on my behalf.»
Then the servants headed off.
Coho and cranberries followed them home.

Then he said, «Go to my sister Calling Raven[28]
to beg on my behalf.»
Sockeye swarmed into the house with the coho and cranberries.

The Creek Woman of Qqaasta was the next
　　to offer something.[29]

The Creek Woman of Qqaadasghu[30]
    made a contribution too.
Food reached to the roof of the house.

The feasting went on until dawn.
And the next day again, and the next day again.
When the guests went home, they say,
ten nights had passed.
But actually, they say, it was ten years.

1020

4

THEN HE WENT WITH HIS FATHER QINGGI, THEY SAY. [4.1.1]
As soon as Qinggi landed at his town,
he gave a feast.
He tried to make the one we speak of eat.   1030
But he would not accept a morsel.

Qinggi gave a feast again the next day,
to make his child eat.
Again he would eat nothing.

Two greedyguts arrived,
and someone grabbed a storage chest of cranberries.
One of the two greedyguts opened up his maw.
They poured in the whole boxful.
They poured one down the other's throat as well.

NEXT DAY, his father gave another feast.   1040
    The greedyguts arrived.   [4.1.2]
Again they poured entire storage chests
    of cranberries into their mouths.

The one we are speaking of ran to the edge of town.
As he was walking there,
cranberries bubbled up out of the swampland.
He plugged the vent with moss.
When another vent formed, he plugged it too.

Then he went back to the house
and asked the greedyguts closest to the door,
«Tell me, how do you manage to eat so much?»   1050
«Sir, don't ask that.
Do you think this is a happy way to be?»

«No, but tell me.
If you tell me, you will eat
at every feast my father gives.
If you don't agree to tell me,
I will plug you up for good.»

«Alright, sir, sit beside me.
I will tell you what to do.
In the morning, take a bath and then lie down.   1060
Rub yourself raw where you feel it most deeply.
By the following day, a scab will form.
You must swallow the scab.»

He followed these instructions.

T HEN, after sitting there awhile: [4.1.3]
    «Father, I'm hungry!»
His father gave a feast without delay.
Again the greedyguts arrived.
Again they upended boxes into their mouths.

He couldn't be filled.   1070
He was famished.
Qinggi gave another feast.
Then he gave another and another, day after day.

At last, the one we speak of went outside.
When he kept picking cranberries out of their turds,

they saw who it was,
and they shut the door in his face.

T HEN he walked away, they say.   [4.2]
  He went around behind his father's house.
«Father, let me come in!»   1080
  No answer.
  They turned him away.

«Father, let me come in!
  I can arrange for you to have grizzly bears.
  I can arrange for you to have mountain goats.»
  He offered his father everything found on the mainland.
«Oh, but my son, their footsteps would keep me from sleeping.»

It was then that he started his singing.
  He was banging his head on the house to keep time,
  and the house began to give way.   1090
  His father came close to letting him in
  when that happened, they say.

Then he got up to leave,
  and they snatched at the things he was wearing –
  black bear and marten, they say.[31]
  After that, he was gone a long time.

T HEN one day at dawn he was sitting offshore   [4.3.1]
  in a harbor-seal canoe.
  He was wearing the hat that belonged to his uncle.
  Seafoam was swirling around on the crown.   1100

After seeing his face,
  the villagers gathered in Qinggi's house.
  And after they talked about what he was going to do,
  Qinggi got dressed.

Xhyuu's housepole at Ttanuu, summer 1903: the villagers are climbing Qinggi's hat. (Photograph by Arthur Church. American Museum of Natural History, Library Services: N° 106695.) *See the note on page 389.*

The villagers wedged themselves into the seams
in the pillar of feast-rings
    on top of the hat that Qinggi was wearing.

WHEN things had stood that way awhile,   [4.3.2]
   the rolling sea began to rise.
As the water got higher, Qinggi got taller.
That made the one we are speaking of jealous.   1110

Then he sliced his father's hat in two.
Half the villagers were killed.
After that, he was gone for a while.

AND then he was there again,   [4.3.3]
   early one morning, they say.
«It's Voicehandler, waiting offshore!»[32]
«Ask him to come in,» his father said.
«I would like to see his face.»

They spread out the mats.
Then his companions came in and sat down.
His father offered him food, over and over.   1120
His father was happy to see him.

AFTER the meal, that evening,   [4.3.4]
   his father sat down near the doorway, they say.[33]
After a time he said,
«Now then, your lordship, my son,
could one of your crewmembers tell us
    a story from mythtime?»

Voicehandler turned to the people beside him.
«Do you know any stories from mythtime?»
«No,» they replied.
He turned to the other side.   1130

«Doesn't one of you know any stories from mythtime?»
«No, we don't.»

Then he said to his father,
«They don't seem to know any stories from mythtime.»
Then Qinggi, his father, said,
«Really? Not even the story called *Raven Travelling*?
    Couldn't one of your crewmembers tell me that story?»

Voicehandler cringed at what people would say,
and he stared at the floor.[34]

A FTER a moment, one of his crew   1140
        who was swarthy and little and sat at his right,   [4.3.5]
leaned back and bellowed,
«Yayaaaaaaaw!
The village of Qinggi, the mythteller!»

The house was as quiet as something
that someone has dropped.

«Yayaaaaaaaw!
    A stipe of bull kelp ten joints long
    grew up in front of the village of Qinggi, the mythteller.
    The gods came out to see it   1150
    and died on the spot!»

«Yayaaaaaaaw!
    A rainbow scratched its back
    right in front of the village of Qinggi, the mythteller.
    The gods came out to watch it
    and died on the spot!»

«Yayaaaaaaaw!
    Last season a reef came out of the sea

in front of the village of Qinggi, the mythteller.
Gull God stood at one end
    and Cormorant God at the other,[35]   1160
tossing humpback whales' tailflukes
    back and forth between them.
The gods came out to watch,
and they died on the spot!»

«Yayaaaaaaaw!
The Harlequin Duck and the Steller's Jay
staged a race in Qinggi the mythteller's village.
The gods came out to see,
and they died on the spot!»

«Yayaaaaaaaw!
A Raven rattle's ribcage came unlaced and flew around   1170
with long, thin songs coming out of its mouth[36]
a season ago at the home of the mythteller Qinggi.
The gods came out to see,
and they died on the spot!»

«Yayaaaaaaaw!
Jilaquns was here a season ago,
doing her weaving in White Quartz Bay,
at the edge of the village of Qinggi, the mythteller.
The gods came out to see
and died on the spot!»   1180

«Yayaaaaaaaw!
Plain Old Marten and the other one, Who Outruns Trout,
chased each other up, down, back and around
at the edge of the village of Qinggi, the mythteller.
The gods came out to see it
and died on the spot!»

Daxhiigang (Charlie Edenshaw). *The Raven and his Bracket Fungus Steersman.*
Argillite plate, 35 cm diameter. ca 1880.
The work has been scraped, broken and badly mended.
(Field Museum of Natural History, Chicago: Nº 17952.)
See the note on page 389.

§5

T HEN HE WENT AWAY, THEY SAY.   [5.1]
When he had travelled for a while,
he came to Facedown Town, they say.

A fleet of canoes was bobbing offshore.   1190
They were fishing for flounder.
The bait they were using was salmon roe.

Right away he wanted what he saw
and started acting like a flounder.
Then he went under the water, they say.
When he had been stealing the roe for a while,
they pulled out his beak and hauled in the line.

Back in the village,
    while they were getting ready to gamble,
they looked at his beak and passed it around.
They handed it one to another.   1200
The one we are speaking of looked at it too.
«Oh,» he said, «it's a scoop for mashed salmon roe.»

He went back of the house
and called the Saw-whet Owl.[37]
He stole his beak
and took it for his own
and gave the Owl something worthless to replace it.

Later on, they went fishing again,
and again he went under the water.
When he had stolen some more of the roe,   1210
a hook went through his beak again, they say.

The one who hooked him hauled him in
and came ashore
and gave him to his child,
and they skewered him for roasting.

When his backside started cooking,
he could hear himself thinking, they say.
«Why don't they run to the edge of the village for something?»

They ran outside right after that, they say.
They left the child sitting there alone.   1220
At that moment, he put on his skin
and flew through the smokehole.

The child started crying for its mother.
«Mommy! My dinner is flying awaaaaay!»

H E never left the town, they say.   [5.2]
    And early one morning
            they started in cooking, they say.
The Crow brought out bark cakes and cranberry sauce.
She set out enough for them all.
They asked even the one we speak of to join them.

He refused to come, they say.   1230
«Not on your life!
You're serving plain old pussytail mussels!»[38]
Then he asked the Eagle to see what it was
they were actually having.

334

The Eagle returned
and said they had bark cakes with cranberry sauce.
«Well, cousin, tell them I'm coming.»

The Eagle said, «His highness is coming.»
«Not on your life!
We're serving plain old pussytail mussels!»   1240

Before they had even started eating,
he headed toward the woods, they say.
He made ten canoes from hunks of punkwood
and filled them with spruce cones for crewmen.
He put flowerstalks of dunegrass
        in the crewmen's hands for lances.

The fleet rounded the point,
and he walked by the tideline, pointing, they say.
«Iixyaaaaay! How can it be?
Canoes rounding the point!
And they bristle with crewmen!»   1250

They dropped their food and flew away, they say.
Then he entered the house
and gorged himself on the bark cakes.
Down on the beach, the canoes kept arriving.
They washed up on shore in a heap.

THEN he left the place, they say.   [5.3.1]
    And as he was leaving,
he picked up his sister, they say.
He left his sister with his wife.
Then, they say, he set off by canoe.   1260

He asked the Junco to serve as his steersman
and took him aboard.
He also took a spear.

The things he had come for were sprawled on the reef
over top of each other.
As soon as they drew alongside,
the Junco went mad.
He brought the Junco back, they say.

Then he asked the Steller's Jay to be his steersman,   1270
and they headed out together.
As soon as they drew alongside,
the Jay started shaking and flapping his wings.
Whoever tried to do it failed.

Then he painted a face on a bracket fungus[39]
and seated it in the stern.
«Look alive there, and backpaddle
as soon as we come alongside,» he said.

Then he headed out with him.
When they drew alongside,
the fungus nodded his head.   1280

The one we speak of speared a large one and a small one,
and he brought the two of them home.
He went ashore there
and called his wife to come
and put one of them on her.

Then he put the other on Siiwaas, his sister.[40]
She started to cry,
and he said to her,
«Yours will be safe, my darling.»

O NCE he left that place behind,   1290
    he married Cloud Woman, they say.   [5.3.2]
And Cloud Woman promised him plenty of salmon.

Then, when they were starting to leave the fishcamp,
as he walked between the drying racks,
salmon ribs caught in his hair,
and his wife was wounded
by the words he chose to use.

«Swim away,»
she said to the dog salmon.[41]
Even the fillets that hung on the drying racks
        started to swim.   1300

Then nothing remained except for some salmon roe
⟨in the box⟩ that his sister was sitting on.
So they left the camp with nothing.

T HEN he made himself look ill.   [5.3.3]
   He went up in the bow, close to the salmon roe.

After they had paddled for a while,
a bad smell reached his sister's nose.
He told her he was picking another scab.

After he had told her this repeatedly,
he tossed the empty food box overboard, they say.   1310
«Siiwaas's empty box skips very very well!»

W HEN they had travelled for a while,   [5.3.4]
    they kindled a fire, they say.
After the yellowcedar he threw on the fire
had showered them with embers for a time,
a burning coal hit Siiwaas in the groin.

337

Then he said there was a medicine.
«Go into the woods and keep saying,
I'm calling my medicine!
If anything answers you,   1320
go there.
If you find a tiny red thing jutting up there,
sit right on top of it.»

After she had called out for a time
the way he told her,
something answered.

When she went looking,
something small and red was jutting up there.
She squatted down on top of it, they say.

She found him – yes! her brother! –   1330
lying underneath her.

T HEN as he was sitting there embarrassed,   [5.3.5]
just doodling with his finger,
a baby started to cry.

He took it along.
He invented the custom of making playpens and cribs.
So the child learned to play.
After that it always followed him around.

Later on, when it went out to play alone,
it disappeared.   1340

Then he started searching.
He dressed in his skin,
and he flew up and down along the tideline.
He did it here and on the mainland.

After hunting and hunting in vain,
he heard it said, they say,
that the gods had arranged it this way
because he had tricked them.
Then he stopped searching.

They say that when the child learned to walk,   1350
lightning flashed around his kneecaps.
His name was Saqaayuuhl, they say.

Much later on, someone came in
    with a cedarbark ring on his head.
«Father, I'm back!»

The one we are speaking of spat in his face.
«Was Saqaayuuhl ever like this?»

As the visitor left, lightning flashed around his kneecaps.
He vanished at once.
And the one we are speaking of cried and cried.

THEN he tucked his sister under his arm   1360
 and headed off with her.   [5.4]
Siiwaas planted ⟨her tobacco seeds⟩ at Xhiina.[42]

When they matured,
he stood on the leeward side of Xhiina
and called a lot of other birds to join him.

They went to get wood for the potlatch, they say.
They came back with it quickly.
When they had brought only a little,
he asked them to stop.
After that they began to get hungry.   1370

Then he invited other creatures.
When they gathered on the water there in front of him,
he dressed himself in something frayed and dirty.
Then he spoke across the water.
They couldn't make him out.

They sent for Porpoise Woman then.
She said, «However would you get along without me?
He wants you to pelt him with abalone and sea urchin.»
They bombarded him with these,
and then he ate them.   1380

Now, since the house was too small,
he held the potlatch out-of-doors, they say.
All the great spirit beings he invited
came in their canoes.

He pierced the noses of many different birds.
The Eagle asked to have his pierced as well.
The Eagle pestered him and pestered him about it,
so he pierced his carelessly, they say.
That's why the Eagle has his nostrils pointing up, they say.

A ND then the one we speak of headed out in his canoe.   1390
  He came to where the sea was boiling.   [5.5]
He loaded herring into his canoe.
Then he dipped them with the bailer
and flung them toward the shore.

«Not even the last people in the world
will find where you are hiding.»   1396

Raven Travelling

Epilogue: Ghandl's Conclusion

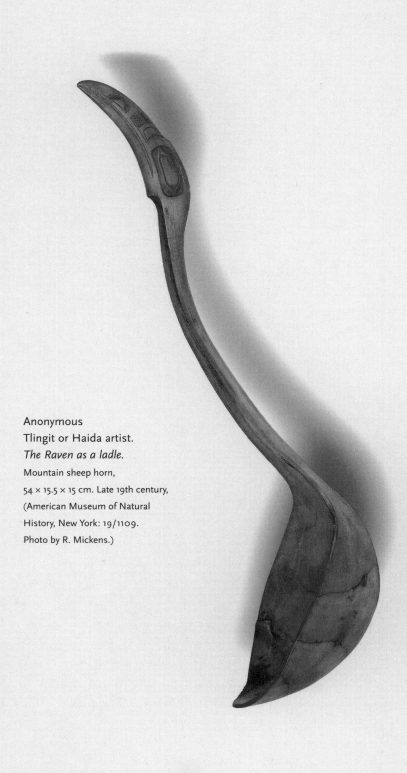

Anonymous
Tlingit or Haida artist.
The Raven as a ladle.
Mountain sheep horn,
54 × 15.5 × 15 cm. Late 19th century,
(American Museum of Natural
History, New York: 19/1109.
Photo by R. Mickens.)

GHANDL:

A

. . . **A**ND THEN, THEY SAY,[1]
        he went to do some fishing for his sister.
He flung the halibut ashore
where it was high and level, they say.
That's the spot known as Halibut Fling, they say.

He went along naming other places too.
«You'll be known as this,
    and you'll be known as so-and-so,»
he said as he was travelling along.

Then he passed one by,
    and it hollered at his back,
«What will my name be?»
    Then, speaking like a southerner, he said,
«You'll have a dandy name: Seawater Rock.»[2]

Then, they say, he was thinking of harpooning Heavy Rain.
He made a harpoon line.
He used the intestines of somebody strong.

He saw Heavy Rain's head go sailing by.
Then he harpooned it, they say,
and was dragged along on his ass.

He hung on for dear life,   20
and it pulled him clear out
to a reef lying seaward, they say.

When he'd skittered along on his butt for a while,
the harpoon head gave way.
A white streak formed along the cliff face
where the line snapped back against the shore, they say.

After that, when he was ready to move on,
he stuffed some eagle tail feathers up his bum as a replacement.
Stuffing in the Eagle's Tail came to be the name of that place.

After that, he started getting woozy
        for his mother's brother's wife.   30
He was making up a love song,
tapping out the rhythm with his head against the rocks.
He went right through, they say, and made a hole there.
Crooning and (Ouch!) Rubbing the Back of the Head
        is that place's name, they say.

This is how it ends.   35

3

A Family Story

The Qquuna Qiighawaay

Anonymous Tlingit artist. *Amulet: Killer whale and human.*

Walrus ivory, 11.5 cm long. Mid 19th century.

(American Museum of Natural History, New York: 19/454, neg. K16492)

[i]

THE VILLAGE of Ttlxingas was still inhabited,[1]   [1.1]
but the sickness had come by that time.
Boss Wren's daughter, Thunder Walking Woman,
    owned a knife that could open its mouth.
And Thunder Walking Woman died at Ttsixhudalxa.[2]
They said that something had carried her off   5
because of the knife that could open its mouth.

They paddled Thunder Walking Woman's body
    back to Ttlxingas.
Then they said that the knife that could open its mouth
    belonged to Disease,
and they paddled it out to the middle.
They fastened feathers to the knife and let it sink.   10
By way of the knife that could open its mouth,
they claimed the sea.

[ii]

LATER, Ttaagyaaw took up hunting with dogs,   [1.2]
and while he was out with one of the dogs,
a black bear attacked him.
It tore off his scalp.

347

They tracked him and found him and carried him in,
and they laid out his body.
With that, they claimed the land as well as the inlets.

Then the Daaghanga Sils family paid them one copper shield
  for rights to the inlet: 20
a copper shield matched against the knife.

He was Waanaghan's son.[3]
He was killed at Kkyaal.

And a Qaagyals Qiigha woman
  gave the Qquuna Qiighawaay a copper shield,
renewing rights to the inlet, because of the knife.

  [iii]

SKILTTAKINGANG too started hunting with dogs.   [1.3]
 At Hlghaay his dogs started barking.[4]
As he started toward them,
he fell on the rock.
The whole of his lower leg was open to the bone.   30
He died there.
Again they claimed the ocean and the inlets and the land.

The Daaghanga Sils family paid another copper shield
  to confirm their ownership of Ghaahlins
and the Qaagyals Qiigha woman paid another copper shield
  to confirm her ownership of Qana.

They claimed all the islets too.
There was no land not already spoken for.

[iv]

Along time later, Waanaghan settled there again.   [2]
Ttawgwaghanat, his daughter, was born
when they were living there at Qquuna.

Then Ttawgwaghanat went to Hlghaay.   40
A woman of the Saw-whet Owl family
    travelled along with her,
and one Daaghanga Silga woman too.
On the way, they capsized.

Both Ttawgwaghanat and the Owl woman drowned.
Then there were tears and tears and more tears.
Sending them food by way of the fire, there in the house,
they claimed the sea and all the Islands.
All of them belonged to the Qquuna Qiighawaay.

[v]

After Waanaghan died,   [3.1]
    when another Waanaghan lived in his place,   50
Gitkuna was born.
Gitkuna built the house he called Gutkwaayda.
He married a Qqaadasghu Qiigha woman.

He was seal-hunting once, out at Gwaaya.
He was creeping toward some seals on the beach
    with his harpoon,
and a small killer whale, a pinto, with two sharp dorsal fins,
    swam up just beyond the seals.
It was handsome.
He harpooned it.

Anonymous artist, probably Haida. *Mortar for grinding calcined shell:
The human in the mouth of the nonhuman.*

Walrus ivory, 4 × 9 × 4.5 cm. Mid 19th century.

(Canadian Museum of Civilization, Ottawa: VII-B-1001, neg 92-762)

Writhing from the wound,
it thrashed across the ocean surface, spouting.   60
At Xhiihlaghut it dived.

The hunters left at once in their canoe.
When they came abreast of Gwiighal,[5]
the open sea beyond them was thick with killer whales.
They were somersaulting over the canoe.

Gitkuna looked toward the south.
The sea was thick with killer whales.
And he looked toward the north.
It was the same there too.

The roof planks of the sea flew toward them   70
and landed right beside them.
The crossbeams of the sea stood up on end
and fell in their direction.
The rafters of the sea fell close to them as well.

After paddling a long time at top speed,
they came ashore at Gwiighal.
They brought the canoe up high above the driftwood.
By then the killer whales were doing tailstands
        even on dry land.

    Soon Gitkuna's crewmen said,
«We'd better think of something.»   80

Big killer whales were spyhopping right there in the cove.
They offered them tobacco.
When they put another offering
        of calcined shell with the tobacco,

a bat scooped up the shell and the tobacco in its jaws.[6]
Then the biggest killer whales moved out to deeper water.
Then the gods went back beneath the sea.

A s soon as Gitkuna got home,   [3.2]
the doctors started diagnosing him.
They told him not to go to sea for four years.
Xhiihlaghut's son was the one he'd harpooned.   90

The doctors told Gitkuna and his father
that the gods were still discussing him:
whether to let him climb up something and slip
or let something collapse on him
or perhaps just to let him capsize.

Four years at most, the doctors told him,
and then they were certain to come for him.

From that time on, he took nothing from the sea.
From that time on, he hunted nothing.

Then Skilantlinda brought him a message: 100

> Hovering near you I see
>   something that shudders.
> For that I will shatter
>   something you love.

After that, they made him a coffin.
He kicked it away with his foot,
and it fell to pieces.
After that happened, Gitkuna lay down.

H E WAS STILL THERE, lying in bed,   [3.3]
    when a silver otter entered Qquuna harbor.
Right away, he asked his father
to say that no one else could have it,   110
and his father gave the order.

Gitkuna took a crew of three men,
and they chased it.
First he tried to shoot it in the harbor.
Then it led him out to sea.
The mist closed in on him at once then.

And then they beat the drums for him at Qquuna
and pounded on the beach logs.

After two days and nights of steady fog,
dawn broke calm and clear.   120
Some went out to search in the direction of Lake Inlet.
Others went to search for him toward Rock Point.[7]
His paddle was the only thing they found.

Again they talked about the sea.
Again they talked about the land.[8]

   [vi]

N OT LONG after that, Gitkuna's father died.   [4]
    Ghwaahldaaw was his successor,
and Gwaahldaaw's son was Tlghakkyaaw.

They had a fishcamp then at Gwaaya,
and the children used to play there.   130
One day a bunch of them went there.
They were pestering the auklets.[9]
They pulled out their feathers and laughed.

After they had done this quite some time,
they made their way down to the foot of Headman Anjusghas.[10]
They lowered Tlghakkyaaw into one of the crevices.
He knocked leaf-barnacles loose with his digging stick[11]
and handed them up to the others.

After a while, he tried to climb out.
His head was trapped between the rocks.   140
The tide was rising.

They went at once to tell his parents,
and his parents gathered face paint, furs and feathers,
and went to where he was.

Then they built a fire,
and all the time they were feeding it what they had brought,
they were talking and talking to Headman Anjusghas.
They asked for their son to be released.

When the offerings had vanished in the flames,
the crevice enlarged   150
and they pulled out their son.
The cliff had closed around him
because he made fun of Anjusghas's auklets.

Later, they went out again to get birds.
They went after the auklets again,
and pulled out their feathers and threw them away.
They laughed at them.

Then they went out to the rim of the cliff in a bunch.
Tlghakkyaaw slipped.
He fell off the cliff.   160

Something caught hold of him partway down.
«Don't move!» they told him.
He moved,
and he slipped once again
and went straight to the bottom.

When the children came home with the news,
his father instructed them not to come into the house.
Then the other children's parents
    started making payments to his father.
They gave him a pile of moose skins.[12]

And then they constructed his coffin.   170
They built him a four-legged death-post –
the one with the tree growing out of it now.[13]

After that, the other children kept away
    from the children of the Qquuna Qiighawaay,
because they had paid them.

   [vii]

B EFORE THIS, powers started coming   [5]
    to a woman of the Qquuna Qiighawaay.
When she started to doctor,
she called on her father
to tie a dancing skirt around her.
He did as she asked.

A god was speaking through her.   180
He promised her ten whales.
After she had fasted for a time,
she went outside,
and something near her spluttered.

When she looked,
what she saw there were California mussels.
Those were the spirit forms of the whales.
She said they would come to the mouth of the creek at Hlghaay.

After ten nights passed,
they went there to look.   190
Humpback whales floated there,
a string of them.
They found ten whales at the creek mouth.
The vertebrae are still where you can see them.

Then she insulted a spirit being, they say.
They say that redleaf seaweed was the cause.[14]

Someone came into Gutkwaayda.
«Something is moving on Turn-of-the-Tide Island,» he said.[15]
«Aiyeee! Aiyeee!»
Then she went out,   200
and she called,
«Who is it? Who's crossing over?
You stay out of here!»

Then they paddled out and looked around.
There was nothing to be seen.
But as soon as they returned,
they wept in Gutkwaayda.
She had insulted one of the spirit beings, they say,
and so she died.

So it comes to a point.[16]   210

APPENDIX, NOTES
&
BIBLIOGRAPHY

Appendix

Haida Spelling and Pronunciation

H AIDA VOWELS are short and long, like vowels in Greek, Latin, Arabic and Hebrew. Short vowels are written once (**a**, **i**, **u**) and long vowels twice (**aa**, **ii**, **uu**). The sounds are approximately these:

a	ranges from the *a* in English *distant* to the *a* in English *art*	**i**	as in English *sit*
aa	like *a* in English *father*, but lengthened: *faaarther!*	**ii**	like *ea* in English *seat*
		u	like *oo* in English *wood*
		uu	like *oo* in English *food*

The diphthongs **aw**, **ay**, **aaw**, **aay** are likewise short and long. Haida *aw/aaw* = *ou* in English *ouch*, and Haida *ay/aay* = *i* in English *right*. Haida vowels are mutable in length, like Hebrew vowels, instead of fixed, like vowels in Greek, so syllable length in Haida is migratory, much like stress in English. For example, the long vowel in the word *llaana* (meaning dwelling or dweller, people or town) shrinks when the definitive suffix is added: *llanagaay* (*the* people or *the* town).

In Haida as in English and many other languages, some basic consonants are represented by digraphs (pairs of letters). Two others are represented by trigraphs. A midpoint is used to separate letters that would otherwise form a digraph. (Thus *n·g* means *n*, then *g*, and not the sound *ng*.) *Sh* and *th*, however, are never digraphs; they always represent the separate consonants *s* or *t* followed by *h*. (The initial sounds in English *ship*, *this* and *thin* do not occur in Haida.)

The consonants are **b**, **d**, **dl**, **g**, **gh**, **h**, **hl**, **j**, **k**, **kk**, **kw**, **l**, **ll**, **m**, **n**, **ng**, **q**, **qq**, **s**, **t**, **tl**, **ts**, **tt**, **ttl**, **tts**, **w**, **x**, **xh**, **y** and the glottal stop, written as an apostrophe (**'**). Another that probably ought to be distinguished, though I have neglected to do so, is ejective or glottalized w (**ẇ**), which in this simplified orthography would be written **ww**.

The letters have roughly the same value in Haida as in English, with the following clarifications and exceptions:

dl voiced alveolar lateral affricate, much as in English *ad lib* or *endless*

g voiced velar stop, as in English *get,* but voiced more lightly than in English

gh uvular *g* (voiced uvular stop), like Tsimshian or Tlingit <u>*g*</u>

hl voiceless alveolar lateral fricative, like the Navajo *ł,* Icelandic *hl* or Welsh *ll*

j voiced palato-alveolar affricate, as in English *judge*

kk glottalized *k,* like the Tlingit or Navajo *k'*

ll glottalized *l*

ng velar nasal, like *ng* in English *wing*

n·g *n* followed by *g* (= *ng* as in English *Wingate*)

n·gh *n* followed by *gh* (uvular *g*)

q uvular *k* (voiceless uvular stop), like the Arabic *qâf,* the Hebrew *qôph,* Tlingit <u>*k*</u>, or the *q* of Inuktitut

qq glottalized *q*

tl voiceless alveolar lateral affricate, like Navajo *tł* or the *tl* in English *exactly*

ts voiceless alveolar affricate, as in English *its;* also often palato-alveolar, like *ch* in English *cheese*

tt glottalized *t,* like the *t'* of Hausa, Tlingit and Navajo

ttl glottalized *tl,* like the Tlingit *tł'* or Navajo *tł'*

tts glottalized *ts,* like the Tlingit or Navajo *ts'*

x voiceless velar fricative, like Russian x, the Arabic *khâ,* the *ch* in German *Bach;* or palatal, like the *j* in Spanish *hijo* or *ch* in German *ich*

xh voiceless uvular fricative, like *ch* in Scottish *loch*

' glottal stop, like the catch in the midst of English *uh oh!*

' smooth pharyngeal stop, like Arabic *'ain* or Hebrew *'ayin* (a northern Haida sound)

To summarize:

- › *doubled vowels are long;*
- › *doubled consonants are glottalized, or ejective* (that is, they are pronounced with a glottal stop superimposed);
- › *the two consonants written with* h (gh *and* xh) *are uvular* (that is, they are pronounced deep in the throat).

Notes to the Text

1 The spelling "Haida Gwaii" was endorsed for several years by the Council of the Haida Nation and thus appears in many publications, including several of my own. In May 2001, the Council adopted the spelling Haida Gwaay.

2 The Haida were not, of course, alone in this experience. Boyd 1999 documents the catastrophic decline of native populations on the Northwest Coast as a consequence of diseases introduced by Europeans. Such a story can be told for nearly every part of North and South America – and for much of Asia as well.

3 An account of this raid and some additional details of Skaay's life, together with notes on the sources of information, can be found in *A Story as Sharp as a Knife*, pp 73–75 & 309–314.

4 Even today, though no one has lived there for 120 years, Qquuna has a headman, resident in Skidegate, who goes by the English title Chief Skedans.

5 These facts and others are known from Swanton's letters to his mentor Franz Boas. The letters are quoted at length in *A Story as Sharp as a Knife*.

6 The terms I like to use in describing these patterns are different from the terms Dell Hymes employs, but it was Hymes who taught me to see and understand this essential characteristic of Native American narrative poetry, and Hymes's work (e.g., Hymes 1981) remains the best introduction to the subject.

7 Letter to Boas, 30 September 1900. Quoted at greater length in *A Story as Sharp as a Knife*, p 69.

8 Altogether, about sixty of the older poles survive, intact or in sections, along with eroded or burned fragments from a dozen more. In the past fifty years, in addition to new poles, about a dozen full-size replicas of older poles have also been raised. A few of these old poles remain in Haida Gwaay. The rest are in museum collections in Canada, the USA, Germany, England and Australia.

9 A few others, including William Myers (long-suffering amanuensis to the photographer Edward Curtis), asked for Haida stories but wanted them in English.

1 Swanton n.d.2: 102–125; cf. Swanton 1905b: 151–172 and *A Story as Sharp as a Knife*, pp 73–110, 173–200. George Emmons's monograph on the Chilkat blanket (1907; best read in the annotated edition of 1993) includes English paraphrases of two stories in which the Woman who Married the Bear is rescued by a creature from the seafloor and taken to his home, where she sees the original *naaxiin* (figured blanket or Chilkat blanket). The first movement of Skaay's Long Poem involves related themes. The central figure has a different history, and the story a different focus, yet the Chilkat blanket remains there on the seafloor (lines 223–232) as a rock-hard, luminous detail.

2 By far the best documentary source on Haida ornithology is the extensive list of bird names dictated by Tlaajang Quuna (Tom Stevens) of the Naay Kun Qiighawaay (Newcombe n.d.3). But the legendary blue hawk or blue falcon (Haida *skyaamskun*) does not appear there. Haida *skyaamskun* is clearly related to Tsimshian *sgyaamsm,* meaning kestrel or merlin – but these birds are known in Haida as *dawghatlxhayang.* The blue hawk, like the thunderbird, is a creature never found stuffed and mounted in museums.

3 The Haida and their neighbors saw them rarely but were certainly aware of the sealskin baidarkas used by peoples to the north. In a text dictated in Tsimshian in 1920, Joseph Bradley mentions Aleut hunters in *xsoom anaasm üüla dił anaasm t'iibn,* "harbor-seal-skin and sealion-skin canoes" (Bradley 1992: 9).

4 The garments called *qwiigalgyaat* (skyblanket) in Haida are *yeil koowú* (Raven's tail) in Tlingit. The Tlingit name has migrated into English through the work of Cheryl Samuel. Her book *The Raven's Tail* (1987) is a study of such robes.

The best documentary source on Haida face painting – a subject of evident interest to Skaay – is Boas 1898. Boas's title for this work (*Facial Paintings of the Indians of Northern British Columbia*) suggests a generic study, but *Facial Paintings* is actually an album of 93 face painting designs by a single artist, Skaay's colleague Daxhiigang. All of these were drawn (on Boas's preprinted forms) at Port Essington in August 1897.

5 Swanton's interpolation, evidently in consultation with Skaay himself (1905b: 151, 171 n 8).

6 Skookum root is *Veratrum viride* (Haida *gwaaykkya*), also known in English as Indian hellebore or cornlily. It is a highly toxic plant once widely used on the Northwest Coast as a ritual purgative (and not at all the same as the edible cornlily of eastern North America, *Clintonia borealis*).

7 Sea-pickles (*Eupentacta quinquesemita* and allies, *ihyaana* in Haida) are small, edible holothurians readily found on Haida beaches. These are the food of the poor – and Wealth Woman is commonly met collecting them. They are also important as sexual metaphors, and are mentioned in that connection in §3.3 of

the Cycle. Their larger relatives (*Parastichopus californicus,* Haida *ghiinuu*) also play an important and seminal role in the opening scene of *Raven Travelling.*

8 Grease (*taw*) is edible grease or oil, especially that of eulachon. It is one of the basic components of Northwest Coast cuisine, eaten like mayonnaise with dried berries or fish, but here it functions purely as metaphor: [*ll*] *gudaagha taw lla gutgaystl,* "he poured grease into [her] mind."

9 Warm salt water is drunk as a purgative before important undertakings.

10 Haida armor was generally made of wooden slats and hide, but Swanton understood this armor to be made of copper. It has thus become customary to identify the younger son's wife as Xaalajaat, Copper Woman. If that is who she is, this is her only appearance in extant Haida literature. Copper, *xaal,* is not mentioned until later in the poem, in an entirely different connection (line 586).

11 Master Carver – in Haida, *Watghadagaang* – is the nonhuman embodiment of artistic skill in painting and woodworking. He lives in the forest, not in the sea. The literal meaning of his Haida name is "Maker of Flat Surfaces."

12 The birthing stake – a handhold for the woman in labor – was widely used on the Northwest Coast.

13 This is not as odd as it may sound. The urine of healthy humans is a sterile fluid, chiefly water, ammonia and carbonic acid. It makes an excellent biological cleansing agent, useful in treating insect bites and wounds. A bath in a grandparent's urine – so long as the donor is free of disease – is therefore not just a ritual honor for the child but a perfectly defensible obstetric procedure.

14 The landward towns (*diidaxwa llaana*) are the villages of Haida Gwaay, which would be seaward from a mainlander's perspective. The seaward towns (*qqaadaxwa llaana*) are those of the mainland.

15 Though the title appears in the Haida manuscript, Swanton's note (1905b: 159) all but guarantees that Skaay himself did not supply it.
  The themes addressed in the second and third movements of this trilogy were favorites with other storytellers, though each one deals with them differently. Swanton recorded two related works in Haida. One was told by Ttsuuna (Jimmy Sterling) at Hlghagilda (Swanton n.d.2: 568–574; 1905b: 341–347), the other by Richard of the Daw Gitinaay at Ghadaghaaxhiwaas (Swanton 1908a: 728–741). The latter work, though told in 1901, is decidedly postclassical: the language and narrative structure both heavily influenced by European usage. The same may be said of a related text written in Tsimshian by Henry Tate (Boas 1912: 192–225) and another published in English more than seventy years later by a Gitksan leader (Harris 1974: 3–23). The Nishga village of Kwunwoq, where this section of the Cycle begins, is also the initial setting for Ghandl's story "A Red Feather" (*Nine Visits to the Mythworld*, pp 179–189).

16 The stick is colored, in other words, like the front of a mallard. Mallards are dabbling ducks, who invert themselves and hang head-down, tail-up to feed. A pole that is painted in such colors can be used to turn the world on its head.

17 The painted housefront is an alternative to a housepole. That it is sewn means that the redcedar planks are drilled and stitched together with cedarlimb line. Structures of this type – representing one of the several architectural traditions native to the Northwest Coast – were once common on the mainland and on Haida Gwaay alike. They were archaic in Skaay's time, but this seems to be the only type of house mentioned in his poem. (The sewn and painted housefront went with the older style of houseframe, using round beams. In MacDonald's terminology, these are type 1 houses. For details, see MacDonald 1983: 19.)

18 Sqaaghahl is the name of a landform on the Tsimshian coast, and of the killer whale spirit who inhabits it. It is the old name for the prominent white cliffs of Skiakl Point, on the west coast of what is now called Stephens Island – and more loosely for Stephens Island as a whole.

19 Skaay of course is pulling Swanton's leg – and everybody else's. Whales have no tailbones.

20 *Hlaay, ghaan, aas,* Skaay says. *Hlaay* are highbush cranberries; *aas* are soapberries; *ghaan* is the name of a class of berries, including salmonberries, (*sqqawghaan*), lily-of-the-valley berries (*siighaan*), currants (*ghaalghaan*) and saskatoons (*ghaan xhawlaa*). Highbush cranberries, which Skaay clearly loved, do grow in Haida Gwaay, but not so well as on the mainland.

   As for the animal foods, it is interesting that moose, elk and caribou are missing from the list. Skaay is an islander; mainland food to him is exotic. It is as though a North American should make a list of French foods and omit pedestrian staples such as beef, pork and potatoes while remembering patés, soufflés and truffles.

21 These are Tsimshian villages. Metlakatla – Maxłaqxaała in Tsimshian, Qaahlaqaahli in Haida – is on the mainland, just northwest of the present Prince Rupert. Qqaaduu is across the channel from Metlakatla, on Guughahl Gwaay (Digby Island). Emptied in the 19th century, Metlakatla was resettled in 1862 by Christian converts led by an ambitious English missionary. Most of this group moved to Alaska in 1887, founding a Christian fortress known as New Metlakatla. The old, pre-Christian Metlakatla and its neighbor Qqaaduu retained their aboriginal identity and importance in the minds of coastal mythtellers. In 1900, for example, the Haida headman Sghiidagits told Swanton that Qqaaduu was the home of Nanasimgit and his mother, the Woman Who Married the Bear. (See *A Story as Sharp as a Knife,* pp 22–23, 124f.)

22 One or two lines of the Haida text have apparently been lost here. This and other textual problems in the first hundred lines of this movement suggest that Skaay, Swanton and Moody had all put in a long day of dictation.

23 This brief cry or song, repeated four times over the course of thirty lines, is adapted from a Nishga or Tsimshian original which Skaay and his earlier Haida audience undoubtedly knew well. Fathoming Skaay's text requires reconstructing that original. To this end, the three most useful analogues are (1) a story that Sgan'sm Sm'oogyit (Chief Mountain) told to Boas in Nishga at Kincolith in 1894 (Boas 1916: 221–225); (2) a story that Henry Tate wrote for Boas in English and Tsimshian about 1905 (Boas 1912: 198–211); and (3) a story told in the 1930s by Joshua Tsibese, with additions by Ethel Musgrave, transcribed in Tsimshian by Gwüsk'aayn (Beynon n.d.: text 70). Boas wrote down only an English paraphrase of the first of these stories, but he did transcribe painstakingly in Nishga the songs that Sgan'sm sang *within* the story.

We can deduce from these sources that Sqaaghahl's Daughter ought to be saying (in Nishga) *Naahl dimt an nakskwhl hlguuhlgwas G̲a'wo?* or (in Tsimshian) *Naał dmt in naksga łguułgas G̲a'wo?* These sentences both mean "Who will marry the child of G̲a'wo?" What Moody and Swanton heard Skaay say is more inscrutable: *Jiinaaaaa nahlguuuuus Gaawaxh.* Here it seems as if an entire Nisgha or Tsimshian phrase has been condensed to a single nonsense word, *nahlguus.* That nonsense word is followed by a name, *Gaawaxh,* and preceded by intoning the word *jiina.* This is the term a Haida-speaking woman would use for a real or potential sister-in-law. (Some mythtellers make the name Sga'wo. Except in this note, I have taken the liberty of restoring her uvular G̲, which I imagine Skaay spoke and Swanton missed. So the name appears in the translation as Ghaawaxh, not Gaawaxh.)

Not only Skaay but also Ghandl and Kilxhawgins used occasional Nishga or Tsimshian phrases in the works they dictated in Haida to Moody and Swanton. In every case, Swanton's transcriptions of these phrases are heavily corrupt. Skaay and Kilxhawgins both had a lifetime of experience interacting with the Nishga and the Tsimshian, and both, I think, had some command of these two languages. Moody belonged to a different generation and had learned English instead. Throughout his time at Skidegate, Swanton made and corrected his transcriptions with Moody's considerable help – and that, perhaps, is the source of the problem. If so, reconstructing the originals into passable Nishga or Tsimshian is a sensible way to proceed. (See also note 5, p 380.)

(A related story that Ttsuuna dictated in Haida in 1901 contains no Nishga or Tsimshian phrases and is disfigured by Ttsuuna's petty moralizing [Swanton n.d.2: 568–574; 1905b: 341–347].)

24 The son of the Moon, in other words.

25 This is the nearest thing in classical Haida literature to an evocation of writing. *Diigii ttluu qqaalang,* says grandfather Moon. The verb *qqaalang* means *to sketch, to draw* and *to paint.* During Skaay's lifetime, it acquired the further meaning *to write,* but in the mythworld, the older meanings rule. The Moon instructs his youngest grandson not to *write a message* but to *draw the figure of a messenger* – and then of course to *tell* that figure what to say.

365

26 Skaay assumes that his listeners know the subtleties of stick gambling. For those who do not, Ghandl's story "The Names of Their Gambling Sticks" may prove a helpful introduction. See *Nine Visits to the Mythworld*, pp 169–177 and the accompanying notes, pp 211–212.

➤ THE QQUUNA CYCLE 2: SECOND TRILOGY ➤

1 Swanton n.d.2: 151–166; cf. Swanton 1905b: 173–189; cf. *A Story as Sharp as a Knife*, pp 169–172. The oral literatures of the Northwest Coast are rich with stories of abandoned youngsters who make good. None of the other stories in the record is quite like this one, but there are several with which this can be usefully compared. These include a fine story told in Haida by Kingagwaaw in 1901 (Swanton 1908a: 460–475) and two others told by Haayas (Swanton 1908a: 475–478, 705–728).

Henry Tate – a lesser talent but a prolific one – wrote a Europeanized treatment of the theme in English and in Tsimshian, possibly based in part on Swanton's translation of Skaay. (Tate's story is published, but only in a modified English version, in Boas 1916: 225–232.)

Around 1913, Boas prepared an analytical study of all the related stories (or "versions" in his terminology) known to him at the time. This is published in Boas 1916: 784–791.

At Alert Bay, only a few weeks before Skaay dictated the Qquuna Cycle to Swanton, 'Nagedzi of the Tlatlasikwala (Charlie Wilson) dictated a fine story to Boas in Kwakwala, involving several themes that are crucial to §2 and §5 of the Cycle (Boas 1910: 38–81). Three decades later, he performed the story for Boas again (Boas 1935–43, vol. 1: 156–168; vol. 2: 153–165). (Boas's note comparing the two performances is in Boas 1935–43, vol. 1: 229f.)

2 To "go outside" or "go to the beach" (*qaaxul*) is a euphemism every bit as routine in classical Haida as "go to the bathroom" is in modern English. Especially at night, tidewater was the normal place to defecate. (A handful of seawater serves very well in lieu of toilet paper and bidet, and tidal action flushes away the feces.) In the mythworld, tidewater is also a place for young lovers and others to conduct a private conversation. Into this story concerned with extremes of feast and famine, genius and ignorance, solitude and community, love and hostility, Skaay has also woven the algebra of humorous extremes that comes with eating and evacuating.

3 I omit here a three-line aside in which Skaay explains to Swanton that mainland headmen join with commoners in splitting their own fish.

4 Tall poles forming the vertical members of the downstream (front) wall of the salmon trap. This wall is in two sections, with the entranceway between.

5 The wings of the fish fence or weir extend from the trap (in midstream) out to the bank on either side.

366

6 Boys are expected to use blunt-tipped arrows (Haida *kkungal*), which are good for shooting small birds. The abandoned boy is using adult arrows (*ttsidalang*) with detachable barbed heads (*juugi*).

7 Line 733 says *Xaal sghahlgaal lla sttagyaangang wansuuga*: "He wore copper amulets on his ankles, they say." This links back to a time when the protagonist was living with his parents and is therefore out of place in Swanton's typescript. I have moved it to precede line 52 (p 107), but its original position in the man-uscript is also of some interest. Good mythtelling is much like playing good jazz but also something like playing good chess. If Skaay spoke the line where Swanton typed it, its position shows him doing one of the things that experi-enced mythtellers do: thinking both back and ahead, and filling in his missing move while he still has time to do so.

8 The eulachon or oolichan (*Thaleichthys pacificus*) is a relative of the smelt. Eula-chons spawn each year in the rivers of the Northwest Coast, from the Bering Sea to the Klamath River in northern California. They are raked in vast num-bers every spring from the lower reaches of the Nass, where they are rendered for their oil. This substance ("eulachon grease") is vital to the cuisine of the Northwest Coast. (In Tsimshian, for instance, edible oils generally are known as *k'awtsi*, but eulachon oil is called *smk̲'awtsi*, "truly edible oil."

9 Haida canoes are landed stern-first, both for the convenience of disembarking passengers and to facilitate a subsequent departure. To land a coastal dugout bow-first is a sign of unseemly haste.

10 The speaker could easily have said "my son whom we abandoned" (*gitghang sta ttalang ttsaasdaghan*). What he says instead is *dalang qiigha*, "one related by birth to you-plural," *sta hl ttsaasdaghan*, "whom I abandoned."

11 The inner bark (phloem) of the western hemlock (*Tsuga heterophylla*, Haida *qqaang*) is an important coastal foodstuff. People living off the land still eat it fresh in springtime. In earlier days, they gathered it in bulk during the sum-mer, then pit-cooked it, pounded it and pressed it into cakes or loaves. These cakes (known formally as *sqingghiist* and informally simply as *qqaang*, like the tree) were dried, stored and served in midwinter, with berries or fish oil.

12 Stories of a bear who married a man are widely told in North America, though not as widely as stories of a woman who married a bear. Daxhiigang told Boas such a story in 1894. (Daxhiigang n.d.2: 10–11 is Boas's English version, pub-lished in part in Swanton 1905b: 186–187.) Another fine performance is the one that Tseexwáa (J. B. Fawcett) recorded in Tlingit at Juneau in 1972 (Dauenhauer & Dauenhauer 1987: 218–243). Skaay again sets the story on the mainland, not in Haida Gwaay.

13 That is to say, the thread – or yarn – or story – of his life. Indigenous people in northwestern North America sometimes kept biographical threads or lifelines

in physical form. For others, the metaphor was enough. (Leechman & Harrington 1921 addresses this neglected subject.)

14 The verb in line 136 is *jiighaa*, "to go for water." It associates readily with *jigaa*, "to copulate, to make love." The echo makes the phrase *gingghang lla ga jiighas*, "he went for water by himself," implicitly funny as well as suggestive. Here there is also an echo of meaning, reinforced by an echo of sound, back to an earlier cadence, where the grizzly sow tells her human partner (line 81), *Gam tlgu dljuughangang*, "No messing around." In this case the verb is not *juugha* but simply *juu*, inflected with the animate prefix *dl-* and negative suffix *-ghang*. (Proclitic *gam* and suffix *-ghang* together make the negative.) Negating the verb, to voice a prohibition, creates a positive evocation of the action it forbids. This is also one of many links back to the opening scene of the Cycle, where proposals of marriage are rejected with the formulaic phrase *Haw jiigha gwawugha*, "Permission to get water is denied."

15 Classical Haida literature includes one other notable meditation on the sapsucker (*Sphyrapicus ruber*). Its author is Kingagwaaw, and the episode occurs in the midst of his performance of *Raven Travelling* (Swanton 1908a: 324f):

> Gaaysta ll qayits dluu
> haw ising xhitiit ahlaang tsaagudan ghan ll qaattlagan.
> Ll sghunsaangan.
> Gam tlagw ll naahlingaay qanggaangan,
> Stluuttsadang haw suugangan.
>
> Xhitiit ga ghan ll qiingwas
> gyaan llaga ttl gwawgangan.
> Wadluu llagu ll naahlingaay gaws dluu
> gwii tlakkwaan·gan ll xitgwan·gangan.
> Wagyaan giina gha naahlingaay da aasgii gwaayaay inggut ll qinsgaayan.
>
> Wadluu hin Yaahl {ll} suudayan,
> «Hlaxaayik gha hl xit.»
> Giina guunaga Hlaxaayik ttaaya gyangan
> ahljiiyahlu gha lla ll suudayani.
>
> «Haw giina gunagaay gyans hl kkudii,
> dang tsin isis ahla,» hin lla ll suudayan.
> Wakkyanan llaga ll hlghwagayan.
>
> Llaga ll hlwaagas ghan aa
> giina guunagas unsadalan dluu,
> «Hahl gwaa ttakkanaay,
> dii kkuuk gha hl naa,» hin lla ll suudayan.
> «Wagyaan dang giidalang gam tsaghagudangghang asga.»

Ahljiiyahlu wiid llagha ll naagan
lla ll tsindas ahla.

When he [the Raven] left that place,
here came another bird with no home of his own.
He was all by himself.
He had no place to live,
the Sapsucker said.

When he perched with other birds,
they drove him away.
And so, having no place to live,
he kept flying all the time.
And he searched the Islands for something to live in.

Then the Raven said,
«Fly to Hlaxaayik.»
He said it because
something dead stood at Hlaxaayik.

«Peck the standing dead thing with your beak.
It's alright; it's your grandfather,» he said to him.
Nevertheless, he was afraid of it.

When the dead thing understood
that he was afraid of it,
it said to him, «Grandson, come here.
Live in my heart,
and your children will not be left homeless.»

That's where he lives even now,
because that is his grandfather.

Hlaxaayik is Yakutat, a Tlingit village well to the north of Haida territory – close, in fact, to the northern end of the range of both the sapsucker and the Sitka spruce.

▸ THE QQUUNA CYCLE 3: THIRD TRILOGY ▸

1 Swanton n.d.2: 186–201; cf. Swanton 1905b: 190–209; Enrico 1995: 118–158. Themes from §3.1 reappear in a story that Henry Tate wrote in English and Tsimshian for Franz Boas (Boas 1916: 116–121). Themes from §3.2 reappear in another story that Taan (Nang Stins or Tom Price) told in Haida in 1901 (Swanton n.d.2: 202–205; Swanton 1905b: 203–206; Enrico 1995: 146, 148, 150–158) and in two stories that Deikinaak'w told in Tlingit in 1904 (one of which Swanton recorded only in English paraphrase: Swanton 1909: 217–219, 272–279).

2 The Sealion Town of this story is Qay Llanagaay, an old village at the site now known as Second Beach, adjacent to Skidegate – not to be confused with the west coast village of Qaysun (Sealion Town or Sealion Roost), birthplace of the poet Ghandl of the Qayahl Llaanas. Ghandl's story "The Names of Their Gambling Sticks" (*Nine Visits to the Mythworld*, pp 169–177) is linked to the same place.

3 Xhaana is a river (now called the Honna) flowing south into Skidegate Inlet. Hlghaayxha is a fishing station on Halibut Bight, north of Skidegate (site 4 on the map, p 31). According to Daxhiigang, this is a place of great importance also to the story of the Raven: the place where the Raven's allotrope Voicehandler has his house, and where the Raven killed his raven (cf. Swanton 1905b: 139). It was just offshore from here, in 1943, that Henry Moody drowned.

4 Guuhlgha was a Haida village close to Hlghagilda (Skidegate), at a site known now as Skidegate Landing. A dogfish oilery was built here in 1876, and other developments have followed. This however is where Swanton lived in the fall of 1900, walking into Skidegate each day to take dictation.

5 Two of the four items carried by this being are easily identified. They are the knot (*ttan* in Haida) – which is probably spruce – and the seaweed (seawrack: *Fucus* spp, *ttal* in Haida). The other two items are perplexing. Maplewood and rose thorns, though based in part on Swanton and Moody's suggestions, are only hypothetical translations for *ghudaang xhuusgi* and *kwii'aw gyaghadang*. Wild crabapple and yew – the hardest woods native to Haida Gwaay – are other possibilities for the former. Maple seems likelier to me not only because it is harder, but because it is exotic: it has to be imported from the mainland.

6 A redundant line – *han lla lla suudas*, "He said to him thus" – appears here in the typescript. Swanton placed it in parentheses. I have omitted it altogether.

7 A shrew in Haida is *jigul awgha*, "sword fern's mother."

8 Mallard oil, feathers, horseclam shells and earthquakes are linked in other works of Haida literature, including Kilxhawgins's history of Ttanuu (*A Story as Sharp as a Knife*, pp 324–325). And the ability of mallards to upend themselves and right themselves again is for Skaay a pervasive, potent notion.

9 An etiological aside appears at this point in the typescript. It seems to me a personal remark, intended quite specifically for Henry Moody. The passage says (lines 186–189 = Swanton n.d.2: 188: 21–22):

> This is why, whenever there's an earthquake,
> people of the Raven side say
>   we should be careful with the mallard grease.
> They're the ones who say it
> because Honored Standing Traveller was a Raven.

Skaay was of course a member of the Qquuna Qiighawaay of the Eagle side. Moody was a member of the Qaagyals Qiighawaay of the Raven side.

10 The capture of a seawolf, using a giant trap baited with a human child, is a much-loved theme in classical Haida literature. Ghandl incorporates it into his story of the Sealion Hunter (*Nine Visits to the Mythworld*, pp 101–103), and Daxhiigang portrayed it in a drawing (Boas 1927: 159).

11 Skaay and Ghandl both imply that Mouse Woman has two separate quadruped identities: mouse and shrew. The differences are obvious enough. Mice have larger eyes, rounder heads, far sweeter dispositions and (like other rodents) two big, chisel-shaped front teeth. Shrews are more closely related to moles than to squirrels, beavers and mice. They have sharply pointed noses, tiny eyes, thorn-like, hooked incisors, potent body odor, and the shrill and friendless nature to which they give their name. Though she may take the form of either mouse or shrew, no classical Haida author speaks of Mouse Woman as shrewish.

12 Across from this point stood the village of Xayna, on the east end of Xayna Gwaay (Maude Island on the present charts).

13 Most of the spirit beings gathered in the house belong to the Raven side. So does Standing Traveller. Like his mother Jilaquns (the Raven's wife), Quartz Ribs belongs to the Eagle side. Although the spirit beings live spread out across the surface of the earth, they also evidently constitute a compact column – the housepole of the world – and they care, of course, who occupies its base.

14 Woman Lips are Licked For (*Jaatgi Gudaqaawgha*) is the personification of the spiny wood fern (*Dryopteris austriaca*), whose rootstocks were a favorite Haida vegetable.

15 *Kkuuxuginaagits*, "Plain Old Marten," is the mythname of the marten. *Taadlat Ghaadala*, "Outruns Trout," is a name applied to many fast creatures, including racing goldeneyes and buffleheads, but in the poems of Skaay and Ghandl, it is the mythname of the swallow. The Marten and the Swallow – reputedly the fastest creatures on land and in the air – often appear in the myths together. Here, however, it is range more than speed that seems important. They are called to run a line from the depths of the earth to the apex of heaven. There is no classical Haida text that quite explains the link, but it appears that this line and its associated pole can be used (like mallard oil in a clam shell) to provoke or measure earthquakes (Swanton 1905a: 12f, 1905b: 208 n 21).

16 Ghangxhiit Point is the southern tip of Haida Gwaay, shown on modern charts as Cape St James (site 20 on the map, p 31). It gave its name to the whole southern region of the Islands and to the people who lived there.

17 The southern Haida, Swanton tells us, were well known for the free use of such names, which other Haida sometimes found insulting.

18 Quartz Ribs is passing down the southeast coast of Haida Gwaay, leaping from island to island. Skaay does not say where his journey began, but the itinerary strongly suggests that he started from Ghaw Quns. This is the home of Quartz Ribs's mother, Jilaquns. The places named in this stanza are all on Qquuna Gwaay (Louise Island) and figure in other stories told by Skaay's colleagues. See for instance *A Story as Sharp as a Knife*, chapter 20.

19 Hlghadan is a Haida village site in the Ghangxhiit region (site 23 on the map, p 31). Quartz Ribs has come to the place where he said he was going.

20 Qqaaghawaay is a rocky islet south of Hlghadan and west of Sghan Gwaay ("Red Rockfish Island," now known as Anthony Island).

21 Archaeological finds on the Northwest Coast suggest that perhaps a thousand years ago, people of both sexes used to perforate the lower lip (rather than the earlobes) and wear labrets. In Haida literature, as in oral and written history, the practice is confined to women of the upper class.

22 It is understood that the creatures of the sea, forest and sky take the form of human beings anytime they enter a domesticated space – that is, a house or a canoe – and that they dress in their animal hides when they enter the wild. While she is in the house, Qqaaghawaay's daughter's five-finned skin, like any outer garment, would be hanging on a peg or folded and stored in a box.

23 Black cod (sablefish, *Anoplopoma fimbria*, Haida *sqihl*) is a rich, oily, deepwater food fish, prevalent along the central west coast of Haida Gwaay. Skaay was a native of the inner coast (east coast) of the Islands, where black cod are rare. He was also a poet with a serious interest in food. He rarely mentions the outer coast (west coast) of the Islands without also mentioning black cod.

24 "Cut me off a head" (*qaaji hla dii qqayt·tlda*) means "Share some of your loot" or "Get some loot for me" – but in this poem it has some other, more prophetic overtones as well. (See *A Story as Sharp as a Knife*, p 313, where Skaay's friend Kilxhawgins comments on the use of a related phrase.)

25 Skaay never tells us outright who or what this mythcreature is, but his description strongly suggests a crab. Taan (Tom Price) explicitly mentions a spirit being in the form of a purple shore crab (*ttsaa'am sghaana*) in his own version of the corresponding episode (Swanton n.d.2: 204; 1905b: 205f). Skaay however is the only classical Haida poet who says, of this or any other crab, *Gu ll hlghana llaagha sqqatliihlgingas*, "He had five dorsal fins."

26 *Kkiijaay*, "the Narrows" – Skidegate Narrows on current charts – is the narrow, shallow channel between the two major islands of Haida Gwaay, Graham to the north and Moresby to the south. Ttsaa'ahl lies at its western entrance. To the east, the Narrows open into a large bay known as Skidegate Inlet. Kkil Point – now called Spit Point – lies on the south side of the eastern entrance to this

Inlet. The drying passage through this point, called Qqwas in Haida, was useful to canoeists. The point has been reshaped to accommodate an airport.

27 *Wagwaahlagaay,* "swimaway," is a nickname for the larger species of sculpin.

28 The fishing ground is Fairbairn Shoals, in the mouth of Cumshewa Inlet.

29 Here at the bottom of p 196 of his typescript, Swanton started a new paragraph with a parenthesis. He typed two long prose lines, then struck them out, never closing the parenthesis, and went on to his next paragraph (line 358f in this translation). There is no trace of this cancelled paragraph in Swanton's own translation. This parenthetical passage appears to be an insertion, supplied by someone other than Skaay, and the text is in part corrupt. (Had he not cancelled the lines, Swanton would no doubt have made corrections in his usual way.) But the insertion is of interest. Restored, the cancelled lines are these:

Gyaan tldaghawaay waadluxhan at hlkkyaan waadluxhan han ll suudas
«Gam dang gyaagha isghanggaaaaang.
Dang tsin·gha quunigaay qqaalang dang sildadagan.
Haw iijaaaaang.»

Then all the [beings of the] mountain and the forest said to him,
«It isn't yours to keeeeep!
Your father's father loaned you his own skin.
That's what it remaaaaains!»

This passage is identical in part – but only in part – to a passage in Taan's treatment of the theme. The differences are substantial, but where the two passages do coincide, they do so down to the inflections. It seems possible, therefore, that Taan is the speaker of these lines. More likely still, the speaker is Henry Moody, who was well acquainted with Taan and liked the way he told the tale. At any rate, this passage constitutes an instance of Haida literary criticism: an exercise in bringing to the surface something present but unstated in Skaay's poem. As such, it is a lesson in listening to myth.

Moody made another, more direct remark about Skaay's treatment of this myth. He mentioned to Swanton (1905b: 208 n 34) that he had never before heard the story of Quartz Ribs end with the death of the hero. When Taan performed the tale for Swanton, he ended with Quartz Ribs's triumphant return to his mother Jilaquns. This was the conclusion Moody expected.

30 "The exact meaning of the archaic words used here," Swanton wrote in 1902, "has been forgotten, but [adultery] is the idea involved" (Swanton 1905b: 208 n 37). The song implies that Floating Overhead's wife is habitually unfaithful.

31 All the places mentioned in this section of the poem are close to Qquuna. *Gaayghu Qqaa'ijuusghas,* "Way Out Seaward," is the most distant of the group of tiny islets offshore from the village.

32 According to Swanton, the Step Aside Trail (evidently an active thoroughfare) led north and west from Qquuna, along the south shore of Cumshewa Inlet. The route of the canoe, in that case, is toward Ghaw Quns, Jilaquns's home.

33 The sea-pickle or white sea-gherkin is a holothurian, mentioned in §1.1 of the Cycle (p 46) and identified in note 7, p 362. Its larger relatives, the sea-sausages or sea-cucumbers, also play a vital role in §1.1.1 of *Raven Travelling*. The choice of a holothurian as a substitute phallus is far from arbitrary. Living holothurians, when handled, have the habit of transforming themselves suddenly from soft to hard or limp to stiff and back again. If handled enough, they will also ejaculate, disgorging their own viscera in apparent self-defense.

34 The text says *staayaay wagha lla isdaasi,* "he put back the labret," though Skaay said earlier that he borrowed *unxhagaay at hlgiidagaay llaagha,* "her sash and dress." The syntax used in mentioning the labret (with no possessive pronoun in the Haida) suggests that Skaay did not intend the inconsistency. (Floating Overhead would have needed sash, dress and labret too for his disguise.)

35 Snowy owls (*Nyctea scandiaca* in Latin, *saqunhl* in Haida) do not breed in Haida Gwaay but visit in fall and winter, just as Skaay implies.

36 In this movement of the poem, Skaay speaks of the Raven only as *Wiigit.* This is the Haida version of one of the adult Raven's Tsimshian names, compounded of *wii* = big + *gyet* = person.

37 Skaay is vivid yet wonderfully discreet in speaking of the shamans. This discretion in the face of the extraordinary is one important aspect of his hunterly reserve, mentioned in the introduction.

▶ THE QQUUNA CYCLE 4: SPIRIT BEING GOING NAKED ▶

1 Swanton n.d.2: 227–243; cf. Swanton 1905b: 210–226. In the 1970s, Solomon Wilson of Skidegate told David Ellis a brief but intriguing story with a related theme (Wilson & Ellis 1980). Ghandl's story "Hlagwajiina and His Family," in *Nine Visits to the Mythworld,* also casts some light on this section of the Cycle.

   The worthless brother's search for strength, a basic theme in §3.1 and again in §4 of the Cycle, also serves as the foundation for a fine work of Tlingit literature: the story of *Dukt'ootl'* told by Taakw K'wát'i (Frank Johnson) at Sitka in 1972 (Dauenhauer & Dauenhauer 1987: 138–151).

   Kingagwaaw gave the same title, *Sghaana ghuunan qaas,* "Spirit Being Going Naked," to a story whose main theme is quite different, but which resembles this section of the Cycle in its closing scene (Swanton 1908a: 417–426).

2 Once again, maple and rose are hypothetical translations for the Haida terms *ghudaang xhuusgi* and *kwii'aw gyaghadang.* (Cf. note 5, p 370.)

3 My reordering of lines 199–327 is based in part on Swanton's own handwritten emendations to his Haida typescript. There may well be underlying errors of

dictation, but the textual sequence on folios 229–231 of the typescript is surely the result of inadvertent transposition during recopying. Some but not all of the required rearrangement is accomplished in Swanton's own translation.

4 Devil's club (*Oplopanax horridus,* Haida *jiihlinjaaw*) is a large perennial shrub growing in thickets in wet and shady places. Stems and leaves alike are covered with venomous spines.

5 Strutting Grouse (*Sqaaw Ttsil*) and Jumbled Wedges (*Ttluu Qqa'andas*) are mountains near Skidegate Narrows and Skidegate Inlet.

6 Here again, a creature who first appears as a shrew has the much more pleasant temper of a mouse on second meeting. (Cf. note 11, p 371.)

7 *Moneses uniflora,* known in Haida as *xilghuga* or *xil awgha.*

8 The knots of branches rotted out of western hemlock trees are the preferred raw material for traditional Haida halibut hooks.

9 The implication of this sentence is that Spirit Being Going Naked did not kill the seawolf by stabbing it in the ears; he merely prevented it from returning before daylight to its underwater realm. What kills it is the raven's call. That is, it dies from being out of place when daylight comes.

10 In the mythworlds of the Haida and their neighbors, people who spend a lot of time alone, either on land or on the water – especially those who are stranded or lost – are in danger of being captured by the Land Otter People and losing their senses. Those who suffer this fate are known as *gaagixiit* in southern Haida, *gaagiit* in northern Haida, and in Tlingit as *kóoshdaakáa.* Kaadashaan, a Kaasx'agweidí Tlingit headman who served as one of Swanton's teachers in early 1904, said that the Raven arranged it that way:

He and the otter were good friends, so they went halibut fishing together.... Finally he said to the land otter: "... Whenever a canoe capsizes with people in it you will save them and make them your friends."...

If the friends of those who have been taken away by the land otters get them back, [the ones recovered] become shamans; therefore it was through the land otters that shamans were first known.... [Swanton 1909: 86]

Some of Swanton's Haida teachers implied, like Kaadashaan, that being "saved" by the land otters was the alternative to (or consequence of) drowning. Others suggested that the *gaagixiit* were not drowned but bushed – that is, deranged by isolation. Yet neither of these simple theories is adequate to Skaay's complex account of Spirit Being Going Naked's tribulations.

Mouse Woman's prophecy, delivered in §4.2.2 (pp 209–210), carries Spirit Being Going Naked only up through the end of §4.2. The whole next movement (§4.3) is the story of his *gaagixiit* phase – and here at the beginning of that movement, he already shows many of the symptoms.

The Haida word *gaagixiit* appears four times in the present text (lines 438, 689, 1018, 1030). In each case, it is translated "the Lost."

There are many stories from the Northwest Coast about land otters and their interactions with humans, and some are substantial enough to cast useful light on this aspect of Skaay's Cycle. Four that I find helpful were dictated in Haida: two of them by Ttsuuna (Swanton n.d.2: 606–609; 1905b: 58–69, 358–361), one by Kihltlaayga (Swanton 1908a: 523–532), and one by an unnamed Alaskan Haida elder (Swanton 1908a: 801–802, 1905a: 251–252). No less important than any of these, however, is a lovely tale written in Kwakwala about 1898 by Q'ixitasu' (Boas & Hunt 1903–5: 249–270).

11 Rhyme and assonance occur in Haida poetry as byproducts of parallel syntax. Now and again in Skaay's work, these features call attention to themselves. Here for instance, in the lament of the Spirit Being of Tears for Spirit Being Going Naked, there is rhyme enough in the Haida to call for some in the translation. The original is this:

> Tlgu ttl dawghan·ghalang tlghawttlxhada stingsi
> ising tlghawttlxhada hlingang gudansi,
> wagwi sghaanaghwa qaaydasi.
> Waghiixhan sghaanaghwa qaaydasi.

This song occurs, by the way, in the middle of the third of five episodes forming the third of five movements of §4 of the Cycle. It occurs, in other words, at the structural midpoint of Spirit Being Going Naked's story.

12 Skaay has allowed us until now to wonder about the identity of the old man living by himself in his depopulated town. He proves to be the bearer of the Haida name *Nang Kilstlas,* "Voicehandler." This is one of the names of the Raven in adult form: a title he inherits in the course of his own poem, *Raven Travelling.* We have of course met him already, in §3.3 of the Cycle, under another of his adult names, Wiigit ("Big Man"), and will meet him again in *Raven Travelling.*

13 Sea Dweller (Haida *Tangghwan Llaana*) is the principal spirit being of the sea. In northern Haida texts, he is often called by his Tlingit name, G̲unaakadeit.

14 *Ttsiida Gwaay,* "Skate Island," appears on current charts as Saunders Island, offshore of the old village of Qaysun. The Skate has other associations as well. Two knowledgeable Tlingit sources, Deikinaak'w and Léek, assure us that the Skate is the canoe of the Land Otter people; Q'ixitasu' agrees (Swanton 1909: 28, 189; cf Boas & Hunt 1903–5: 266).

15 Spirit Being Going Naked and his wife, Sea Dweller's Daughter, are on the west coast of Haida Gwaay, a region famous for its oil-rich black cod. The irresistible attractions of Haida west coast living are embodied in this fish.

16 *Sttling Nang Gyuugins,* "Spines for Earrings" or "The One Who Has Spines in His Ears," is Sea Dweller's doorkeeper. In one of Ghandl's poems, he guards the

door of another house in White Hillside (Ghadaghaaxhiwaas – now Masset). See *Nine Visits to the Mythworld*, p 52.

17 Skaay does not tell us who this woman is, but she lives in the back bedroom of Sea Dweller's Daughter's house, reached by passing through a star. Swanton understood her to be the daughter of Sea Dweller's Daughter, and thus Spirit Being Going Naked's own stepdaughter. The nature of the dialogue (and the way her bedclothes fall) suggests that she is instead the lame companion, Spirit Being Going Naked's junior wife.

18 Skaay says he steered into *Kkiijis*, "The Gut." This is the east end of Skidegate Channel, widening eastward into Skidegate Inlet and narrowing westward into the East Narrows. Spirit Being Going Naked has come from the west coast by passing through Kkiijaay (Skidegate Narrows) into Kkiijis.

➤ THE QQUUNA CYCLE 5: BORN THROUGH HER WOUND ➤

1 Swanton n.d.2: 262–269; cf. Swanton 1905b: 227–234. Ghandl's stories "The Way the Weather Chose to Be Born" and "Hlagwajiina and His Family," in *Nine Visits to the Mythworld*, help to set this section of the Cycle in perspective. As mentioned above (note 1, p 366), there are two transcribed performances of a work by the Kwakwalan mythteller 'Nagedzi which echo themes from both §2 and §5 of the Qquuna Cycle. In 'Nagedzi's story, the injured child abandoned by his people is a boy. He nonetheless gives birth, like the girl in Skaay's story, to a supernatural child.

2 The wood of choice for bows in the Haida world is yew – so much so that bow and yew are the same word: *hlghiit.*

3 Blunt-tipped arrows are preferred for shooting small birds – the traditional first quarry of Haida boys.

4 The One Who Wanders Inland (Haida *Diidaxwa Nang Qaaghuns*) is one of the principal Forest People (spirit beings of dry land) in Haida mythology, yet no one told Swanton a well-developed version of his story. What Swanton did hear was a short account by Xhyuu (the headman of Skaay's lineage), supplemented by an older man named Giikw (Swanton n.d.2: 278–280; 1905b: 235–237; cf. Enrico 1995: 172–177). According to Xhyuu, the One Who Wanders Inland was formerly a human who, as headman of Tla'aal (now Tlell), bore the traditional title Qunaats. Because of his cruelty to his people he was ousted by his nephew. The nephew then assumed the title Qunaats, while the ousted tyrant was transformed into Diidaxwa Nang Qaaghuns.

   As a political leader himself, Xhyuu specialized in stories of this kind, told with a clear political moral (cf. *A Story as Sharp as a Knife*, chapters 20 & 22). If Skaay or Ghandl had told Swanton "the same" story, it might have taken quite a different shape, revealing something more about the newly minted spirit being's nature.

(Swanton's translation of Xhyuu's tale is unfortunately troubled by some confusion over the names.)

5   Rice lily or rice root (*Fritillaria camschatcensis*, Haida *inhling*) is an important native food plant up and down the Northwest Coast. The edible bulblets are known in Haida as *inhling ttsin*, "rice lily teeth." There may be an implied pun here with *tsiin*, the Haida term for salmon in general – but in this section of the poem Skaay never uses the word *tsiin*. With his usual hunterly precision, he mentions only particular species: coho (which in Haida Gwaay usually run in late September) and dog salmon or chum (the last species to run – as a rule in late October). Rice root was usually harvested in summer, after the sockeye run in Haida Gwaay and shortly before the coho and chum.

6   Skaay's descriptions of the spawning coho and chum are brief and precise. The sides of spawning coho are red; those of spawning chum are vertically streaked. ("How are the prows of their canoes?" is not a question about *noses* but about distinguishing characteristics.)

7   The syntax of line 444 all but requires previous mention of a cane, and such a mention does appear in Swanton's own translation, though not in his Haida typescript. Skaay may have spoken such a line, and Swanton may have written it down but failed to retranscribe it.

8   The brown creeper (*Certhia americana*, Haida *qaydang gut tldang*, "clings to his tree") is a largely solitary, secretive, well-camouflaged small bird – but far more often met in Haida Gwaay than his more colorful cousin the nuthatch.

▸   RAVEN TRAVELLING: THE FLYTING OF SKAAY & XHYUU   ▸

1   Swanton n.d.2: 43–45; cf. Swanton 1905b: 129–131; Enrico 1995: 58–62 (versos) & 69–73 (rectos). Skaay and Xhyuu staged this little jam session the day before Skaay actually began dictating *Raven Travelling*. The circumstances are described in *A Story as Sharp as a Knife*, pp 213–220. Daxhiigang also told this tale – but like Skaay, he chose to keep it separate from *Raven Travelling* proper. His version, handsomely told even through the veil of double translation, is in Daxhiigang n.d.2: 30–32. Swanton, who was determined to make whole cloth out of separate elements where the Raven Cycle was concerned, fused what both Skaay and Daxhiigang had chosen to keep separate (Swanton 1905b: 143–145).

    The expedition to tame the Southeast Wind was also a favorite among Kwakwala-speaking mythtellers, and three early versions are published in that language. One was dictated to Boas in 1894 by Q'omgilis of the Nakumgilisala, as part of a cycle of stories about O'meł (Boas 1910: 226–229). Two others were written by Q'ixitasu' (Boas & Hunt 1903–5: 350–353; 1906: 98–103).

2   Warm salt water, the old standard Haida purgative, works swiftly to produce both vomiting and diarrhoea. Skaay says nothing about a ritual toilet but does imply that in Fishing God's house there is a container – or perhaps a hole in the

floor – for ritual vomiting. If Fishing God vomits up whole halibut and catches them again, perhaps his vomit box is actually the sea.

3 It is not perfectly clear from Swanton's manuscript where the change of speakers occurs. In his own translation, Swanton makes the break at the boundary between episodes, assigning these four lines to Xhyuu, while his handwritten emendations to the Haida typescript suggest the allocation given here.

4 The euphemism in Haida is the same as it is in English: *dii kkinggagaaya*, "I'm all warmed up," from *kkiinaa*, to be hot or warm.

5 Swanton put these lines in brackets in his Haida typescript (Swanton n.d.2: 45). It seems likely that they were spoken after the fact, perhaps by Henry Moody.

> RAVEN TRAVELLING: THE OLD PEOPLE'S POEM >

1 Swanton n.d.3: folio 1 & n.d.2: 23–42; cf. Swanton 1905b: 110–150; Bringhurst 1995; Enrico 1995: 14–105. For a discussion of the poem, see *A Story as Sharp as a Knife*, pp 213–294.

Several other early performances of *Raven Travelling* are available for comparison. These include: (**1**) In Haida and English, the versions told to Swanton in 1901 by Kingagwaaw and Haayas (Swanton 1908a: 293–329); (**2**) In Nishga and English, the versions told to Boas in 1894 by Moses Bell and Philip Latimer (Boas 1902: 7–71); (**3**) In Tsimshian and English, fragmentary versions told to Gwüsḵ'aayn by William Smith, Arthur Lewis and others in the 1930s (Beynon n.d.: texts 81, 95, 119 & 135); (**4**) In English only, (**a**) Boas's account of the version told to him in Chinook Jargon by the Haida artist Daxhiigang in 1897 (Daxhiigang n.d.1: 2–8; Swanton 1905b: 138–147); (**b**) a paraphrase by Swanton and Don Cameron of a version told to them in Tlingit by Deikinaak'w at Sitka in 1904 (Swanton 1909: 3–21); (**c**) Swanton's account of a version told to him in English by Ḵaadashaan, a fluent Tlingit speaker, in 1904 at Wrangell (Swanton 1909: 80–154).

2 Sea-cucumbers or sea-sausages (Haida *ghiinuu*) are intertidal holothurians, *Parastichopus californicus*, the nearest thing to freely living phalluses to be found on Haida beaches. Lambert 1997 is a useful guide. (Cf. note 7, p 362; note 33, p 374.)

3 The mythcreature behind the invitation is called *dang tsin·gha quunigaay*, "your grandfather the great." The word *quuna*, great, does not mean the same thing as "great" in the English phrase "great-grandfather," but it is equally idiomatic. *Quuna* is used alone to refer to a father-in-law, who is necessarily a senior male of the same moiety. In the Haida kinship system, a person's own father belongs to the opposite side; so does one's mate. The father-in-law is always therefore of the same side. Among grandfathers, one's mother's father is always of the opposite side, and one's father's father always of the same side. *Tsin quuna* means "male ancestor, older than a father, of the same side." The relationship

between a younger male and such an ancestor is, therefore, potentially one of reincarnation.

4 Aldo Leopold's brief essay "Clandeboye" concerns western grebes on a fresh-water marsh in Manitoba, not pied-bill grebes on the North Pacific coast, but it answers better than anything else I know to the question "Why a grebe?" See Leopold 1949: 158–162.

5 *Goosga sagaytweel txa'nii gya'wn!* means "Come do everything right now!" What Swanton wrote is *Gū'sga wagēlai'dx̱ạn hā-ā-o*, or in my orthography, *Guusga waghiilaaydxhan haa-aa-aw*. This is not a bad approximation of the sound pattern of Tsimshian, but it makes no Tsimshian sense. So there are sev-eral possibilities: (1) Skaay didn't speak Tsimshian but knew what it sounded like and simply uttered a parody; (2) Skaay spoke Tsimshian well enough, but Henry Moody, who didn't, corrupted the result; (3) the Raven himself, as Skaay conceived him, couldn't speak Tsimshian, so Skaay put Tsimshian-sounding nonsense in his mouth. Dell Hymes's studies of the speech of tricksters (e.g., Hymes 1996) lend some credence to option three, but other things are against it – especially line 160 of Skaay's poem: *Gyaan kilghat kihlghagi ising lla saawas*, "Then he spoke again in the Tsimshian language." Overall, the second option seems to me the likeliest. (See also note 23, p 365.)

6 The people out to seaward (*qqaadaxwa xhaaydaghaay*) are those who live on the mainland (the Tsimshian and Nishga in particular); the people here to land-ward (*diidaxwa xhaaydaghaay*) are those who live in Haida Gwaay.

7 The Nuxalk and Heiltsuk country – surrounding the present village of Bella Coola – is known in Haida as Lalgiimi (from Tsimshian *Laałgyiimiil*).

8 Beach pea (*Lathyrus japonicus*) and giant vetch (*Vicea gigantea*), which grow side by side in many spots along the coast, are both known in Haida as *xhuuya tluugha*, "Raven's canoe." Ripe beach pea pods are usually 7 or 8 cm long, vetch pods roughly half that length.

9 Ghaw Quns, "Big Bay" or "the Great Vagina," is a modest place of large im-portance in Haida mythology. The diminutive woman whom the Raven brings to live there is Jilaquns, "Big Bait" or "the Great Attraction." Skaay does not name her in this poem, though he describes her with some care. She also plays a crucial role in §3 of the Qquuna Cycle. Gumsiiwa dictated a story about her to Swanton only a few days after the latter's arrival in Haida Gwaay (Swanton n.d.2: 490–493, translated in Swanton 1905a: 94–96 and in Enrico 1995: 160–168). Daxhiigang also told her story to Franz Boas (Daxhiigang n.d.2: 13–14; Swanton 1905b: 316–317; Enrico 1995: 168–169). In his ethnography (1905a: 23), Swanton says a bit about her importance to the Haida social order.

10 Like the tentacles of the sea anemone – which in Haida mythology is the em-bodiment of the clear sight and skill required by hunters.

11 Skaay will confirm later on that Stlgham is the Eagle. This name or title is widely found, but in mutable forms, on the Northwest Coast, and I do not know its etymology. When the northern Haida poet Haayas performed *Raven Travelling* for Swanton in the spring of 1901 (Swanton 1908a: 296f), he used the form Stlaqaam – but Haayas gave this name not to *Ghuudaay*, the Eagle, but to *Kalgaayagangaay*, the Butterfly.

12 What is implied in this episode is actually an offer of artificial insemination. In the traditional medicine of the Northwest Coast, the juice of tree roots is regarded as an analogue of semen, and coastal folklore has it that root juice will make a woman pregnant if she swallows it while preparing her materials for weaving. Kingagwaaw, Deikinaak'w and Léek all refer to this belief in the context of stories they told to Swanton (Swanton 1908a: 642; 1909: 42, 193).

   The Raven's final word to the Eagle, *qal ghahaw ll xhiilugha,* "it came from a tap in an alder," is another marvel of perversity, and it too rests on a shared motif. Alders grow in wet locations – shorelines, streambanks, floodplains – yet alder is the one tree in Haida Gwaay that will *not* give sap when tapped. When the Nishga mythteller Philip Latimer told *Raven Travelling* to Boas in 1894, he said the Eagle goaded the Raven into *trying* to getting water from an alder. The Tsimshian writer Henry Tate says much the same (Boas 1902: 17; 1916: 65, 69). Skaay turns the tables but alludes to the same joke. (Swanton heard *qqaal,* "clay," instead of *qal,* "alder.")

13 The Skeena is the major river in the Tsimshian country. Like the Nass (the major river of the Nishga) and the Stikine (the major river of the Tahltan and the southern Tlingit), it begins among the creeks in the high Spatsizi Plateau, hundreds of miles north and east of Haida Gwaay.

14 This aside was probably introduced to force a temporary closure – a resting place in the performance. It is useful for clarification nevertheless. This is the only place in this movement of the poem where Skaay mentions the word *ghuut,* which is Haida for eagle.

   Hlaaghahlam is probably derived from Tsimshian *lgu'ałaan,* a term of polite address used when a male speaks to his brother-in-law. (The suffix *-m,* meaningless in Haida, is the first-person plural possessive in Tsimshian.) But in Nishga and Tsimshian versions of the Raven story, the Raven's companion is commonly called by a similar name, Lagabuulaa. (Early examples include the version that Philip Latimer told to Boas in Nishga in 1894 [Boas 1902: 16–24] and a rather oafish version that Henry Tate wrote for Boas in English and Tsimshian in 1905 [Boas 1916: 68–70]). *Lagabuulaa* is a play on the Tsimshian verb *buu, gabuu.* In reference to whales, this means to spout or blow; with reference to humans, it means to come (in the sexual sense).

15 This means that his grandfather placed his own feet over those of his grandson, then took hold of his grandson's hands and pulled him upward, stretching him to make him grow up tall.

16 Kkuuxuginaagits, "Plain Old Marten," and Taadlat Ghaadala, "Outruns Trout," also appear at the conclusion of §3.1 of the Qquuna Cycle. (Cf. note 15, p 371.)

17 Qadajaan is a mountain on the south side of the Nass Inlet. The spirit being or killer whale living in this mountain is the guardian or owner of the eulachon. The name is probably of Tsimshian origin. Other Haida mythtellers have given it as Qajang or Qaattsigan.

18 The wooden screen behind the fire, dividing the owner's private quarters from the rest of a Haida house. Qadajaan's eulachons are kept behind this screen.

19 Sword fern (*Polystichum munitum,* Haida *snaanjang*) is widely found on the northern Northwest Coast, and its rootstocks are an important seasonal food. Skaay is alluding here to an episode that he doesn't actually tell: one in which the Raven scatters Swordfern Woman's armpit hair, and so distributes ferns, much as he has just distributed eulachon.

20 In the old Haida calendars, months were counted by the half year, equinox to equinox. The Raven suggests a shorter year, perhaps to make life easier for humans, who must harvest food and store it, and build houses and make clothes. The dog insists on a longer year but an easier life. (One such calendar – rather grandly published as *the* Haida calendar – is described in Swanton 1903.) One of the stories that Henry Tate wrote for Boas in English and Tsimshian also links the Dog to the formation of the calendar. (Tate n.d. is the original text; Boas 1908 is a retranscription with German interlinear translation; Boas 1916: 113–116 is a looser English version.)

21 "Someone's grave" is all Skaay says – but no one other than a shaman would be buried this way, exposed to the elements in an isolated location.

22 *Gyaan lla at gu lla taydyaasi*: "then her/him with there he/she lay," or slept, or went to bed. This is Skaay's usual phrase for sexual activity. The euphemism is exactly the same in Haida as in English.

23 In the world of Haida mythology and in traditional Haida life, an affair between a man and his father's sister is not a cause for scandal; the lovers, after all, are from opposite moieties, and a paternal aunt can teach her nephew much. But an affair between a son and his own mother strikes at the kinship system's heart.

24 *Qqaytsgha Llaanas,* The People of the Strait, are a lineage of spirit beings or killer whales living at House Point (now charted as Rose Spit, the northeasternmost extremity of Haida Gwaay). See *Nine Visits to the Mythworld,* p 106.

25 The door implied is a hanging door or winter doorflap, hinged at the top and weighted at the bottom.

26 Haida *qqayskkut.* Tlaajang Quuna used this name (Newcombe n.d.3) for both the bufflehead and the hooded merganser. The hooded merganser breeds in Haida Gwaay while the bufflehead probably does not, but hooded mergansers

prefer fresh water. Neither, of course, subsists on whale, but either could be drawn by other food to the vicinity of the carcass.

27 Sinjuugwaang, "Sniffing the Wind," lives in the headwaters of the Tlell River, on the east coast of Graham Island.

28 Yaahl Kingaangghu, "Calling Raven," lives near Qquuna – in the headwaters of what is now called Skedans Creek.

29 Qqaasta is a salmon stream southeast of Hlghagilda, shown on recent charts as the Copper River. There was formerly a village at the mouth of the creek. Skidegate people still use the area as a fishcamp.

30 Qqaadasghu is a creek and an old village site on the north shore of Qquuna Gwaay (Louise Island). Skaay lived here briefly after the evacuation of Ttanuu.
   All four of the creeks alluded to in this passage are south of Ghahlins Kun, or Highflat Point, the home of Big Surf (Sghulghu Quuna), in whose house the feast is being held. The creeks are more or less centered on Skidegate Inlet. They are also the main salmon streams found in between the homes of the spirit beings Sghulghu Quuna and Qinggi. The distance between these major landmarks is about 60 sea miles direct, more like 100 miles by canoe.

31 Marten and black bear live in Haida Gwaay; grizzly and mountain goat do not. There is, moreover, a proverbial relation between the former two: *Kkuuxu haw taan ghan kwaayang, wansuuga*: Marten is black bear's elder brother, they say.

32 This is the first time in the fourth movement that the Raven is actually named, and the only time in the poem that anyone calls him Voicehandler (Nang Kilstlas) instead of Voicehandler's Heir (Nang Kilstlas Hlingaay).

33 This is not where the head of the house would normally sit. Qinggi has ceded his spot behind the fire and come out to join the audience of villagers.

34 The trickster's inability to learn to sing a song is a widespread theme in Native American mythology (discussed in Hymes 1996). Here we have a complex parallel: the trickster's inability to tell his own story.

35 The common cormorant in Haida waters is *Phalacrocorax pelagicus*, the pelagic cormorant, called *kkyaluu* in Haida. The cormorant mentioned here is *sghiitghun*. This is *P. auritus*, the double-crested cormorant, which visits the Islands in the fall.

36 A very interesting passage. Raven rattles are used by all the native nations of the northern Northwest Coast and are known by cognate names in all the northern coastal languages: *sheishóoxw* in Tlingit, *haseex* in Nishga, *sasoo* in Tsimshian, *siisaa* in Haida. They are carved in two parts: belly and back. The Raven's head, wings and tail are part of the back. So is the humanoid passenger which the rattle usually carries. The belly (Haida *qan*, meaning breast or ribcage) does not look like it could fly, and it seldom has any discernibly avian

elements. It is shaped like half an egg or a short canoe, and is usually engraved with the face of the Raven's marine allotrope, Ttsam'aws, the Snag. Dance etiquette and conventional wisdom on the Northwest Coast require that Raven rattles should be carried belly up most of the time, because they cannot fly away when held in that position.

37 *Aegolius acadicus,* the northern saw-whet owl, called *sttaw* in Haida, is the only owl that breeds in Haida Gwaay and the one most frequently seen and heard. As owls go, saw-whets are tiny: smaller than robins. The beak is black but hardly adequate in size to replace that of a raven. It is, by the way, proverbial in Nishga that *Sagawsa t an naxn̓ał huuxw; laasatkw t an ga'ał xbilgantkw:* "Good luck comes to those who hear the saw-whet owl; bad luck to those who see the screech owl." (Cf. Tarpent 1986: 51.)

38 *Ghal* are blue mussels, *Mytilus edulis.* Though a delicacy elsewhere, they are basic winter food on the Northwest Coast, available at each low tide to rich and poor alike. Another reason for regarding them as workaday food and not a feast dish is that no skill is needed to prepare them. They are set beside the fire to roast; when they open, they are ready. The pussytail or pubic hair is the byssus or holdfast of the mussel.

39 Bracket fungi are nearly as rare in Haida literature as they are in the literatures of Europe, but the Raven's choice of bracket fungus here is not fortuitous. The principal recorded use of bracket fungi by peoples of the Northwest Coast is as a medium for carving shamans' effigies and grave markers. They are known also for their insulation value and are used as protective pads when handling live coals. (Cf. Blanchette et al 1992; Compton 1993.)

40 The northern Haida poet Haayas calls the Raven's sister Suuwaas rather than Siiwaas (Swanton 1908a: 303f). Randy Bouchard has recently identified another variant of the name, used by Johnny Wiiha of Skidegate, who told a Raven story to Boas in the 1880s (published in Boas 1895). Boas heard this name as Shuwaash and wrote it as *Cuwā'c* or *Cuva'c.* This neither looks nor sounds like Haida; nevertheless, as Bouchard points out, it twice appears in Boas's Haida wordlists, once defined as "crow" and once as "loose" (an error, possibly, for "loon"). Boas glossed it in *Indianische Sagen* as *die Lumme* (properly "guillemot" but to Boas usually "loon"). The usual Haida words for guillemot, loon and crow are *sghaaxhaaduwa, taadl* and *kkaaljida.* Skaay speaks of *Kkaaljida,* the Crow, at line 1227, just before the Raven's sister is first mentioned.

41 *Oncorhynchus keta,* called *skkaagi* in Haida and dog salmon or chum salmon in English, are the last species of salmon to run in the fall.

42 Skaay does not say what Siiwaas planted. Native tobacco (Haida *gul*) is much the most likely possibility and the only precolonial one. Potatoes (*sgaawsiit*) – the first crop adopted from Europeans – would be the next most plausible choice.

1 Swanton n.d.2: 53–54; cf. Swanton 1905b: 138; Enrico 1995: 80, 82, 87–88.

2 As Skaay suggests at the outset of §3.2 of the Qquuna Cycle, the Haida of the Ghangxhiit region were known for condescending and self-deprecating names. (Cf. note 17, p 371.) This passage has at times been misconstrued to mean that the Raven speaks "in southern dialect." That however is not what Ghandl says.

➤ THE STORY OF THE QQUUNA QIIGHAWAAY ➤

1 The Haida text is published with Swanton's own translation in Swanton 1905b: 87–93. The structure of the poem, which proves quite intricate, is discussed in *A Story as Sharp as a Knife*, chapter 15. Ttlxingas (site 14 on the map, p 31) is on the southwest side of Qquuna Gwaay (Louise Island).

2 Ttsixhudalxa is salmon stream and fish camp in the Qquuna region.

3 Waanaghan is a hereditary name normally used by the nephew and heir of the headman of the Qaagyals Qiighawaay of the Raven side, who was also, in the 19th century, usually head of the village of Qquuna. The bearer of this name should thus be a suitable father for the heir to the headship of Skaay's lineage, the Qquuna Qiighawaay of the Eagle side.

4 Hlghaay is a bay south of Qquuna, and the salmon stream that feeds it.

5 Gwaaya and Gwiighal are small islands south and east of Qquuna, charted now as the Low Islands (Low and South Low).

6 A bat may seem a curious creature to meet in an offshore storm accepting offerings on behalf of a killer whale – but bats routinely feed by skimming over water, and some populations live in close association with the sea. At least four species live in Haida Gwaay. The biggest of these is the silver-haired bat (*Lasionycteris noctivagans*), which is known for its long marine migrations. Another, Keen's bat (*Myotis keenii*), is endemic to the British Columbia coast. On Ghandl Kkiin Gwaayaay (Hotspring Island), near Ttanuu, Keen's bats and little brown bats (*Myotis lucifugus*) roost together in a naturally heated intertidal cave. Skaay's word for bat, by the way, is *quutgadagamhlghal,* possibly related to the Tsimshian word for bat, *ts'ogat'axtxayl.*

7 They went north and south, in other words, looking far and wide. Lake Inlet (Suu Qaahli) is the head of a large bay some 50 miles south of Qquuna (charted now as the head of Skincuttle Inlet). Rock Point (Ttiis Kun) – also mentioned in §3.2.5 of the Qquuna Cycle – is probably the place now charted as Gray Point, about ten miles north of Qquuna.

8 Reeves 1992 – a text dictated in Tsimshian in 1938 – is another story of a hunter led to sea by a silver otter. In Reeves's story, however, the hunter's crime is minor, and after two years on the seafloor he is permitted to return.

9 These are Cassin's auklets (*Ptychoramphus aleuticus*, Haida *hajaa*). They spend the autumn and winter at sea, coming ashore in spring to nest in shallow burrows in the slopes above the tideline. There the eggs, the young and even the adults are easy prey for humans, gulls and other predators.

10 This is the name of the point at the east end of Gwaaya – and, of course, the hereditary name of this landform's resident spirit being or killer whale.

11 Leaf barnacles (*Pollicipes polymerus*, Haida *ttlkkyaaw*) and acorn barnacles (*Balanus nubilis*, Haida *ghaawdawal*) are both important foodstuffs on the Northwest Coast, accessible at each low tide. Leaf barnacles are the smaller of the two but have much lighter armor and are easier to get.

The name of the leaf barnacle, *ttlkkyaaw*, is made of two components which mean "thin-&-flat" and "sharp." It rhymes semantically and acoustically with *Tlghakkyaaw*, "Sharp Ground," which is the name of the barnacle harvester. This makes the story sound like literature, not history, but it may still be both. It is quite possible that Tlghakkyaaw was given this name only after his death.

12 Traditional Haida practice would require the families of those who happen to be present at an accidental death to pay the family of the deceased. There are of course no moose in Haida Gwaay, and their skins could only be obtained by trading with people from the mainland.

13 Double mortuary posts were frequent in the northern Haida villages but much rarer in the south. Triple and quadruple mortuary posts were rarer still. George MacDonald records only one triple mortuary post (at Yaakkw on the northern coast) and one quadruple post (the Iidansaa mortuary, built for Gwaayang Gwanhlin's uncle, which is still in place at Kkyuusta). But there were more. George Dorsey, for example, saw a quadruple mortuary post at Qang in 1897 (Dorsey 1898: 11), which is missing from MacDonald's survey, and there is no reason to doubt Skaay's claim that a mortuary with four pillars was built at Qquuna for Tlghakkyaaw. Nor is there any doubt about the meaning of his words: *Ll xhaada llagha ttl hlgiistansingdaayaghan*: "His grave-post for-him they made-pillarlike-fourfold." If this death-post really had a tree growing out of it in 1900, one might expect to find it in the early photographs – but no such structure has yet been identified.

14 The seaweed is *Porphyra perforata*: red laver in English, *sghyuu* in Haida.

15 Turn-of-the-Tide (Dalqqaay Hlgahlging) is one of the group of islets just outside Qquuna harbor.

16 The last line in Haida is *Haw tl kunju*. This is the only occasion on which Skaay uses this closing formula – one associated generally with history (*gyaahlghalang*) and clan legend (*qqayaagaang*) rather than with myth (*qqaygaang*).

Notes to the Illustrations

▸ FRONTISPIECE ▸

George Emmons bought the remains of this superb Haida rattle in the Tlingit community of Sitka sometime after 1884. He described it as "one spirit within another, both singing." (Cf. Wardwell 1978: 84–85; 1996: 246.)

▸ PAGE 36 ▸

Among contemporary weavers, skyblankets are now widely known as Raven's Tail robes. The Swift Robe (named for the mariner, Capt. Benjamin Swift, who purchased it on the coast of southeastern Alaska about 1800) is one of the best preserved early examples and the only one designed to give the appearance of being two blankets rather than one. Cheryl Samuel has described the construction of this textile in detail (Samuel 1987: 94–103).

▸ PAGE 174 ▸

Ngiislaans (John Cross, c.1858–1939) was not an artist on a par with Skaay and Daxhiigang, but the story of Qqaaghawaay and Quartz Ribs was one in which he took a particular interest. He explored the theme in several relief carvings and drew a Qqaaghawaay tattoo design in pencil at Swanton's request (reproduced as plate xx.17 in Swanton 1905a). Bill Holm has published a brief but very lucid discussion of his style (in Abbott 1981: 192–193).

▸ PAGE 196 ▸

This is one of a series of 18 drawings (possibly more) that Daxhiigang made for Franz Boas at Port Essington, near the mouth of the Skeena River, in August 1897. Boas was then employed by the American Museum of Natural History in New York, and the drawing is on a sheet of Museum letterhead. The museum's printed address has been deleted in the present reproduction. (So has a rubber stamp, added to the drawing by museum staff.) The story that Daxhiigang told in conjunction with this drawing concerns not only a seawolf but also a carping mother-in-law who masquerades as a shaman. Boas's paraphrase of the story, which is all that he recorded, is in Daxhiigang n.d.2: 16–17, published in Swanton 1908a: 623–624. Ghandl weaves the same theme into his story "The Sealion Hunter" (*Nine Visits to the Mythworld,* pp 95–110).

> ▸ PAGE 198 ◂

Daxhiigang made few masks, and only two surviving examples have yet been identified. One is an elaborate transformation mask, now in the Pitt-Rivers Museum at Oxford (reproduced in Swanton 1905a: 145). This is the other. It is a great deal more subtle than most Gaagixiit masks. The nostrils are upturned, and the lips protrude, as usual, but the face is not extensively deformed, and the lips and cheeks are not riddled with spines, as in many recent examples. Instead, the Lost Man's desperation and derangement are concentrated mostly in his eyes. Swanton commissioned this mask in 1901. It was completed in 1904 and sold, to the museum that still owns it, for $6.00. (These and other details are in Edenshaw 1904, a letter from Daxhiigang's cousin.)

> ▸ PAGE 246 ◂

Daxhiigang's uncle Gwaayang Gwanhlin (Albert Edward Edenshaw) sold this mortar to George Dawson at Kkyuusta in the summer of 1878. There is a discussion of the work in Duff 1975: 144–149.

> ▸ PAGE 272 ◂

Raven stories – especially those involving the trickster's insatiable greed – are favorite subjects for Haida goat horn spoons, and Skaay must have known these three spoons well. Swanton's unpublished notes confirm that they belonged to Xhyuu's uncle and mentor Gitkuna, whose house in Ttanuu was Skaay's home for many years. The spoons were used, in other words, in the house shown on p 328 of this book and on pp 104–107 of *A Story as Sharp as a Knife.* On Gitkuna's death in 1877, the spoons passed to one of his female relatives, then to her son. The deceased son's wife sold them to Swanton in the spring of 1901. (Cf. Swanton n.d.5: 14–18; n.d.6: 6; 1905a: 137.)

The themes portrayed are, from left to right: (1) the Raven struck in the chest by a spring salmon (an episode that forms §2.2 of Skaay's *Raven Travelling*); (2) the Raven clutching his lost beak, then re-emerging in raven form from the body of a flounder, and the child who sees this transformation happen (events that Skaay places in §5.1 of his poem); (3) the Raven and the Beaver (evoking a much-loved story that Skaay explores at length in §2.3).

> ▸ PAGE 282 ◂

Though smaller in scale than the original, this pole is closely modelled on an early or mid 19th-century pole from Sghan Gwaay Llanagaay (catalogued as Ninstints 12 in MacDonald 1983). It was carved by Bill Reid with the assistance

388

of Doug Cranmer. The eroded and sectioned remains of the original pole, removed from Sghan Gwaay in 1957, are now in the same museum.

At the top of the pole are three watchmen. Below them are three figures which constitute one reincarnation cycle for the Raven. The uppermost of these is *Xhuuya* (Tsimshian *Txaamsm*), the Raven in multivalent adult form, with human arms and hands as well as corvine wings, and a face in his feathered tail. He is perched on the head of *Tsaaghan Xuuwaji* (Tsimshian *Midiigm Ts'm'aks*), the Sea Grizzly, who carries on his chest the infant Raven. The pole was moved indoors in 2001. For a photo of the whole pole in its former location, see Bringhurst & Steltzer 1992: 73.

➤ PAGE 328 ➤

Skaay lived in this house for half his life – roughly 1845 through 1886 – but when the photograph was taken, house and village had been empty (apart from occasional use as a campsite) for over 15 years. The housepole, raised in 1878, shows Qinggi holding the Ravenchild in human form and the Ravenchild holding a young grizzly (one of the gifts he offers to Qinggi). Most of the pole is occupied by Qinggi's people climbing his tall hat. The lowermost figure, partly obscured by vegetation, is a huge Raven in stylized avian form. The finial is a smaller, more naturalistic image of the same. Earlier photographs of the house are reproduced in *A Story as Sharp as a Knife*, pp 104–107.

➤ PAGE 332 ➤

Over the years, Daxhiigang carved at least three versions of this subject, all as low-relief argillite tondos. The latest of the three (now in the National Museum of Ireland, Dublin) was carved in the early 1890s. Another version (now in the Seattle Art Museum) precedes the Dublin plate, but not by many years. The version shown here (now in Chicago) is the earliest and may date from circa 1880. The three works are nearly identical in size, and all have been broken and mended. The three are shown together in McLennan & Duffek 2000: 207.

Select Bibliography

THE ABBREVIATIONS used here are as follows:
AES = American Ethnological Society (New York)
AMNH = American Museum of Natural History (New York)
APSL = American Philosophical Society Library (Philadelphia)
BAE = Bureau of American Ethnology (Washington, DC)
NAA = National Anthropological Archives (Washington, DC)

Abbott, Donald N., ed.

1981   *The World is as Sharp as a Knife: An Anthology in Honour of Wilson Duff*. Victoria: British Columbia Provincial Museum.

Banfield, A.W. F.

1974   *The Mammals of Canada*. Toronto: University of Toronto Press.

Beynon, William [= Gwüsk'aayn]

n.d.   "The Beynon Manuscript." Columbia University Library, New York. [Individually paginated holograph texts numbered from 5 to 253, with some omissions. In Tsimshian with Gwüsk'aayn's interlinear English translation.]

Blanchette, Robert A., et al.

1992   "Nineteenth Century Shaman Grave Guardians Are Carved *Fomitopsis officinalis* Sporophores." New York: *Mycologia* 84.1: 119–124.

Boas, Franz

1895   *Indianische Sagen von der Nord-Pacifischen Küste Amerikas*. Berlin: Asher.

1897   "The Decorative Art of the Indians of the Indians of the North Pacific Coast. New York: *Bulletin of the American Museum of Natural History* 9: 123–176. [Revised as chapter 6, Boas 1927; reprinted in Boas 1995.]

1898   *Facial Paintings of the Indians of Northern British Columbia*. Jesup North Pacific Expedition 1.1. New York: AMNH. [Reprinted in Boas 1995.]

1902   *Tsimshian Texts*. Washington, DC: BAE Bulletin 27. [Actually Nishga.]

1908   "Eine Sonnensage der Tsimschian." *Zeitschrift für Ethnologie*. Berlin: Behrend: 776–797.

1910   *Kwakiutl Tales*. Columbia University Contributions to Anthropology 2. New York: Columbia University Press.

1912   *Tsimshian Texts (New Series)*. In one volume with John Swanton, *Haida Songs*. Publications of the AES 3. Leiden: E.J. Brill.

1916   *Tsimshian Mythology*. Washington, DC: BAE Annual Report 31.

1927   *Primitive Art*. Oslo: Aschehoug. [Reprinted, Harvard University Press, 1928.]

1935–43 *Kwakiutl Tales (New Series)*. 2 vols. Columbia University Press Contributions to Anthropology 26. New York: Columbia University Press.

1995   *A Wealth of Thought*, edited by Aldona Jonaitis. Seattle: University of Washington Press.

Boas, Franz, & George Hunt [= Q'ixitasu']

1903–5 *Kwakiutl Texts*. 3 vols. Jesup North Pacific Expedition 3.1–3. New York: AMNH.

1906   *Kwakiutl Texts: Second Series*. Jesup North Pacific Expedition 10.1. New York: AMNH.

Boyd, Robert

1999   *The Coming of the Spirit of Pestilence*. Seattle: University of Washington Press.

Bradley, Joseph

1992   *Ndeh Wuwaal Ḵuudeex a Spaga Laxyuubm Ts'msiyeen: When the Aleuts were on Tsimshian Territory*. Suwilaay'msga Na Ḡa'niiyatgm 5. [Prince Rupert, BC: Tsimshian Tribal Council.]

Bringhurst, Robert

1995   "Raven Travelling, Page One: A Lost Haida Text by Skaai of the Qquuna Qiighawaai." Vancouver: *Canadian Literature* 144: 98–111.

1998   *Native American Oral Literatures and the Unity of the Humanities*. The 1998 Garnett Sedgewick Memorial Lecture. Vancouver: University of British Columbia.

1999   *A Story as Sharp as a Knife: The Classical Haida Mythtellers and Their World*. (*Masterworks of the Classical Haida Mythtellers*, vol. 1.) Vancouver/Toronto: Douglas & McIntyre; Lincoln: University of Nebraska Press.

Bringhurst, Robert, & Ulli Steltzer

1992   *The Black Canoe: Bill Reid and the Spirit of Haida Gwaii*. 2nd ed. Vancouver/Toronto: Douglas & McIntyre.

Cahalane, Victor H.

1947   *Mammals of North America*. New York: Macmillan.

Calder, James A., & Roy L. Taylor

1968   *Flora of the Queen Charlotte Islands*. 2 vols. Ottawa: Department of Agriculture.

Campbell, R. Wayne, et al.

1990–2001   *The Birds of British Columbia.* 4 vols. Vancouver: UBC Press.

Canada. Department of Fisheries & Oceans

1991   *Sailing Directions: British Columbia Coast,* vol. 2 (North Portion).
            12th ed. Ottawa: Canadian Hydrographic Service.

Carl, G. Clifford

1960   "Albinistic Killer Whales in British Columbia." Victoria: *Provincial
            Museum of Natural History and Anthropology Report for 1959*:
            B29–36.

Chowning, Ann

1962   "Raven Myths in Northwestern North America and Northeastern
            Asia." Madison, Wisconsin: *Arctic Anthropology* 1.1: 1–5.

Compton, Brian

1993   Upper North Wakashan and Southern Tsimshian Ethnobotany.
            Ph.D. dissertation, University of British Columbia, Vancouver.

Dauenhauer, Nora Marks, & Richard Dauenhauer

1987   *Haa Shuká, Our Ancestors: Tlingit Oral Narratives.* Seattle:
            University of Washington Press.

Daxhiigang [Charlie Edenshaw]

n.d.1   Myths and interpretations of artworks dictated to Franz Boas.
            Typescript. BAE ms 4117-b(4), NAA, Smithsonian Institution,
            Washington, DC. [pp 1–8, 18–22 & 33–34. Boas's English
            translation of texts dictated in Chinook Jargon at Port Essington in
            1897. Completed by Daxhiigang n.d.2.]

n.d.2   Myths and interpretations of artworks dictated to Franz Boas.
            Typescript. Mss file 1901-31, Dept. of Anthropology Archives,
            AMNH, New York. [pp 9–17 & 23–32. Boas's English translation of
            texts dictated in Chinook Jargon at Port Essington in 1897.
            Completed by Daxhiigang n.d.1.]

Dorsey, George A.

1898   *A Cruise among Haida and Tlingit Villages about Dixon's Entrance.*
            New York: Appleton.

Douglas, George W., Gerald B. Stanley, Del Meidinger & Jim Pojar, ed.

1998–   *Illustrated Flora of British Columbia.* Victoria, BC: Ministry of
            Environment, Lands & Parks. 8 vols.

Duff, Wilson

1975   *Images Stone B.C.* Saanichton, BC: Hancock House.

Durlach, Theresa Mayer

1928   *The Relationship Systems of the Tlingit, Haida and Tsimshian.* New
            York: Publications of the AES 11.

Edenshaw, Henry [Kihlguulins]

1904   Letter to John Swanton, dated Vancouver, B.C., 6 October 1904.
            Mss file 1905-57, Dept. of Anthropology Archives, AMNH, New
            York. [One page, transmitting a mask made by Daxhiigang.]

393

Ellis, David W., & Solomon Wilson

1981   *The Knowledge and Usage of Marine Invertebrates by the Skidegate Haida People of the Queen Charlotte Islands.* [Skidegate, BC]: Queen Charlotte Islands Museum Society.

Emmons, George T.

1907   "The Chilkat Blanket." New York: *Memoirs of the American Museum of Natural History* 3.4: 327–401.

1993   *The Basketry of the Tlingit and the Chilkat Blanket.* Annotated ed. with appendices by Nora Marks Dauenhauer et al. Sitka: Sheldon Jackson Museum.

Enrico, John

1995   *Skidegate Haida Myths and Histories.* Skidegate, BC: Queen Charlotte Islands Museum Press.

Ford, John K.B., & Graeme M. Ellis

1999   *Transients: Mammal-Hunting Killer Whales of British Columbia, Washington, and Southeastern Alaska.* Vancouver: UBC Press.

Ford, John K.B.; Graeme M. Ellis; Kenneth C. Balcomb

1994   *Killer Whales: The Natural History and Genealogy of* Orcinus orca *in British Columbia and Washington State.* Vancouver: UBC Press.

Ford, John K.B., & Deborah Ford

1981   "The Killer Whales of B.C." Vancouver: *Waters* 5.1 (special issue).

Ghandl of the Qayahl Llaanas

2000   *Nine Visits to the Mythworld,* translated by Robert Bringhurst. (*Masterworks of the Classical Haida Mythtellers,* vol. 2.) Vancouver/Toronto: Douglas & McIntyre; Lincoln: University of Nebraska Press.

Handbook of North American Indians

1978–   20 vols. Washington, DC: Smithsonian Institution.

Harris, Kenneth B.

1974   *Visitors Who Never Left: The Origin of the People of Damelahamid.* Vancouver: UBC Press.

Holm, Bill

1965   *Northwest Coast Indian Art: An Analysis of Form.* Seattle: University of Washington Press.

1981   "Will the Real Charles Edensaw Please Stand Up? The Problem of Attribution in Northwest Coast Indian Art." In Abbott: 175–200.

Hymes, Dell H.

1981   *"In Vain I Tried to Tell You": Essays in Native American Ethnopoetics.* Philadelphia: University of Pennsylvania Press.

1990   "Mythology." In *Handbook of North American Indians,* vol. 7: Northwest Coast: 593–601.

1995   "Na-Dene Ethnopoetics, A Preliminary Report: Haida and Tlingit." In *Language and Culture in Native North America,* edited by

Michael Dürr, Egon Renner & Wolfgang Oleschinski. München: Lincom: 265–311.

1996   "Coyote, the Thinking (Wo)man's Trickster." In *Monsters, Tricksters and Sacred Cows: Animal Tales and American Identities,* edited by A. James Arnold. Charlottesville: University Press of Virginia: 108–137.

Kilham, Lawrence

1989   *The American Crow and the Common Raven.* College Station, Texas: Texas A&M University Press.

King, J.C.H.

1977   *Smoking Pipes of the North American Indian.* London: British Museum.

Kuhnlein, Harriet V., & Nancy J. Turner

1991   *Traditional Plant Foods of Canadian Indigenous Peoples.* New York: Gordon & Breach.

Lambert, Philip

1997   *Sea Cucumbers of British Columbia, Southeast Alaska and Puget Sound.* Vancouver: UBC Press.

Leechman, J.D., & M.R. Harrington

1921   *String Records of the Northwest.* Indian Notes and Monographs [n.s. 16]. New York: Museum of the American Indian.

Leopold, Aldo

1949   *A Sand County Almanac.* New York: Oxford University Press.

Levine, Robert D.

1977   The Skidegate Dialect of Haida. Ph.D. dissertation, Columbia University, New York.

MacDonald, George F.

1983   *Haida Monumental Art.* Vancouver: UBC Press.

McLennan, Bill, & Karen Duffek

2000   *The Transforming Image: Painted Arts of Northwest Coast First Nations.* Vancouver: UBC Press.

Matson, R.G., & Gary Coupland

1995   *The Prehistory of the Northwest Coast.* San Diego: Academic Press.

Nagorsen, David W., et al.

1993–   *The Mammals of British Columbia.* 6 vols. Vancouver: UBC Press.

Newcombe, Charles F.

n.d.1   "Notes of a Journey Round the Southern Islands of the Queen Charlotte Group, British Columbia, in the year 1901." Dept. of Anthropology Archives, AMNH, New York.

n.d.2   "List of plants collected by Dr John R. Swanton." Latin and Haida. Ms 4117-A(2), NAA, Smithsonian Institution, Washington, DC [where it is catalogued as Swanton's].

n.d.3   Annotated checklist of British Columbia birds, with Haida names
         supplied by Tlaajang Quuna [Tom Stevens]. Ms 4117-A(3), NAA,
         Smithsonian Institution, Washington, DC [where it is catalogued
         as Swanton's].

Pojar, Jim, & Andy MacKinnon, et al.

1994   *Plants of Coastal British Columbia.* Edmonton, Alberta: Lone Pine.

Reeves, Henry

1992   *Adawga Gant Wilaaytga Gyetga Suwildook: Rituals of Respect and
         the Sea Otter Hunt.* Suwilaay'msga Na Ga'niiyatgm 2. [Prince
         Rupert, BC: Tsimshian Tribal Council.]

Reid, Bill

2000   *Solitary Raven: Selected Writings,* edited by Robert Bringhurst.
         Vancouver: Douglas & McIntyre; Seattle: University of
         Washington Press.

Samuel, Cheryl

1982   *The Chilkat Dancing Blanket.* Seattle: Pacific Search Press.

1987   *The Raven's Tail.* Vancouver: UBC Press.

Scudder, Geoffrey G.E., & Nicholas Gessler

1989   *The Outer Shores.* Skidegate, BC: Queen Charlotte Islands
         Museum.

Skutch, Alexander F.

1996   *The Minds of Birds.* College Station: Texas A&M University Press.

Swanton, John R.

n.d.1   Haida notebooks. 2 vols. Holograph. BAE ms 4162, NAA,
         Smithsonian Institution, Washington, DC.

n.d.2   Skidegate Haida texts. Typescript with holograph corrections.
         Ms Boas Ling. Coll. N1.5 = Freeman 1543. APSL, Philadelphia.

n.d.3   Skidegate Haida texts. BAE ms 7047, NAA, Smithsonian Institution,
         Washington, DC. [Uncorrected carbon of Swanton n.d.2.]

n.d.4   Masset Haida texts. Typescript with holograph corrections.
         Ms Boas Ling. Coll. N1.4 = Freeman 1544. APSL, Philadelphia.

n.d.5   "List of articles purchased from the Indians at Skidegate."
         Holograph notebook. Mss file 1901-31, Dept. of Anthropology
         Archives, AMNH, New York. [37 pp, written in 1901.]

n.d.6   "List of Haida spoons." Typescript. Mss file 1901-31, Dept. of
         Anthropology Archives, AMNH, New York. [9 pp, based on n.d.5.]

1903   "The Haida Calendar." Lancaster, Penn.: *American Anthropologist*
         n.s. 5: 331–335.

1905a   *Contributions to the Ethnology of the Haida.* Jesup North Pacific
         Expedition 5.1. New York: AMNH.

1905b   *Haida Texts and Myths: Skidegate Dialect.* Washington, DC: BAE
         Bulletin 29.

1908a   *Haida Texts: Masset Dialect.* Jesup North Pacific Expedition 10.2.
         New York: AMNH.

1908b   "Social Conditions, Beliefs and Linguistic Relationships of the
         Tlingit Indians." Washington, DC: BAE Annual Report 26: 391–486.
1909   *Tlingit Myths and Texts.* Washington, DC: BAE Bulletin 39.
1910   *Haida: An Illustrative Sketch.* Washington, DC: Government
         Printing Office.

Tarpent, Marie-Lucie
1986   *Haṅiimagooṅisgum Algaxhl Nisga'a.* New Aiyansh, BC: School
         District 92.

Tate, Henry
n.d.   "Sun and Moon: A Tsimshian Text." BAE ms 2048b. NAA,
         Smithsonian Institution, Washington, DC. [Holograph, 16 pp
         numbered 195–210, written for Franz Boas. Retranscribed and
         translated as Boas 1908.]

Turner, Nancy Jean
1974   *Plant Taxonomic Systems and Ethnobotany of Three Contemporary
         Indian Groups of the Pacific Northwest.* Victoria, BC: *Syesis 7,*
         Supplement 1.
1995   *Food Plants of Coastal First Peoples.* 2nd ed. Vancouver: UBC Press.
1998   *Plant Technology of First Peoples in British Columbia.* 2nd ed.
         Vancouver: UBC Press.

Turner, Nancy J., & Roy L. Taylor
1972   "A Review of the Northwest Coast Tobacco Mystery." Victoria, BC:
         Syesis 5: 249–257.

Turner, Nancy J., et al.
1993   "Edible Wood Fern Rootstocks of Western North America."
         Flagstaff, Arizona: *Journal of Ethnobiology* 12: 1–34.

Wardwell, Allen
1978   *Objects of Bright Pride: Northwest Coast Indian Art from the
         American Museum of Natural History.* New York: Center for Inter-
         American Relations.
1996   *Tangible Visions: Northwest Coast Indian Shamanism and Its Art.*
         New York: Monacelli.

Welty, Joel Carl
1979   *The Life of Birds.* 2nd ed. Philadelphia: Saunders.

Wilson, Solomon, & David Ellis
1980   "The Haida Story of Sea Lion Village: The Supreme Power Who
         Walked About." Skidegate, BC: *The Charlottes* 5: 4–6.

Two main text types are used in this book. The serifed type is Aldus, designed for Mergenthaler Linotype, Frankfurt, in the early 1950s by Hermann Zapf. The unserifed type is Scala Sans, designed for the Vredenburg Concert Hall, Utrecht, in the early 1990s by Martin Majoor.

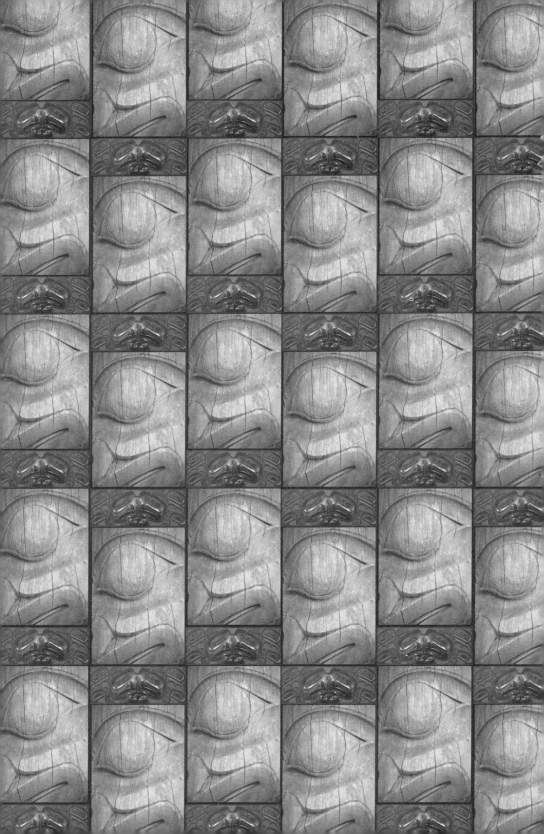